Buried Beneath the Lies

A Pearl Girls Novel

Gina Heron

This is a work of fiction. All of the characters, organizations, and events portrayed in this novel are either products of the author's imagination, or are used fictitiously. Any resemblance to actual persons, living or dead, business establishments, events, or locales is entirely coincidental.

For Granny Lucille

ACKNOWLEDGMENTS

This book has been such a fun ride to work on, and I've had the chance to do the work with some of my very best friends. How lucky am I?

THANK YOU TO:

Melissa Freeman, as always, for your editorial expertise and forever friendship. You know.

Heather Bell Adams, for your friendship, savvy reads, encouragement, and grace. I'm so glad we're on this journey together!

Kristin Kisska, for your fantastic feedback, your friendship, and, well, this pearl around my neck that I'm never taking off. #writingsistersforlife

Gina Evans, for your thorough reads, insightful questions, amazing sense of humor, and faithful friendship.

Mama, for your copy edits, beta reads, and for being my Mama. And for giving me the green light on another one. Love you!

Terry Lynn Thomas, Kasey Corbit, Kimberly Brock, for your friendship, support, and encouragement through every page.

Kate Rock and Susan Peterson, two of the most amazing book bloggers / book lovers / supporters of authors out there. Thank you for cheering me on!

My Foxtale Book Shoppe family! Karen, Mama Jackie, and Gary, I love y'all so much!

Brandi Rogers, the list is long. xo

Michael Krajewski, thank you for once again making stellar cover art to wrap around my words. You're one of the best friends a human could have, and I love you so.

My kids and my extended family, for putting up with me.

And to the readers taking a chance on these books. Thank you from my whole heart.

GINA HERON

Beneath every fear lies the pearl of hope.

—Gabriella Godda

CHAPTER 1

When her husband slammed through the back door cussing a blue streak, Reva Patterson froze where she stood in the living room with one shoe on, one shoe lost, and a mouth full of spit, toothbrush and toothpaste. She rolled her eyes, abandoned the hunt for the missing shoe (which could only be missing because Tommy knocked it out of its place taking off his dirty work boots the night before) and hustled back to the bathroom.

She checked her phone for the time: 1:18. If she left in the next twelve minutes, she'd have just long enough to make the drive over to Blossom Hill and get the cake set up for Bay's baby shower at two.

And this cake was a beauty. Not what she'd have designed herself, if given the opportunity, but she'd baked and decorated it to the precise specifications of her mother-in-law, Amelia. Well, she'd made it an exact replica of the one Amelia had chosen from a random Pinterest board. Reva wasn't particularly enthusiastic about the design—a simple, round, two-layer hombre affair with thin pink ruffles graduating from light to dark, all painstakingly crafted with a batch of finicky icing that she'd have to keep from melting in the August heat. She prayed that Amelia wouldn't mind the personal touches she'd added, a sprinkling of candy pearls and a delicate butterfly perched on the top, as if it had just landed, or was about to take flight. Reva had been dreaming about butterflies for weeks, and, remembering the necklace Bay wore, the addition felt right.

Reva had tossed more than a serving or two of hope into this cake, including the hope that this baby shower would be a high point in an otherwise crappy weekend. It had been raining since early Friday, and between feeling trapped indoors by the late summer storms and listening to Tommy carry on about all the daylight he was losing on his new job site, time with the girls was

1

exactly what she needed. Of course, it would have been nice if she felt like she was part of this particular group of girls, since the Pearl Girls consisted entirely of the married women in Tommy's family, excluding her.

Something else she kept hoping for, in spite of herself, was to be part of that circle. Reva held the dubious distinction of being the only woman to have married into the family and not received a pearl on her wedding day, which would have signified her status as a Pearl Girl. She'd never known the reason for the snub, which made it difficult for her to know what she should rectify. So, she'd spent the last ten years trying to get better at pretty much everything.

Reva rinsed her mouth out and shut off the faucet, grabbed her favorite tinted gloss from its spot in her meticulously organized makeup drawer, and swiped some on her lips. She ran a brush through her chestnut hair before deciding to secure it in a hair tie at the nape of her neck, rather than curling it into a more sophisticated style as she'd imagined. No time for that today. Readjusting her snug knit top, she thought she might better skip the cake at the shower. She'd sampled plenty of batter from the bowls the day before. Gran had been wrong all those years as Reva worked alongside her in the kitchen, she thought, tugging at her pants. Those calories did count. And they ended up right on her hips, if she wasn't careful.

In the quiet of the house, she could hear Tommy barking into the phone.

"Don't matter what day it is, the trailer's sunk a damn foot in the mud. I got the skidder and loader moved before they got too far gone, but you left a trailer full of wood sittin' in the way, and I ain't got another rig to pull it this morning. Get your ass up and out there so we can get moving."

Twisting the knob as gently as she could, Reva eased out of the bathroom and down the hall. She could see Tommy leaning against the kitchen counter, his lanky frame hunching under his constant worries over missing workers, blown ten thousand dollar tires, busted equipment, and the price of fuel. He scratched at the three or four days' growth of stubble on his chin, and Reva made a mental note to schedule him a haircut. Tugging at her ponytail, she remembered that her regular appointment for a trim was scheduled the following week. Maybe she'd ask for something different, maybe highlights. Or layers.

Or maybe she'd keep it the same. No muss, no fuss, and one less decision to make.

She found her missing left shoe jammed under the edge of the sofa. The shoes—the pair she wore more often than not—were sensible black leather wedges she'd bought on sale at the outlets in Bluffton. They gave her a little extra lift without causing her any distraction as she trudged through her days at Lawson, Park & McKinley, where she pulled triple duty as office manager, paralegal, and legal assistant for the local satellite office of the Charleston-based firm.

Tommy turned and caught sight of her, so she waved and pointed to the door as she slid her foot into the shoe, hoping he wouldn't have time to get off the phone and stop her before she could escape. He gave her a dismissive wave and continued yelling into the phone. The flash of heat in his blue eyes that used to leave her knees weak now left her feeling defeated. Lately it seemed he was angry all the time, and no matter what the source of his anger was, eventually it landed squarely on her.

It had been a hard year for them both, though. Her gran's passing away three months earlier, and the toll it had taken on Reva as her caregiver, had strained their relationship. And the record-breaking rain and heat that had come with the summer had added financial worries for Tommy's business. It was a rough patch was all. It would pass.

Reva carefully lifted the cake box from the counter, took her keys from their hook, shouldered her purse, and hurried through the back door and out into the fresh drizzle that Tommy brought back with him.

In the car, she blasted the air, tuned the radio dial to the local country music station, and exhaled as much frustration as she could force out through her nostrils. She'd started singing along to Miranda Lambert's latest hit when her cell phone rang.

"Dammit Tommy, can I have a minute's peace?"

She reached into her purse with her right hand and snagged her phone from its spot in her organizer, then checked the display. Not Tommy.

Reva tapped the screen to send Crystal's call to voice mail and slid her phone back in its pocket. Whatever her sister wanted could wait until after the shower, and hopefully by then Crystal's momentary crisis would be long forgotten, because the only time Crystal called Reva these days was when she needed crisis management, otherwise known as *money for pills*.

An undercurrent of sadness tugged at Reva's heart whenever she thought about her baby sister. Crystal infuriated her, but at the same time she worried. She didn't have the bandwidth for that worry today.

The phone rang again, and Reva swore through gritted teeth. She answered this time, but before she could get a word in, Crystal's gravelly voice, textured from years of smoking and general hard living, rushed through the speaker phone. "Reva, we need you over at Mama and Daddy's. You gotta hurry."

"What's wrong? Are they okay?" Reva slammed on the brakes and jerked the car into a gas station parking lot she was almost too far past, cringing when her front bumper scraped against the uneven curb.

"The sheriff is here with the fire marshal, and they're taking the house."

"Wait—what? But it's Sunday." Reva's panic that one of her parents was dead or dying was immediately replaced by what she was ashamed to acknowledge as a deeper dread: they'd been found out. Her family's dark, dirty secret had somehow come to light, and now they'd all be exposed. She swung her car around in the parking lot and took a left back onto the road, heading toward the wrong end of town rather than straight to Blossom Hill, where she should already have been.

CHAPTER 2

The little white house leaned more toward gray than Reva remembered, so much paint had peeled away from the plank siding. The front porch, which ran the length of the house, held cardboard boxes stacked haphazardly atop each other, with the ones furthest from the door sagging, weathered, as if they'd been waiting there to be opened for a dreadful long time—way too long. Reva knew there were windows, but she couldn't see them for all the stacks of boxes. Had her mother's catalog and magazine orders backed up to this point, where they sat on the porch for ages, unopened? She'd likely graduated to ordering online, which sent a shiver of fresh dread through Reva's body. There was no sign of the white rockers she and her daddy would escape to when she used to visit occasionally, no flowers blooming in the three hanging pots that twirled lazily from their chains in the wind, nothing that spoke of life, of welcome.

A rush of guilt flooded up her throat from her belly, and Reva covered her mouth with both hands, as if she could physically press it back down. How had things gotten so out of hand? It had seemed impossible to Reva to curb Darlene's hoarding tendencies, so she'd found a way to put it out of her mind, to pretend it wasn't her problem to solve. Darlene stopped letting her come inside years ago, and so Reva let her choose the hoarding over the family, like always.

But Reva realized now that she should have tried harder. She should have at least seen to it that Willie had a place to sit outside of the chaos. From the looks of it, there didn't appear to be anything at all of comfort left here, nothing except a world of heartache and hurt. The whole place seemed to be waving a dingy white flag, defeated.

Three taps on her window startled Reva out of her momentary

despair. The girl doing the knocking stepped back and pulled at Reva's door handle, not waiting for her to help herself out.

"Hey, Miss Reva," the girl said, her earnest voice barely above a whisper. "Sure is good you came over. I don't know what y'all gonna do now." The girl shook her head, sending the hood of her jacket sliding down and her tight black curls bouncing around her shoulders.

"Caprice?" Reva said, questioning the child's identity and knowing it all the same. Caprice was their neighbor from across the street, though she was a toddler when Reva moved out, which meant she had to be twelve or thirteen now. On the rare occasions Reva had dropped by after she got married, Caprice was always around somewhere, sharp and attentive, studying every scene and waiting for a chance to tell a good story to anyone who would stop to listen.

And Reva always listened to Caprice when she had a chance. She felt a kinship with the girl over having what was likely the most unfortunate pair of first names in the county. Darlene had named Reva after her favorite character on a soap opera, and she'd never been able to escape the jokes in school. Rumor was that Caprice had been named after her father's Chevrolet, though no one around New Hope had ever really known who that father might be. Caprice's mother had left town for a while and come back months later with a baby in tow. Everything else Reva knew about that was rumor. Regardless, Caprice was a delight, and Reva hoped the rumors hadn't trickled down to her generation.

"Been a long time," Caprice said, a brilliant grin spreading between her flawless tawny cheeks. She threw her shoulders back and stood as tall as she could, topping Reva's five feet five by two or three inches, easily. "I grew a little."

"Indeed, you did," Reva said, smiling up at the young lady she had to look up to, even as she stood. "I guess you saw the commotion?" she asked while giving Caprice a tight squeeze.

Caprice followed Reva's gaze to the front yard, where the deputy's car sat by Crystal's old beater in the driveway. "Boy, did I ever," Caprice began, then launched into her detailed account of the morning's events, ignoring the drizzling rain.

"I was inside this morning sitting at the desk right there by the window, playing a game on my computer," she said, pointing behind them to the big bay window by the front door of her mother's double-wide. "Anyway, first thing, there was this man who pulled up in a big truck and got out with a laptop or tablet of some sort. Your daddy came out and they talked for a minute, and then it looked like they started fussing. I tried to focus back on my own business and not listen too hard. Next thing I know, I look up, and there's a police car pulling up in front of the house. I didn't want to be nosy or nothin', but I was worried something might be wrong, you know? So, I slid on out front right when Miss Crystal was stepping outside to talk to 'em. I wondered, ya know, if maybe..."

Reva nodded her understanding that Caprice wondered if the police were there to pick up Crystal.

"Anyway, I snuck in a little closer, in case Miss Crystal needed my help or anything, you know? But then she started screamin' at those two officers, telling 'em they ain't had no business coming in the house uninvited, that they needed a warrant or something, and that fella without the uniform pulled out some kinda paperwork that she snatched right outta his hand, Miss Reva. And then that deputy, he placed his hand right on the door knob and scooted her on out the way, like so," Caprice said, acting out the deputy's role in dramatic fashion for Reva, "and Miss Crystal shoved him back with her shoulder, like this." Caprice shifted her body to the opposing angle and thrust out a shoulder. "And then he told her something 'bout not wanting to have to cuff her and sit her in the back seat of that cruiser."

Reva squinted at the car in the driveway, but Caprice shook her head.

"Then Miss Crystal bounced outta his way with a quickness and let 'em on in."

Reva nodded. "You hear anything else?"

"All I heard was what the little fella without the uniform said."

"And that was?" Reva prodded when Caprice didn't continue.

"That they had to do an inspection on the house to make sure the place is safe for the folks living in it," Caprice answered. She'd fixed her gaze on the front door, eyebrows raised as she chewed the side of her thumb.

Even though Reva knew without a doubt Caprice had never stepped foot in her parents' home, the girl was inquisitive enough to have gotten some idea of the state it was in. And she could see the front porch, along with anyone else who happened to ride by. The thought left Reva's cheeks burning. There was no way that the house was anywhere near passable on the inside.

"Where's the guy who was in the truck?"

Caprice shrugged. "Looked like they told him to leave."

"You got a phone?" Reva asked Caprice.

The girl pulled an ancient flip phone from the pocket of her shorts. "For emergencies."

"I'm going to give you my number, and if you ever see anything strange going on over here again, please call me immediately. Can you do that for me?"

Caprice's eyes lit with her smile.

"Yes, ma'am, I'm glad to keep an eye on things for you." Caprice tapped away at the keypad on the phone as Reva recited her cell phone number.

"Thanks, Caprice," Reva said, giving the girl's arm a squeeze. "I'll take it from here today."

Caprice gave Reva another quick hug and skipped across the road, not pausing to look for traffic. Thankfully, there rarely was any. "See you later, Miss Reva!"

Reva waved a hand in the air as she forced one foot in front of the other.

"Hey, sis."

Crystal's voice stopped Reva in the middle of what felt like a death march toward the house. She closed the front door behind her and came down to the second step, leaned against the wobbly wooden railing, and lit a cigarette.

"Hey, Crys," Reva said. She tried to keep her expression neutral, to not let her brow furrow with the usual worry that overcame her every time she saw her sister.

Crystal had always been a beauty—tall, willowy, with big blonde hair and big hazel eyes and big boobs to match. If they'd have been from a different kind of family, Crystal would have likely been a beauty queen, maybe could have gone to college on scholarship based on her looks alone. Unfortunately, she'd used her good looks to escape in other ways that had worn her down instead of built her up. At twenty-six, she was two years younger than Reva, but she looked older. Somehow, though, she was still pretty beneath the wear and tear, even if she was too thin, too anxious, too tweaked out to function. If she was clean and sober, as she supposedly had been for the last eight months, she was hanging on by a thread. Reva wished that her sister would somehow settle into her body, and into a normal life, with maybe her own place, friends who weren't junkies, and a man she wasn't using for a place to stay and who wasn't using her for sex.

She should have known better than to throw her hope in the ditch like that, but she'd spread it thin enough to cover Crystal, anyway.

"Sorry to call you out here like this. I know you hate being here," Crystal said, blowing smoke in Reva's direction.

And there was gut punch number one. The urge Reva had felt to wrap her arms around her baby sister vanished. She bit her lip and made a conscious effort to absorb it and not swing back. "You wanna tell me what's going on?"

Crystal nodded her head toward the door and took a long drag on her Virginia Slim, a flip-flop slapping against her foot as she bounced a leg furiously, a nervous habit. "Why don't you go on inside and find out for yourself?"

Reva looked past Crystal to the front door, the faded red paint, the darker area around the door knob where it hadn't been wiped down in ages. She would rather be dragged out back and beat than walk through that door, and her sister knew it. But old habits die hard, and Reva would be damned if she'd show weakness at the first sight of Crystal in months. She steeled herself and marched up the steps, onto the porch, and grabbed the door knob, noting that it wasn't only grungy, it was loose. Anyone could likely walk right in at any time, but who would want to?

"Not me," Reva muttered under her breath. "Definitely not me."

But she made herself open the door.

CHAPTER 3

Reva didn't realize she'd been holding her breath until she felt the air leaving her lungs in a rush, as if she'd actually been punched. It wasn't that she didn't know what to expect when she walked through the front door of her parents' place. It had been bad for a long time. Still, the amount of stuff crammed into the room around her was impossible to process. She could move maybe three steps to her left or right before she ran into a wall of boxes, bags, newspapers, and…God knows what was in there. From the sharp, musty smell of it, she wasn't sure she wanted to know. Was there even any furniture still in the room, buried beneath the piles of Darlene's hoard?

Closing her eyes, Reva fought the sting of tears threatening to roll down her cheeks, which burned hot with embarrassment for her family, that someone from the outside had come in to see it like this. From somewhere deep inside, she called up a memory of what this place had once been: a home to her family. She and Crystal had played over by the fireplace, where there was a child-sized pink table and chairs for them to have tea and cakes with their dolls. The smell of cinnamon toast from the kitchen mingled with the earthy scent of wood smoke from the Squire stove that kept their spot by the hearth so warm. On the walls, there were framed prints from the local furniture store hanging on the walls, and brass sconces with real candles that Darlene would light when company came. There had been laughter here, and love.

Hadn't they been happy?

When she opened her eyes, the memory fell away as quickly as it had enveloped her. Once she'd re-oriented herself to the current state of the space, she found a path that led down the little hallway to the kitchen, where she heard someone speaking in a quiet, soothing voice. By sheer force of will, she took quick steps to cover the distance, stopping short of entering the room. Sweat trickled down her back, both from nerves and the stuffiness of the over-packed space. She pulled at the hem of her shirt to no avail. "Now, Mr. Tucker, we can help you line up some folks to make the cleanup easier." A man in plain clothes addressed Reva's father, Willie, whose gaze had drifted to where Reva stood. When their eyes met, the pain in his seemed to somehow deepen. The deputy and fire marshal turned and greeted Reva. She shook hands and mumbled her name, unable to look them in the eye or hear what they said in return. Her parents' house was outside town limits, and she said a silent prayer of gratitude that she didn't know either of the men personally, even though she recognized the fire marshal from somewhere.

Reva forced herself to look around the kitchen. One of the few blessings of her mother's hoarding had been that it hadn't spiraled beyond junk to filth before, but Reva had always been afraid there would be a tipping point when food and trash would start to pile up, too. Every surface in the kitchen was covered in clutter— empty plastic containers, wads of plastic bags, mail, stacks and stacks of plastic cups and papers plates—but at least there wasn't an obvious food or garbage issue. There were some packaged foods scattered around the counters, but there was no mountain of dirty dishes piled up or half-eaten TV dinners or smelly trash bags in sight. At the moment, Reva figured she would take whatever relief she could find.

"Where's Darlene?" she asked Willie, reaching out to give his hand a gentle squeeze. He squeezed hers back a little harder, rolling her fingers like he did when she was a kid.

"She went to her room to rest. This all might be the death of her," he answered, leveling a cold stare at the fire marshal.

"With all due respect, if she continues to live in this house in the condition it's in, it'll be the death of her," the fire marshal responded.

"We've gotten along fine without any help from anybody, and ain't caused a soul any trouble. I don't see how it's suddenly y'all's business what we keep in our house."

"Mr. Tucker—"

Willie waved off the man's interruption, a look of disgust crumpling his face. "It ain't right, y'all bustin' in here like this, judgin' us, telling us we got to do this or that or else lose our home. We been gettin' by fine—"

"I'm sorry, can someone explain to me exactly what's going on?" Reva broke in, unable to stomach the rising distress in Willie's voice.

"I'm assuming you're the other daughter?" the deputy asked.

"Yes, I am."

"Ma'am, we had a report of possible elder endangerment at this address, due to the condition of the house here."

"From who?"

"The source of the report is confidential," the fire marshal answered.

"How can it be confidential when the jackass called you from our driveway?" Willie spat out.

"Who, Willie?" Reva asked.

"This fella who come up here this morning, saying he was from the census bureau. You could tell it when he come in here he was nosy as all get-out. Even asked me if I needed some help around the place, but—" Willie flung his hands up again and shuffled to the door leading outside from the kitchen. "I'll be out in my shop. See these fellas off," he said, then slammed the door behind him.

Reva and the two men stood in the silent chaos of the kitchen for a minute. This, she thought, was one reason she stayed away as much as possible. She had no desire to be in charge of this, wanted nothing to do with it, in fact. But she'd always known that as soon as she moved an inch too close to her family's circle, it would turn tornado on her and snatch her right up into the middle of it, and this would be her mess to clean up.

"So, Darlene knows about this?" she finally asked.

The deputy nodded. "Yes, ma'am, we spoke with your mother briefly."

"I guess that went well," Reva said with a laugh.

The men exchanged a look.

"And some guy at the census bureau called you today?"

"I'm sorry, but it was a confidential call. I can tell you, though, that the report was filed out of pure concern for your parents' well-being. I imagine you and your sister share some of the same concerns, Miss Tucker," the deputy said.

Reva fanned her burning face with a hand. "It's Mrs. Patterson.

And, of course I'm concerned about my parents, but what y'all don't seem to understand is that my mother is ill. She has this compulsion, and—"

"And I'm guessing y'all don't know what to do about it," the fire marshal broke in. "I've worked with a hoarder or two before, and I do understand that some folks aren't in good control of their impulses, which makes it hard for a family to take charge of the situation. We have some names and numbers back at the office I can give you, people who can help with this kind of thing. If you'll give me your number, I'll call you with the information."

Reva shook her head, overwhelmed at the thought of people in the house, and how Darlene would react. "Darlene won't ever let some stranger in here moving around her stuff."

The fire marshal handed her his phone. "Enter your name and number in there anyway. I'll send over the information. Maybe you could at least get some tips to get y'all started in the right direction."

"What is it you're requiring us to do, exactly?" Reva asked.

"When we check back in thirty days," he began, "we need to see that the walkways have been cleared, and that all the things piled up that might be a hazard have been moved, and that the walls, switches, and outlets are accessible. I need to be able to check the safety of the structure, the electrical, plumbing, your basics of a home inspection, really."

"So y'all are expecting us to have this whole house cleaned out in thirty days?" Reva asked, spreading her arms to indicate the enormity of the job.

Both men nodded. "Yes, ma'am, that would be the requirement."

"And what happens if the house isn't livable to your standards by then?"

The deputy took his turn fielding the question. "At that point, we would have to start the process of having the house condemned, if it remains unlivable. At the end of that process, it would be seized by the county, cleaned out, and demolished."

Reva threw her hands up. "Well, shit."

"Mrs. Patterson, the last thing we want to do is take your folks' home from them. This property would be pretty useless to the county, house or not, but the fact remains, we can't leave it in this condition now that we're aware of the situation. It's not safe for them, and if there was a fire or a medical emergency, it wouldn't be safe for our EMTs and firefighters coming in here trying to work. This has to be resolved."

The deputy edged his way toward the door that exited through the carport.

"I can't argue the point. I don't know how we're going to make this happen without having to literally snatch things from Darlene's cold, dead hands by the end of it."

"Like I said, I'll send you some contacts. If you need help, ask for it. Lord knows, I would," the fire marshal told her as they followed the deputy outside.

"Sorry to rush out," the deputy said, "but I was supposed to be back at the correctional facility for a pickup at two. If we're done—"

"What time is it?" Reva's voice hitched up a notch as she looked for somewhere to check the time.

"It's 2:28," the deputy answered. "I'm already running behind."

"You and me both," Reva nearly choked out, pushing past the two men and pin-balling back down the hall and out the front door as fast as she could.

Bay's shower had started half an hour ago, and the cake was sitting in the passenger seat of Reva's car, in the midday heat. The temperature outside was in the nineties. She didn't want to think about what that meant for the temperature inside her car.

"Where are you—"

"I gotta go," Reva yelled, without turning to say goodbye to Crystal.

"Sure, you do," Crystal hollered back. "Go ahead and leave us in your dust one more time and hurry home to your perfect little life, Reva."

"I'll be back," Reva said, jerking open her car door and sliding inside. She didn't have time for the same stupid games they'd been playing all their lives. She didn't have time for any of this.

But she'd make the time. After she fixed things with Amelia and the Pearl Girls.

CHAPTER 4

Where are you? Are you on the way?

Reva groaned at the lone message from her mother-in-law that displayed when she pressed the home button on her phone, received forty-two minutes ago. She hit the call button and braced herself.

"Are you on the way?" Amelia asked when she answered, her voice barely above a whisper. Reva could hear the chatter of the gathered women in the background.

"Almost. Something came up that I had to take care of and—I'll be right there," Reva answered, her words coming out in a rush.

"This is why I said you could have come up to Owl's Roost to work on the cake. I could have brought it from there on my way. But I had no idea where you were, and I don't have a key to your Gran's place anyway."

Reva winced at the layered jabs from Amelia. More and more, she pushed Reva to work with her at Owl's Roost, the popular café that anchored New Hope's Main Street, hinting at adding specialty cakes to the menu, and other items they could add if they had the extra hands full time. Amelia kept on with the hinting, and Reva kept on with the dodging. She didn't want to bake cakes all day. For special occasions like the shower, sure. She loved making them. For stress relief, yes. For a job?

Reva had bigger plans. But she couldn't exactly tell her mother-in-law that she had no interest in taking over her café someday, at least not until she was ready to explain why.

And then there was the matter of the withheld house key. When Reva and Tommy lived beside his parents, Amelia always had a key. Reva intentionally forgot to have an extra made when she and

Tommy permanently moved to Gran's house. Something else she'd have to continue to creatively dodge.

"Something came up with my parents, and..." she trailed off, not sure how to explain that she lost track of time because, as much as she might get annoyed with Amelia, by comparison her own family was a train wreck. "It doesn't matter. I'm almost there."

"Well, hurry it up," Amelia said. "Bay's opening her gifts."

"I will," Reva said. "I'm sorry about this, Amelia."

"No use fretting. Just get over here."

The line went dead as Amelia unceremoniously hung up on her. Reva could admit that Amelia's frustration with her was justified this time, but her abruptness still stung. She could only pray the picture-perfect cake on its way to the shower—if late—would make up for it.

Twelve minutes later, Reva tapped three times and eased the front door open at Blossom Hill. "Hello?" she whispered, peeking her head around to peer into the impeccably kept living room of the LaFleur home. What looked to be more than two dozen women crammed into the space around Bay Ramirez, who sat to the left of a pile of pink baby paraphernalia the likes of which Reva had never seen.

"You made it!" Amelia spotted Reva and hurried over to greet her at the door, snagging the cake box from her hands.

"I did," Reva said, almost out of breath. "I hope the cake's okay."

Reva hurried to the kitchen behind Amelia. "I can't believe I lost track of the time and left the cake sitting in the heat like that. But Crys called and when I got there, everything was a mess, and—nevermind that, though. Let's see about the cake."

"Oh, is everything okay with your family?" Amelia asked, her brow furrowing as she set the cake box down on the counter.

"It will be," Reva lied. The last thing she wanted to do was share the extent of Darlene's hoard with her mother-in-law.

Violet LaFleur, Bay's mother, came in from the other room.

Amelia sucked in a breath as she pulled the top of the cake box open.

"Wh—what?" Reva asked, eyes going wide as she watched Amelia and Violet both cover their mouths with their hands—a gesture so similar they could be sisters rather than cousins—as they stared into the box.

"Don't worry about it, hon," Violet said, pushing down the lid. "Mel already ran over to the Pig to see what they have in the bakery. I'm sure he'll be back any minute with something that'll work."

"What's the matter? Did it—it..."

Violet looked to Amelia, who shrugged her shoulders. "Melted. Honey, it melted."

Reva edged around the counter slowly, not really wanting to see all the work she'd put into that cake melted in a puddle, but morbidly curious. How bad could it be?

The answer: pretty damn bad. Not one ruffle of hand-mixed pink icing was left on the cake, which had collapsed into a corner of the box, burying the delicate butterfly beneath the layers that somehow had turned to mush when the icing melted.

"Oh—oh, no," Reva croaked, closing her eyes and willing the image of the smashed-up cake to reassemble itself into the beautiful concoction it had been a few hours ago.

"It's totally fine," Violet said, wrapping an arm around Reva's shoulders. "Really, Mel will be back any minute and no one will be the wiser."

"I'm so sorry," Reva whispered. "I can't believe I let this happen."

"Reva, what exactly is going on with your parents?" Amelia asked, folding her arms across her chest. "This isn't like you."

Reva's eyes darted from Violet to Amelia and back as she scrambled to come up with the right thing to say. "It—it's—nothing really. Nothing to worry about."

"It has to be something for you to be late getting here for the shower, and—"

"Amelia," Violet broke in, "let's not make it worse. Mel's pulling up now. Y'all go join the ladies in the living room and I'll set up dessert."

"I'm—"

"Concerned, I know," Violet interrupted again with a stern look, nudging her cousin. "Go."

Reva and Amelia followed orders and headed back to the living room, where they stood to the side to watch as Bay finished opening her gifts.

The minutes dragged on as Reva stood there by her mother-in-law, feeling the weight of Amelia's stare every time it drifted her way. She bit her lip and tried to focus on Bay, on the joy her friend was experiencing in the moment, but she couldn't keep the disappointment she was feeling from welling up and pressing into her lungs, making it hard to breathe, to hold her emotions in check. She'd been so excited for this day, even though she knew everyone else around her was concerned about how she'd handle a baby shower, given her history. Amelia hadn't said anything to her directly, of course—she always relayed touchy messages through Tommy—but she'd considered letting someone else make the cake, and leaving Reva out of the shower entirely, thinking it might be too much for her, celebrating Bay's daughter who'd be coming any day now.

Reva had insisted she would be fine, and she'd meant it. She was fine. She was excited for Bay and Scott. If she'd learned nothing else from her Gran, she'd learned to not let your tragedies rob you of your joys, and for Reva, a friend's joy was as good as her own.

So, she poured that joy into the cake that sat in a sad, melted heap, hidden away in the kitchen. She'd allowed herself a little of that joy, and a little hope. She tried so hard, but this was how it had always been, how these days seemed to always turn out. History repeating itself once again, her past, her family, coming back to bite her in the ass every time she thought she was making progress. She clung to hope, even when it dragged her face first through the dirt.

As Violet presented the ladies with a tray of grocery store cupcakes that were nowhere near a replacement for the cake Reva had painstakingly decorated and subsequently destroyed, Reva slipped into the kitchen where Mel was starting to clean up.

"Hey, sweet Reva," Mel said, grinning at her. "Cake crisis averted."

"Ugh," Reva covered her face with her hands. "I'm so sorry."

"Mind if I…"

Mel tapped the top of the cake box with his index finger and raising his eyebrows to complete the question.

Reva shrugged her response.

"Huh," he huffed, opening a drawer in the island, grabbing a fork, and digging into the cake box. He lifted a big bite of cake that he'd swirled in the pool of icing and put it in his mouth. "Delicious. Really. Selfishly, I'm glad it melted because I wouldn't have gotten any otherwise."

Reva laughed as he took another big bite, then joined him at the counter as he handed her another fork.

The cake was good. It was as delicious as she'd hoped it would be. At least Mel would know.

"Hey, thank you so much for the beautiful blanket," Bay said, coming into the kitchen as she wrapped Reva in a hug.

"You're so welcome," Reva said. "It's one of the last ones Gran made. I'd put it aside for you last year. I'm so sorry about the cake, and for not actually being here for most of the shower," Reva said.

"Don't even worry about it," Bay said, stepping back and holding her by the arms. "Everything okay?"

Reva nodded. "This day has given me whiplash. I was in a rush, and then I had to run take care of a thing with my family. It was a hell of a day for me. I really am sorry."

Amelia gave Reva a weak smile when she caught her eye over Bay's shoulder from where she was helping Violet with the dishes. "These things happen, hon. It all worked out."

"Come on in here and help me load Bay's haul into her truck," Leigh Anne said, grabbing Reva by the arm on her way to the living room.

Leigh Anne was Bay's sister-in-law, married to her older brother, Ethan, and also happened to be Reva's cousin. Reva knew that Leigh probably wanted to get her alone to find out what was going on with her. They both had the same fine line to walk, though Leigh had been much more successful at it to date.

"I'll help, too," Bay said.

"You will do no such thing." Amelia pushed Bay onto a barstool. "That baby needs to bake a few weeks longer."

Mel slid the cake box toward Bay and handed her a fork. "Eat some of this cake. It's amazing."

Reva was relieved to hear the laughter in the kitchen as she followed Leigh Anne into the next room.

"How mad is she?"

"How mad is who?" Leigh Anne asked as she began piling Reva's arms full of boxes.

"Amelia," Reva whispered. "How mad is she about me being late and ruining the cake? What was she saying before I got here?" Leigh Anne gave a wave of her hand. "She seemed fine to me. The cupcakes weren't bad."

"Well, the cake was gorgeous before it sat in out in this heat."

"I'm sure it was," Leigh Anne said, laughing as they stacked the first load of presents into the back of Bay's SUV.

"I know I won't hear the end of it now," Reva grumbled as they gathered the next load of gifts. "She already pointed out, if I'd used the kitchen at Owl's Roost, she could have grabbed it. Or if she had a key to our house now... Today's been a disaster on top of a disaster, and now I'm going to have to make up for this somehow. I feel like I've spent my entire marriage trying to make up for one thing or another. And then there'll be the questions about what's happening with my parents—"

"I'm sorry if I was butting in, Reva. I was concerned about your family. I mean, you're my family, too."

Reva's heart stuttered in her chest at the sound of Amelia's voice behind her. She straightened quickly as Leigh Anne turned to her, eyes wide, before scurrying back outside with a couple of bags she snatched in her haste to exit the room.

"I didn't mean—I know you were worried, and I appreciate it," Reva said, facing Amelia. "I'm sorry I disappointed you, and I know—"

"I understand exactly what you meant. Again, sorry if I overstepped."

Amelia turned on her heel and stalked from the room.

"Well, if she wasn't pissed with you before, she is now," Leigh Anne observed from where she was lurking near the front door, hands on her hips.

Reva groaned. "I let myself believe for a minute this day couldn't get worse."

"What's going on with your folks, Reva?" Leigh Anne asked.

Reva began stacking the rest of the gifts methodically and shook her head at Leigh Anne's question. Leigh Anne had done everything she could to distance herself from their family when she married Ethan LaFleur, much like Reva had when she and Tommy got together. "You don't want to know."

"Is there anything I can do?"

"How open are you to committing arson?" Reva asked as they worked to fit the last of the gifts into Bay's back seat alongside the car seat that had already been installed for the new baby.

"How likely are we to get caught?"

Reva laughed. "Unfortunately, we probably can't get away with it now."

Leigh Anne shrugged. "Well, if there's something I can do..."

"Nothing to worry over," Reva said, squaring her shoulders and lifting her chin. "I'll handle it." She nodded toward the house. "Tell them again I'm sorry. I have to go."

"Reva," Leigh Anne called after her.

But Reva didn't stop. She was smart enough to know to cut her losses with Amelia for the day, to let things settle. And, given the way her day had gone up to this point, it was likely best to eliminate any opportunity to make things worse.

"Hey," Tommy mumbled to Reva from his recliner as she came in.

"Hey." Reva slid off her shoes and put them in their place, then made a show of picking up Tommy's boots and setting them on his rack just outside the door.

"I was gonna get him," he said, rolling his eyes.

"Sure, you were," she replied.

Reva set down the cake box and crossed to the medicine cabinet and grabbed some ibuprofen, got some water from the fridge, and downed four.

"Mama called to check in on you. What happened with the shower today?"

Reva rubbed a hand over her face. "She didn't tell you?"

Tommy got up from his recliner and stood behind her at the kitchen counter, rubbing her shoulders. "She said you were late because of a family emergency you obviously didn't want to talk about, and that the cake didn't make it."

"Sums it up," Reva said, exhaustion and defeat heavy in her voice.

"You wanna tell me what happened?" he asked, reaching around her to lift open the lid of the cake box. She fought the urge to grab it and fling it across the room, because then she'd have more mess to clean up.

Reva studied what was left of the cake. After dealing with her parents' crisis and then the cake catastrophe, she didn't have the energy left for a fight with her husband. And any discussion about her parents, about how they lived, would start a fight. He'd say something insulting, and true or not, she'd get defensive, and it would spiral from there.

She was tired of fighting with Tommy. It seemed like the only way they knew how to communicate with each other anymore. What he wanted at any given moment seemed in direct opposition to what she wanted, all the time. And they were both all compromised out. So, they fought instead. They fought about the bills, closet space, whether they'd stay in Gran's house or sell it, trying for a baby again, who unloaded the dishwasher last, why he refused to put up his own boots. All things big and small, it seemed.

What was the next phase, she wondered? What was left when they were done compromising, and fighting, and nothing had changed?

"My parents have to clean up their house," she said.

"No shit," Tommy said, laughing. "They've needed to clean up their house since we met, Reva, but we both know they won't."

Reva clinched her hands into fists and slid away from him. "My head is pounding," she said, not taking the bait. "We can talk about this tomorrow. Goodnight, Tommy."

"So, you're not even gonna tell me what happened over there today?"

She slipped quietly down the hall to their bedroom, ignoring him as he called out to her, pretending not to hear. She shut the door and leaned against it, knowing he wouldn't come to bed—he rarely did—and that they'd march into tomorrow morning pretending nothing had happened.

Except it had. Maybe finally too much had happened. Even though it was still early, she walked through her nightly routine and fell into bed, hoping it wouldn't be an entirely sleepless night. Reva sensed a shift, something foreboding, in the way the day had unfolded. She'd been so prepared, everything lined up perfectly for the shower.

Until Crystal called, and in her panic she'd forgotten about the cake in the car. It was unthinkable, meticulous as she was, that she'd make that kind of mistake. Sure, had she remembered the cake, or done it at Owl's Roost so Amelia could have taken it with her, it wouldn't have prevented the calamity at her parents' place. But the rest of it could have been salvaged. She could have gotten the cake to the shower, avoided hurting Amelia's feelings, and maybe even enjoyed an evening of quiet with her husband. And, if she looked at it honestly, had she forced herself to deal with her parents' situation years ago, rather than run from it, that would have been avoided, too.

Tomorrow, she would get up, and she would figure out how to fix all of this, even if she had no idea where to start.

GINA HERON

CHAPTER 5

A low fog hung over the tidal marsh beyond the yard, tempering the light as the sun broke through the heavy clouds above the tree line. The air was near dripping with heat, amplifying the briny scent of the wind. Reva sipped her coffee as she watched Lucy stalk through the reeds, searching for fish.

She loved this old swing of Gran's, the one her grandfather had framed and cemented into the ground, intending it to withstand the coastal storms that blew through. The swing, and the sturdy old house behind it, were both built to last. Their marriage had been, too.

It occurred to her as she sat there in the peace and quiet, watching the morning unfold, that no matter how many sunrises she witnessed from the same spot, no two were ever the same. The world around her changed every day, in ways she could see and feel. She wondered whether the internal shifts she felt changed what she saw, too. As within, so without? Somebody said that once, she was sure. Where had she read it?

The great blue heron first joined Reva for her morning coffee a few days after her grandmother passed away two months earlier, and she'd come back to visit every day since. Reva took the bird's arrival as some sort of sign from her gran. After Reva and Tommy moved in to help take care of her, Gran and Reva had a cup of coffee together every day. Gran would take a few quick sips from her cup, then look up at Reva with a sweet little grin and a gleam in her eyes. *"What's the truest thing you know today, darlin'?"* she'd ask, and Reva would rack her brain for a more creative answer than the one she'd given the day before.

"What's the truest thing you know today, Lucy?" Reva whispered. Their morning communion had been such a solace that she'd felt compelled to name the bird. She settled on Lucy because of Gran's great love for all things related to Lucille Ball. Reva wondered as she sat that morning whether herons migrated, if Lucy would be leaving her in the fall. She'd have to look it up.

Lucy's head pivoted and her wings fluttered, then she lifted away and over the water. She must have felt the rumble of Tommy's return seconds before Reva sensed it, then heard the screech of his brakes on the big truck, the slow hiss of exhaust. He'd gotten up in the middle of the night to start his work day, and would be in and out as his crews kept things moving, trying to keep ahead of the storms that seemed endless.

The last time Reva and Gran had a serious conversation, it was about her marriage to Tommy. Gran sensed the trouble between them, even before they'd begun staying with her. But Reva was firmly rooted in her denial of any real problem. She'd convinced herself it was a rough patch they'd get past, not one that would linger. When Gran questioned her about her happiness, Reva told her that maybe she wasn't as happy as she could be, but that she was secure.

"Oh, Reva, if the relationship isn't a happy one, what's the use feeling secure in it? Who wants to be secure in their misery?" Gran had asked her.

Reva had laughed off her concern, and reassured her that she was happy in her marriage, or at least as happy as anyone else she knew. It might not be exciting, or full of joy, or much inspiring, but it was safe. And that was enough.

At least she'd convinced herself it was enough.

Reva sighed. "Security is an illusion," she said, looking in the direction the bird had flown. "That's the truest thing I know."

Dumping the tepid remains of her coffee into the bushes, she hurried to stash the mug in the dishwasher, grab her bag, and get to the car before Tommy was close enough to speak. Avoiding him wasn't the right way to handle their lingering fights—and there were plenty of them—but Reva had enough to deal with for a Monday morning, as it stood.

Starting with her parents. As she drove back to their house for the second time in two days, Reva tried to formulate some sort of plan to deal with Darlene's hoard that didn't involve burning the house to the ground. Having not come up with any great ideas on the way, when she got there, she let herself in through the unlocked kitchen door and turned in a circle where she stood, trying to take in the full extent of the clutter around her. It was hard to focus on specific things when there was so much excess. How many bowls, bags of corn chips, plastic bags, mason jars, empty microwave soup bowls, or sets of cutlery could two people possibly need? And then there were the stacks and stacks of magazines on the floor, newspapers, even tabloids. Why would her mother want those things in the first place, much less keep them piled up around the house?

Then she was looking from the kitchen across the hallway, at the door of her parents' bedroom. She closed her eyes for a moment, then took the necessary number of steps to get her across the hall to the door. She laid her hand against the dark wood and listened hard. Darlene was inside, she knew, even though all was quiet after the drama of the day before, when she'd been able to hear the sobs and whimpers out in the hall. It would take Darlene months to recover from a day like yesterday.

Reva thought that maybe she should go in, try to comfort her mother or offer words of encouragement. But she knew she wouldn't get very far before Darlene started in on a rant about the unfairness of it all. It had been the same thing every time Reva— or anyone else—had approached Darlene about cleaning out the cluttered house. She would need those things when she was ready to reopen the store, she'd say. Or she needed to check all the papers and magazines for items she might want to order, stock for the imaginary store. She'd have a different idea every now and then. First it was a costume jewelry shop, and then maybe she'd open a used book store, and then maybe a gift basket boutique. Reva would always ask why she didn't go back to running a plain old dress shop, and Darlene would get a faraway look in her eyes. But she never would answer.

Reva was ashamed to admit it, even to herself, but most times she brought up the dress shop to shut Darlene up when she was going on about the next thing she thought she'd do. Reva didn't believe Darlene was ever going to leave that house to go further than the Right Way Thrift on the edge of town. Willie drove her there every Saturday morning first thing, before the bins of new items were picked over or there was a crowd—not that the Right Way Thrift ever drew an actual crowd. This was where Darlene would start the odd collections of glass turtles or porcelain birds,

Japanese decorative plates, and McCoy bowls. Of course, just about everything she picked up there was chipped or cracked or in some other way damaged, but Darlene was sure every piece of it could be salvaged and sold off in her shop that was never going to be.

As her hand slipped from the door, Reva decided she wasn't ready to face Darlene yet, even though a part of her wanted to see her mother, to tell her that she was here to help, and that they could work through this together. She thought again about knocking, but instead turned on her heel and headed through the kitchen and out back. On her way through, she couldn't resist giving a good kick to the stack of old tabloids that nearly tripped her. The pile shifted awkwardly, then slid unceremoniously into what little path was clear in that spot. Reva didn't bother to straighten them.

There was at least a little relief to be found in the small back yard, which was neatly kept, as always, by Willie. Reva checked the time—she was already a half hour late for work—and hustled to the little shop situated at the corner of the property. Its welcoming porch and clean white vinyl exterior sat in stark contrast with the house it belonged to. Reva's heart squeezed at the thought that a backyard shop was all that her Daddy had for himself, all that he'd been able to salvage of his meager dreams.

She tapped her fingernails against the glass windowpane in the door to the shop, then stepped inside. Willie sat in one of the rockers that had been relocated from the front porch, apparently. Like Crystal, he seemed thinner, smaller than the last time Reva had seen him. The lines around his dark eyes spoke of perpetual sadness, as did the downturn of his mouth. He wore a blue uniform top and navy pants, even though he'd retired from welding a few years earlier. Willie had always been a man of habit, had relied on his routines. Reva was a lot like her father in that way, she knew. Consistent, steady. She didn't know how he'd managed to survive with Darlene for so many years, in the chaos. Living with Darlene's ever-expanding hoard, Reva had felt for the longest time like she was drowning. And yet somehow, Willie had managed to stay with it, to keep his head above water, and Darlene's, too.

The shop had always been an escape for Willie, and Reva noted a few new additions that indicated it had become even more so. A single bed, neatly made, stood against the back wall, beneath a little window. There was a bedside table with a small lamp, Willie's Bible, and a Zane Grey novel stacked beneath his reading glasses. A mini fridge stood at the end of the little counter where a sink had been installed. Had Willie been relegated to living in his shop? A fresh lump formed in Reva's throat. It wasn't fair.

"Hey, Willie," Reva said, her voice softer than usual.

"Hey, darlin'," he answered, not quite meeting her gaze. "I'm sorry about all this."

"I didn't realize..." Reva didn't know how to finish the sentence, because whatever she said, it wouldn't be true. She had realized, had known, that things were getting further and further out of control at her parents' house. It was the reason that, when Darlene stopped inviting her inside, she'd simply stopped coming by, rarely called, and tried to push it out of her mind. It had been easier to let it go than face the fact that they'd been teetering on the brink of this disaster for so long.

Willie shook his head. "It's been going downhill a long time, gal. A long time."

Reva pulled out a stool from beneath Willie's workbench and sat. "So, you're sleeping out here now?"

Willie nodded. "Ain't really nowhere to sleep inside for me, especially now that Crystal's back home. I had a little bed in her old room, but she needed it worse than me. Besides, it's fine out here with the fan and the window unit. And it's quiet."

Reva's eyes went wide. "Wait, Crystal is staying here?"

"Don't go gettin' all wound up over your sister, now," Willie said. "She ain't caused no trouble here lately."

"She ain't been no help here, either." Reva winced at how easily she picked up the cadence of her former self when she was around her family.

Willie almost smiled. "She gives me a little break with your mama, if nothing else. I reckon she's doing her best. Anyway, I'd rather her be staying here than takin' up with another man who'll get her all juiced up again. I swear, I believe she'd be fine if not for these men around here messing with her."

"Crystal is nearly twenty-seven years old. And that's old enough to take some personal responsibility for whether or not she stays juiced up."

"Well, I'm holding out hope that this last rehab took. At least with her home I can keep an eye on her."

Reva closed her eyes and counted to ten. Now was not the time to get into it with Willie over Crystal, or to point out that, this last rehab, she'd only completed eight of the thirty days it required, at a minimum. It wouldn't do any good to upset him further.

"Explain to me what happened with this person coming to the house yesterday."

Any humor left in Willie's face vanished into shadow. "It was that damn census bureau asshole came around here."

"Why would somebody be here from the census bureau?" Reva asked.

"Said they'd sent us some kinda paperwork that we was required to fill out, by the law," Willie started, getting to his feet to pace the length of the shop. "He came around with this fancy computer thing, tellin' me that since we didn't do those papers and send them in, we got to let him fill them out right here. I kept him out front of the house, sat on the steps to fill out the thing with him, but then Crystal decided to flounce herself outside to see what she could see, and I could tell he got a good look inside, and your Mama, she was standing in the hallway watchin' out the door. He got to asking me about who lived here, and if we was getting any assistance or needed any. And I told him hell no, we didn't."

Reva let her chin drop to her chest. "Oh, Willie, you didn't."

Willie got up from his chair and stood across from her, pounded his fist on the workbench. "Wasn't none of his business peering into our home like he did, or asking questions about things he don't understand, or calling the damn sheriff on us. How do you think we'll get your mama to clean this place out in thirty days? It ain't likely we'll get her back out of the bedroom by then." He started to pace the small room, another habit Reva had inherited from him.

"Maybe it's a blessing in disguise, because we have to get Darlene to clean some stuff out now. A lot of it."

Willie covered his eyes with his hands. "They can't come and take everything from her, can they? They can't take the house?"

Reva shrugged. "Unfortunately, they can, if the fire marshal says it's not fit for living in. They'll condemn the house and they'll take everything that's left in it."

"Can't you talk to them lawyers where you work, darlin', and see if they could do something?"

Reva hesitated, then lied through her teeth. "I'll talk to Macon today and see what he thinks. But the law as I know it is clear on something like this. Now that they've issued a citation, we have to comply with it. Willie, we have to clean this place up."

She would absolutely not be asking anyone at the firm about whether her parents' house could be seized because of her mama's filthy hoarding habit. No one at Lawson, Park & McKinley knew anything about Reva's family, or their situation, and no one would, unless it was over her dead body.

Looking at her watch again, she realized that her boss might actually kill her dead if she didn't shake loose and get over there. She'd sent him a text claiming she had an appointment she'd forgotten, but still, she wanted to make it in before her absence sparked any curiosity with him.

And there was one more stop she intended to make before she could go in to work.

Reva kissed Willie on the cheek and told him she'd be back soon. She almost felt guilty for relief she felt, leaving home again.

No, she would not ask anyone at the firm about this. She would deal with it quietly, on her own time from now on. No one else needed to know where she came from—or what she came from—when she'd worked so hard to forget it herself.

GINA HERON

CHAPTER 6

Reva pulled into the empty parking lot of the nearly abandoned strip mall near Old Town in Bluffton. Many of the businesses in this part of the town had shuttered, or relocated to the newer, more accessible shopping centers on the main highway leading to Hilton Head. It was an odd location, she thought, for a government office—even a temporary satellite branch—but she double-checked the address and spotted the small sign for the US Census Bureau taped in the window of the second storefront from the left end of the strip.

Ignoring her rational internal voice that suggested she take a moment to gather her thoughts, to consider whether she really needed to confront this man who'd reported her parents, Reva strode across the lot and flung open the door, sending the little strip of bells hanging on the handle into a frenzy. She didn't have much time, and after her talk with Willie, she was almost as agitated as he had been.

Once her eyes adjusted to the dim florescent light of the room, Reva took in the two desks situated on opposite sides, one of them stacked with rows of folders, the other occupied by the largest, most intimidating bearded man she'd ever laid eyes on.

Until he smiled.

"Wow," the man said, leaning forward at his desk, pushing the laptop he had been working on out of the way.

For a second, Reva forgot why she'd walked into this office. She reached a hand up to check her hair, which she'd forgotten was knotted up in a disheveled bun at the nape of her neck. It was too late to do anything about that, though. At least she was dressed okay, she thought. She glanced down to check what she had on— practical black dress pants and a blue top someone once mentioned made her eyes pop. She wondered briefly what he must see, taking in the entire picture.

And then she remembered. This was likely the man who had called the fire marshal on her family. The frustration, shame, and anxiety of the last two days rushed back through her in angry waves. His open smile and kind eyes didn't mean much, given what he'd done.

How dare this man be attractive?

"What do you mean, wow?" she asked, fumbling for the thread she'd meant to pick up with him on the drive over.

"I think you're the first person who has voluntarily walked through that door since I took this gig, not counting a couple of friends who've stopped in. You know this is the census office, right?" His smile hadn't faded at her clipped tone, or the icy stare she tried at. She'd had to avert her eyes quickly, though, as she found something about his face warming her from the inside out. As if it wasn't hot enough in South Carolina in late August.

"I—it's—this isn't exactly a voluntary drop-in," she finally managed. "Are you the guy who does the home visits? The one who comes out to collect data or whatever?"

"Yes, ma'am, I am. Billy Simpson, by the way. My friends call me Simpson. And you are?"

Billy Simpson held his hand out to Reva, and she fought the urge to take it, twisting both of her hands behind her back.

"Not your friend, Billy."

His smile faltered for the first time, and Reva stood a little taller.

"Do I know you, Miss…?" he asked, letting the question hang.

"Mrs. Reva Patterson. Reva Tucker Patterson," she answered. "I believe you met my parents, Willie and Darlene Tucker, yesterday. They live over in New Hope. Ringing any bells for you, Billy?" she said, surprised at the venomous tone dripping from her own tongue.

"Of course, the Tuckers," he said, laying his hands flat on the desk in front of him. "Are they alright? I was concerned when—"

"Oh yes, Billy, we know how concerned you were. Everyone is very well aware of your concern over my parents."

"Okay, Reva, you're losing me here a little—"

"Mrs. Patterson."

"Mrs. Patterson, my apologies," he said, picking up a pen with his left hand. She noticed that it shook a little.

"Yeah, you should be sorry, and scared," she said, looking pointedly at his shaking hand. "I work for one of the biggest law firms in this state, you know. I could likely have your job for what you've done to my family."

Reva fought to keep her voice from shaking as she leveled the empty threat. She likely could not have his job, and would rather actually die than bring the issue of her parents to someone in the firm. But she needed someone to lash out at after the chaos of the day before, and, from where she stood, he was the most deserving target.

Simpson dropped the pen back on the desk and watched it roll toward the edge. A look passed over his features—something like thunder, something that sent her heart fluttering with its intensity—and just as quickly smoothed over. She wasn't sure what she'd seen there, but it was all at once frightening and exciting.

"Listen, Reva, I'm not scared of you. I have a slight tremor in my hand, nerve damage from a shrapnel wound." He looked her up and down, as if sizing her up. She squirmed. "Scared is not a thing I get these days. But you might be pissing me off a little bit."

"Oh, you're mad? That's rich. You con your way inside my parents' home—two people who might have some flaws, but aren't hurting a soul but themselves, and maybe me and my sister, but—" the way he was looking at her scrambled her thoughts. "What you did is going to disrupt their entire lives, you know. And mine."

"Good," he said. The bark of his voice made Reva jump. "From what I saw in that house, their lives needed a disruption, so if I forced one, I'm glad. If you're looking for me to apologize to you for doing something you should have likely done years ago, lady, you came looking behind the wrong door. Somebody had to do something. It's a damn shame for anybody to live that way."

"Don't you think I know that?" Reva shouted at him. Tears she could no longer hold formed streams down her cheeks. Her hands balled into fists, and she pressed them against her eyes, trying to regain a little control. But she'd completely lost it. "Don't you think I've tried? For my whole life, I've tried to understand it, to fix it, to reason with her—with Darlene—to convince Willie to do something, anything. Nothing I say or do gets through to them. It never has. She got sick and our lives—"

Reva forced herself to stop talking. The room was quiet, and she knew without looking at him that Billy Simpson was waiting for her to continue. But she wouldn't give him the satisfaction. "This was a mistake," she whispered, taking a step back toward the door. "Hey, hold up," Simpson said, standing up and rounding the desk. "I didn't mean to upset you."

"People don't understand what it's like, living day in and day out with something—with something that's broken, that you can't fix. And they wonder why you don't do something about it—like, somebody should do something about it. Just clean it up, right? Make her stop. Don't let her buy things. Throw them out in the middle of the night. Get rid of it. But what nobody gets is that the broken thing isn't on the outside, it isn't what they can see. Something is broken in her, and we can clean that house 'til kingdom comes, and it won't make one damn bit of difference. The house isn't what's wrong with her. It's the inside."

"Reva, look at me."

"Mrs. Patterson," she whispered, turning her eyes up to meet his. Her gaze didn't make it past his mouth.

"Mrs. Patterson," he said, a quiet thread of irritation straining his level voice, "look at me. Really, look at me."

Reva let her eyes wander over his face. Deep brown eyes, nearly black, strong brow, prominent nose, olive skin, a neatly trimmed beard, less neatly trimmed hair. Toned chest evident beneath an Army tee, tight torso, thick, veined, tattooed arms, strong legs—

It was then that she noticed the prosthetic. Her eyes snapped from it back to his face, and he smiled.

"I get it. You could patch up the outside, but what's broken on the inside would still be broken."

"Wait, you're Billy Simpson. That Simpson, the one who was with Scott Ramirez—"

He nodded. "Yes, I'm that Simpson."

"I'm—"

"Don't you dare say that word to me, Mrs. Patterson. I almost like you a little bit, but if you say that word to me I'll never forgive you for it. Deal?"

Reva nodded, shaken at the sudden realization that this was Billy Simpson, Scott's teammate in Special Forces, the very one who had been with Scott when he was captured by the Taliban, the one who'd been wounded. Had lost his leg.

She was about to tell him she was sorry, but she wasn't sure if that was the word he meant, so she thought it would be best to keep her mouth shut and let him talk.

"Like I said, Mrs. Patterson, I get it. Your mother—and maybe your father, too—they're resistant to the idea of changing their external situation because then they have to deal with all that internal shit, and that's the part that really hurts. Even for you, right?"

Reva let the long, silent pause answer his question.

"The bitch of it is, you have to deal with one to get to the other. And, for them, that external shit could literally kill them. Maybe it's something you haven't been able to convince them to do. Maybe it's too hard for you to deal with it yourself. I'd understand if it was. That doesn't mean they should continue to live like that, though. I took it upon myself to make that welfare call not because I wanted to make trouble for them, or for your family. I was trying to see that they got help that they need."

"Are you always so generous?" Reva asked, rubbing the back of her neck, hoping the headache that was forming there would ease a little.

"No, I'm a stingy bastard in general," he said, smiling. "I've been lucky enough to have a few people in life be this kind of generous for me. So, I like to pay it forward where I can."

"Really, you shouldn't have," she said.

"You're welcome."

Simpson leaned against the edge of the desk, and Reva allowed herself another look at him. A hundred questions rested on the tip of her tongue, but she couldn't bring herself to ask even the first one of them. They studied each other for a long moment.

"Afghanistan," he said.

She nodded. "I know," she said. "You were with Scott."

"Good, then. You know the story."

Reva nodded. "You don't like to talk about it."

He shook his head and smiled, standing a little taller. "I like to be about it."

Reva laughed, and was awarded with the most devious grin she'd ever seen.

"There it is," Simpson said. "I got a smile outta you. Now, Reva, what's the situation with your parents?"

She sighed. "Mrs. Patterson. We have twenty-nine days to clean up Darlene's hoard."

"And after that?"

"After that…well, if the house is still unlivable, the county takes it. They lose everything."

Simpson's face contorted with concern. "That's not gonna happen?"

Reva laughed again. "I will do everything in my power to see to it that it doesn't. And, when I'm done, my parents will have a clean house for a minute, and Darlene will likely remain locked away in her own head. And Willie will resign himself to living with it that way. Per usual, he'll cave to whatever Darlene wants to keep her semi-stable. The house will start to fill up again, and they'll live in their precarious circumstances until the census bureau good Samaritan shows up next time and turns them in."

"What's your plan?"

"The fire marshal graciously suggested some services to come in and clean up, but I'm pretty sure we can't afford them, so I guess I'm going to roll up my sleeves and do it my damn self. And that's probably going to push Darlene right over the edge."

"Holy shit," Simpson mumbled.

"You cuss a lot."

"So do you. You're holding back because we just met."

Reva couldn't help another smile. "Whatever, Billy."

"Whatever," he said with a roll of his eyes. "Worst word in the history of the human language. Okay, Reva, what can I do to help out?"

Reva shook her head. "Mrs. Patterson. And no thanks, I think you've helped us enough. Maybe in the future, before you decide to pass on the intervention or whatever it is, check to make sure that the people you're intervening for want the help. Or at least that it's not gonna blow up in their faces."

His expression did that weird thundercloud thing again. "Interesting choice of words there. Unfortunately, though, that's not how it works. People who need an intervention never want it."

"Well then, at least try to find a way not to make a bigger mess than the one you found. Because this," Reva said, bringing her hands to her temples, "this is going to make a mess of my life. Starting with my job, which I have neglected to clock into at all this morning. Shit."

"See, potty mouth."

"Shut up, Billy. And please, for the love of God, don't help us anymore."

GINA HERON

CHAPTER 7

"Mrs. Patterson, how good of you to grace us with your presence before your lunch break today."

Reva let the heavy front door of the office, which she had just unlocked at 10:20 a.m., slam behind her.

"I left you a message, Macon," she called as she walked past the door to his office. She circled her desk, tossed her bag beneath it, thumped the day's stack of mail down on the credenza, and powered up her computer. She patted the new Mac affectionately. The firm had finally gotten around to upgrading the systems in the satellite offices a few months ago, after years of letting them lag behind. Reva took a little credit for it, having sweet-talked their IT guy into suggesting it would improve their overall network performance if all of the offices were running similar systems. She didn't know if it was true or not, but it didn't matter, as long as the partners bought it.

"It's not my job to pull messages from the machine, dear. It's yours."

"I also sent a text to your cell. And I know you got it from the read receipt." She hustled down the hallway with her shoulders squared, chin up. She flipped on lights, started the copy machine, opened the active file cabinets, and started a pot of coffee in the little kitchenette.

"And now I'll pull the messages from the machine, dear," she said, rolling her eyes as she walked back by Macon's door.

He laughed. "Carry on, then."

Reva had been working at the New Hope office of Lawson, Park & McKinley for eight years. Macon had been there with her for three of those. She loved her job, and she was good at it. She'd established the rhythm of the work, and for the most part, Macon followed her lead when he replaced the attorney she'd worked with her first five years at the office after his retirement. From the beginning, she set the tone, the pace, and the standard to which their little office performed. And it performed well. There were six satellite offices in four counties, and the New Hope office was only outperformed by the Florence crew, but that was because Florence was the personal injury claim capital of the whole freaking world.

In the few years Macon had been the lead in the New Hope office, he and Reva had managed to develop what she considered a productive professional relationship, even if he did grate on her last nerve at times. At first, she'd worried that the fact that he was married to one of Tommy's cousins would complicate matters, but as it turned out, Macon and Elizabeth weren't much on socializing with folks around town, including Elizabeth's family. So, aside from their work, they only seemed to run into each other at the occasional family dinner Macon didn't bow out of. It kept things simple between them, just the way she liked it.

Reva finished transcribing the last of the messages on the machine and sent them to Macon via their chat app. As she began to sort through her stack of filing and checked for transcription on the machine, Macon wandered out of his office and over to her desk. He could have held a conversation with Reva from his own desk in his office without even raising his voice—her desk sat in the open area right across from his door, facing him—but he appeared to be feeling chatty on a day when Reva was decidedly not. She fought the urge to roll her eyes at him again and refused to look up from the file she'd started organizing. Reva had spent enough years around lawyers to know some of their tactics, and this was one of Macon's that annoyed her no end. Standing over her, almost in her space... he had questions, and he meant to get the answers.

"What is it, Macon?" she asked.

"Why were you so late this morning?"

Reva shrugged. "Like I said, I forgot I had an appointment this morning."

"Okay, well...it's not like you is all."

"Am I ever late, Macon?" Reva asked, her voice tweaked with irritation she couldn't mask.

He laughed. "Today you were."

Reva sighed. "Before today, have you had issues with me being on time, opening the office, having everything ready when you get here to start your day?"

"No, you are extremely reliable, Reva. It's one of my favorite things about you," he answered, nodding his head at her.

"Good. I'm glad we're on the same page with that."

Macon took a sip of his coffee. "Everything okay at home?" he asked.

"Yes, everything is fine at home. There was a family matter I had to see to with my folks this morning, and I'd forgotten is all," she clipped out, shooting a glare at him as she turned her chair toward her keyboard. "Nothing for you to worry about."

Macon shifted his body to half sit on the surface of her desk, taking up more space. "Hey, hey, I'm sorry, Reva. I'm concerned is all. I didn't mean to upset you."

Reva took a deep breath and let it out slowly. "I'm sorry I'm snapping at you, Macon. I'm a little stressed, and I hate being late. I need a minute is all."

"I was wondering, since you said it was a personal thing. I haven't seen Tommy around lately, not that I get out that much with work and all. Just wanted to check in and make sure all's well with y'all."

He paused, an obvious effort to leave space for Reva to spill something about trouble between her and Tommy. Trouble or not, though, Macon McKinley was the last person she'd be sharing any confidences with about her family. If he said anything to Elizabeth, and Elizabeth mentioned anything to Amelia...

She couldn't stomach the thought. "Tommy and I are fine. Always have been, always will be."

Macon nodded his approval. "Glad to hear that. You seem like the type of girl who knows to put her husband first, and knowing how that family is, I'm sure Tommy expects it. Probably well matched. Anyway, I need to run over to the house for a walkthrough with the contractor today at one, so let's grab lunch on the way and swing over there."

"I just got here, Macon. I need to catch up on all of this transcription and filing. You're fine to drive, right? The doctor released you last week." Reva forced her voice to a neutral tone.

Macon had been milking his rotator cuff surgery for all its

worth, using Reva as a personal chauffeur when he needed to run errands or check in on the house he and Elizabeth were building in a shiny new gated community near Bluffton.

He made a show of stretching his right shoulder until he grimaced. "Still uncomfortable as hell. And it won't kill you to get out of the office with me for a little while, right?"

But I might kill you, she thought.

"What if somebody comes by, or the home office is looking for you? We don't need to both be out of the office so much at the same time. Maybe we need to see about a part-time runner, to drive you for the next few weeks."

Macon laughed. "Don't worry so much, Reva. If anybody asks, I'll answer for the both of us. And we'll both have our cell phones, right? Nobody's going to give you grief for giving me a ride. I mean, I'm the boss, right?"

It took a good half a minute and all her effort for Reva to squeeze out a response. "Right."

A few seconds later that felt like years, he pushed off of her desk, went to his office, and shut the door. Reva closed her eyes and pressed a hand against her pounding heart. She didn't know why, but every time Macon's sexist, chauvinist side started to show—and it showed often—her heart nearly beat its way out of her chest. The other attorneys she'd worked with in the past were men, too, but they'd never given her any grief. And the worst of it was, Macon didn't even seem to know the way he talked to her sometimes was a problem.

It made her mad as hell, but also scared as hell. She'd spent all those years working at this firm, gaining experience, working on her bachelor's degree, and she finally had what she needed to get to the next step: a degree, with honors, and a high enough LSAT score to get into damn near any law school she'd like. All she was waiting on was the acceptance letter from the University of South Carolina School of Law, and she'd throw her name in the hat for the firm's annual grant. If it had been any of the other attorneys she'd worked with at the firm, she would have already told them about her LSAT score and her application to law school. Hell, two of them had written her referrals to the school. But something in her gut told her that Macon could be a problem.

Reva couldn't afford more problems today, so she bit her lip where he was concerned and soldiered on.

CHAPTER 8

Bumping down the dirt lane to the house as night began to fall, Reva silently cursed Tommy and his stupid trucks for making a mess of the driveway. After the recent storms, they'd left ruts so deep she was afraid her little Ford would bottom out before she got it around back to the parking pad. She made a mental note to see about having gravel poured, as if she could afford that.

Taking in the house itself, she felt a sense of comfort she couldn't find anywhere else, especially on days like this one. The old farmhouse was well-kept—Reva should thank Tommy again for giving the exterior a fresh coat of paint and keeping the hedges neatly trimmed, even if he was destroying the driveway—and as welcoming as could be. It was situated at the top of a little crest and framed by a wide front porch that wrapped around both sides of the house, right up to the chimneys that bookended it. Dense potted ferns and red geraniums sat scattered between rocking chairs, just the same as when Papa and Gran called this place home. Reva's only additions to the porch were ceiling fans and white twinkle lights that she kept on a timer for 7:30. They were already on as she rounded the side of the house to find Crystal's car parked in her spot.

"Noooo," Reva moaned, letting her head fall against the steering wheel. She'd escaped any real conversation with Crystal the day before, and after the hell of a Monday she'd had at the office, she wasn't up for a second run-in. She had been near desperate to get home, though, so she trudged up the back steps and kicked her shoes off on the screened porch before stepping inside, making a mental note to brush them off and bring them in later.

The first thing that struck Reva as odd about the scene in her living room was the sound of Tommy's low, rumbling laugh blending with Crystal's giggles. The TV was on, but the sound was muted. Usually Reva had to ask Tommy to turn the damn thing down as she walked in the door.

The second thing that tweaked her was Crystal's lanky frame sprawled out on her sofa, her legs completely exposed in cutoff jeans, her boobs damn near exploding from the cheap tank top she wore. Rather than make any move to get up as Reva came through the door, Crystal stretched liked a cat, arching her back and throwing her hand over her head.

"I almost fell asleep waiting on you, Sis," she said, grinning.

"I see that," Reva said as she walked through to the kitchen and flipped on the lights. "I guess I don't have to ask what brings you over tonight, after all this time."

Crystal grunted as she sat upright on the couch. "I wanted to talk to you about the plan for this whole thing with Mama and Daddy."

"What's on for dinner?" Tommy called from his recliner.

"Pot roast," Reva called without turning around.

"Smells good," Crystal said, coming to stand by Reva as she started to transfer the roast from the crock pot.

"Of course, it smells good." Reva allowed herself to smile for the first time that day. "There's tea in the fridge. Help yourself and have a seat," she said, nodding toward the bar stools on the other side of the kitchen peninsula, which overlooked the living room. "We'll talk while I finish up, and you can eat dinner with us."

Crystal leaned over the roast and breathed in deeply. "All this crap's so fattening, though."

Reva rolled her eyes. "I'll cook some brown rice, and steam some extra veggies. You look like…" She paused to pull back the words that were about to rush out—*a very hungry junkie.* "Like you haven't had a decent meal in a month of Sundays."

"Nobody cooks at mama's and daddy's anymore. Just microwave crap."

"Why don't you do some of the cooking?"

Crystal barked out a raspy laugh that ended in a coughing fit. Reva waited patiently for an answer to her question, thinking emphysema was probably already eating out her sister's lungs from all the shit she'd smoked.

"Did you see the kitchen when you were there yesterday? Ain't no way you can cook in there without lighting the whole damn place on fire."

Reva thought about Willie hidden safely away in his workshop. "Would that be such a tragedy?" she said under her breath.

"What?"

"You could clean it up," Reva said too loudly, almost shouting. "I said you could clean it up. Consider the labor as rent for a roof over your head."

Crystal jerked the refrigerator door open and thumped the pitcher of tea onto the counter. "Really? How much did you pay for this roof up over your head?" She turned her eyes to the tongue and groove ceiling. "Oh, right, it was give to you free, by family."

The house was a sore spot between the sisters, and between Reva and Darlene, too. Gran had little to leave behind when she died, mainly the house and its contents, which she'd deeded to Reva long before her death. A small insurance policy was left to Willie, but it was barely more than enough to cover her funeral costs.

Reva wouldn't allow herself to feel guilty about that, though. It never occurred to Crystal or Darlene to consider how Gran was able to get out of the house during the last few years, or keep up with the household bills. Reva took responsibility for all of that when Gran began to lose her sight. When she could no longer drive, it was Reva who picked her up for church, took her shopping on Saturdays, and made sure she got to all of her appointments. Willie came over to spend time with Gran when he could make a way, but in the end, Reva was the one who'd taken over her care, and not because it was a burden left to her, but because she wanted to.

Because it was Gran who had taken care of her all those years.

Reva stopped what she was doing and pressed the heels of her hands against her stinging eyes. Missing Gran snuck up on her like this, in the moments her mind wandered back to when she was living. Then it would hit her that she'd never see her again, hear her laugh, or see the pure joy on her face at the sight of her granddaughter. No one else had ever loved Reva quite like Gran had. She didn't know if she'd appreciated that enough before she was gone.

"When was the last time you saw Gran before her funeral, Crystal?" Reva asked, returning to her work at the stove.

"I was in rehab, for Christ's sake," Crystal answered.

"Before you were in rehab, then. When was the last time you saw her before you went to rehab?"

"You and Tommy moved in here with her, Reva. It makes sense you would'a seen her more than me. I guess I should have pounced on the chance before you took everything over."

Reva threw a steam bag of vegetables in the microwave and slammed it shut. "Took everything over? You mean the responsibilities? Yes, I did take those over, while you couldn't be bothered to drive ten minutes to check on Gran. You'd have driven ten times as far to find a dealer."

"See, this is why I can't talk to you about one damn thing. You always got to drag up my past—"

"We can call it your past when you've been clean for longer than a few—"

"Hey!" Tommy's voice boomed over the two sisters'. "If y'all gotta fight, how about take it in the yard? I'm watching the game in here, and there ain't no need for the bitching over things that's said and done, anyway. It sounds to me like you got bigger fish to fry at the moment, with what's goin' on at your mama's."

The sudden outburst from Tommy after his total silence since she walked in startled Reva out of the argument with her sister.

"So, I guess Crystal filled you in on the situation."

Tommy nodded, not taking his eyes off the television.

"He thinks we ought to send Mama somewhere for a few days and go in there with shovels, clear the place out completely so they can start over."

Reva put the roast down on the bar in front of Crystal. "Well, I guess the two of y'all got the whole thing worked out, then. I'm happy to let you take care of this mess."

Crystal slammed her open palm down on the counter. "Why you gotta be such a—"

"Watch how you speak to me in my home, baby sister," Reva said, going deadly quiet. "Don't think I've outgrown dragging your ass outside and whoopin' it."

"There still ain't no talkin' to you, is there?" Crystal pushed back the bar stool and stomped to the back door, snatching it open.

"Don't worry about Mama and Daddy. I'll take care of everything over there, and you can keep on sittin' pretty in your free house and your fancy job and your—your—ugh!"

Reva waited, listening as her sister stalked off the porch, then back up the steps.

Crystal flung the door open and stepped inside. "I forgot my—"

Reva raised her arm and pointed to Crystal's bag, sitting between the sofa and Tommy's chair. Tommy laughed.

Crystal snatched up the bag and repeated her exit.

Reva stared Tommy down. Finally, he looked up at her. "What?" he asked.

"Think she'll come back?" Reva asked.

Tommy shrugged. "Nah, she'll wait for you to come on over there and do what you do."

"And what is it I do, exactly?" Reva asked him, her head cocked to one side.

"You tell everybody what to do and how to do it, and then when they don't do it like you want it done, you do it for 'em."

Reva opened her mouth to argue, but thought better of it. "I can't help it my entire family is incompetent."

Tommy laughed. "I reckon not."

"Want dinner?"

"Yeah, I want dinner," he said.

Reva pulled down two plates. She filled Tommy's first, poured a glass of tea, and took both to him.

"Thanks," he said, taking the plate as she sat the tea on a coaster on his side table.

"You're welcome," she said, putting on her best smile. She'd make an effort with Tommy tonight, to smooth things over. "Maybe I'll give you a little dessert later."

He shook his head, keeping his eyes on the TV. Reva stood over him and watched as he mindlessly shoveled a forkful of roast and rice into his mouth.

"Or not," she mumbled on her way back to the kitchen.

Reva ate her dinner alone at the bar, her back to her husband and the glare of the television. After she was done, she gathered their dishes and loaded them in the dishwasher.

"Did you get the mail?" she called to Tommy, but he didn't

hear her. "Never mind, I'll get it myself."

Reva slipped on her sneakers and wandered down the hall to the front of the house. The night air held the first hint of fall. She paused to wrap up in Gran's old sweater that still hung on the hook by door. The scent of lavender and peppermint still clung to the yarn, at once a comfort to Reva and a painful reminder of her loss.

As she picked her way down the muddy lane to the mailbox by the road, she wondered what Gran would tell her to do about the current state of her marriage. Gran had never been Tommy's biggest fan, but she wasn't exactly in favor of divorce, either, so she'd tried to give Reva a positive spin on their problems. The last couple of years, though, it had been harder to do, even for Gran.

Reva and Tommy had their bumps in the road, but they'd dug into a serious rut after they lost Tee Jae. It was their third pregnancy to end in miscarriage.

The first two babies they'd lost late in the first trimester of each pregnancy, so by the time Reva started spotting at twenty-nine weeks, she had let herself relax a tiny bit, believing that this time would be the time. Surely God wouldn't take a third baby from her, not one whose gender she knew, not one she had named.

She had been wrong about that.

It was hard for Reva to believe it had been almost two years since they buried their baby boy. And just as hard to believe that she could barely let Tommy touch her since.

Reva grabbed the mail from the box as it began to drizzle rain again. Hugging the stack close to her body, she jogged back up to the house. She locked the front door behind her and ducked into her little office. As she flipped through the junk mail, she stopped short at one particularly thick envelope. It was from the University of South Carolina School of Law. She lifted the envelope from the pile and held it in both hands, testing the weight of it, the thickness of it.

"Please be a yes," she whispered. "I need a yes today."

She flipped the envelope over and gently pulled the flap away. The letter was thick, and once she had it open, she could see that there were several sheets of paper folded together inside.

"If it wasn't a yes, there wouldn't be more than one sheet of paper," she whispered. "It has to be a yes."

Reva closed her eyes and unfolded the letter, laying it out flat on the desk in front of her. She took a few deep breaths, and when she felt steady enough, opened her eyes and started to read aloud: "It is our pleasure to welcome you to the University of South Carolina School of Law Class of..."

She leapt to her feet and ran down the hallway squealing with joy.

"What in the devil has got into you, woman?" Tommy asked when she bounced her way into the den.

"I got in!" Reva waved the letter over her head. "I did it!"

"You got in to where?" Tommy asked, his face scrunched with confusion. "What are you going on about?"

Reva quit her flailing and came to a dead stop at the end of Tommy's recliner. She dropped to her knees between his feet. *It's better to ask forgiveness than permission.* That's what Gran had told her. It was time to test out that theory.

"I did a thing." Reva refolded the letter and held it in her lap.

"What is it?" Tommy said, an edge of irritation clipping his words. He leaned so he could look past Reva to the television.

"Tommy, this is important," Reva said. "I need you to listen, and I need you to be happy for me, okay?"

He gave her a hard look. "I can't promise you how I'll feel over something I don't even know about. Spit it out."

"Remember when I pulled that three hundred dollars out of the bank account a few months ago for the continuing education class I was going to?"

Tommy nodded. "Yeah, I remember. You were gonna get the office to reimburse it, but I haven't seen it come back yet."

"Well, I haven't asked them to reimburse it yet. I had to wait and see how things turned out."

"Reva." Tommy looked at her, exasperated.

"It's good news, babe. Can you let me have my moment, please?"

"I've let you have about twelve now," Tommy said. "Can you get to the point?"

"I used the three hundred dollars to pay my application fee to the University of South Carolina School of Law." Reva unfolded the letter and held it out to Tommy. "And I got in."

Tommy continued to stare at Reva—or through her, more like it. He didn't move to reach for the letter.

"Aren't you going to congratulate me or something?" Reva asked, after waiting forever for him to speak.

"Or something," he answered. Tommy shook his head and rubbed a hand over his face, a habit he had when he was frustrated or angry.

Reva pushed herself up off the floor and folded the letter back up. "You know how much I want this, Tommy. How long I've wanted this."

"Yeah, I know you want it, Reva. You want all kinds of things…a law degree, a bigger house—"

"I'm happy in this house. I love living here," Reva interrupted. It was true, when they lived in the double wide by Tommy's parents, she'd kept a Pinterest board full of house plans, family homes she could imagine raising their future children in. But now that they were settled in Papa and Gran's old house, Reva couldn't imagine being anywhere else. This was her home.

Hers, she thought. Not theirs. One of the key issues hanging in the air between them every minute they spent in this house.

"Well, I'm glad one of us is happy in it." Tommy slammed the foot of his recliner down and pushed past her. He turned back to her before disappearing down the hall. "Reva, where in hell do you think we're gonna get the kind of money it'll take to get you through law school? You can't work and do that, and I'm still trying to get my business off the ground. You ain't been out of school but a little bit, and itching to go back. Can't you just appreciate the good job you got and let it go?"

"I do appreciate the job I got, Tommy. I've been working it for years, right through school, and we didn't take out one loan. I graduated summa cum laude, at the top of my class, and I aced the LSATs. I'm a shoe-in for the firm's grant money—"

"What makes you so sure of that? What if you ain't shit to them, Reva? What if they prefer to keep you right where you are, and ain't willing to foot the bill for you to move on elsewhere?"

"That's not how it works, Tommy."

Tommy grimaced, then ran his hands through his shaggy hair. "You got no clue how the world really works, Reva. Somehow you bought in to all the 'if you believe it you can achieve it' bullshit. Why can't you be happy with what you got?"

Reva sighed. "This letter is proof that I *can* do this, Tommy. I got in, early acceptance and all. Maybe we need to talk about it, come up with a plan or something to make it work, but for now, can't you muster a little excitement for me?"

Tommy shook his head. "I'm going out. I need a beer."

Reva clutched her acceptance letter over her heart and let her chin drop to her chest as she listened to the door slam behind him. She inhaled deeply, picking up on Gran's scent again from the sweater she still wore. Pulling it tight around her, she let the tears she'd usually hold back roll down her cheeks. "You'd be happy for me, Gran." She sat down at the bar and wiped her eyes, then read the letter again.

"I did it," she said to the empty space around her. "I really did it."

But it hurt, if she was honest with herself, to spend a moment she should be celebrating so completely, utterly alone.

GINA HERON

CHAPTER 9

Reva was beginning to think God had changed his mind and sent another great flood to rid the earth of ever-escalating human-generated foolishness. Even so, it was difficult to consider ducking into her parents' open front door as refuge from the storm.

"Hope there's not a tornado," she grumbled over her shoulder to Tommy as thunder boomed behind them. "They'll never find us in the rubble."

"I can't believe I let you drag me out here for this on a Saturday I didn't have work," Tommy said, leaning close to her. "Always something with your family."

Reva landed an elbow in his gut. "That's not so. You haven't been here in years. We can't let them lose this house, Tommy."

"Hell, a tent would be an improvement, in my opinion," he offered, taking in the two front rooms of the house.

"My dad's already living in his workshop. We can't let it get worse than that, and if they lose this place, where do you think they'll end up?" Reva gave him a pointed look.

"Oh no," Tommy's eyebrows lifted nearly to his hairline. "We are not living with no more of your family, Reva. I'm drawing the line with that."

"And that's why we're here, to help make sure that doesn't happen. You wouldn't want to leave them with nowhere else to go, right?"

Tommy ran his hands over his stubble and responded with a guttural noise.

Reva would never tell him, but she took a perverse pleasure in forcing him out of the recliner and into the mess at Darlene's and Willie's with her. On Saturdays when he couldn't work in the woods, like this one, he'd spend the whole day in front of the television, watching ridiculous reality shows and smoking himself into a stupor. He resisted as long as he could that morning, but Reva finally made it plain that he would help her or learn to eat his own cooking until this whole ordeal was over.

"Hello?" Reva called as she picked her way gingerly down the hall.

"We're back here, in the kitchen," Crystal yelled.

"Is this where we're starting, then?" Reva asked, stepping past a stack of HSN boxes that she didn't remember from a few days ago. All hope that they'd gotten started without her dwindled as she took in the room. Nothing had been touched. If anything, the mess she witnessed earlier in the week had been added on to. Even the stack of tabloids that had scattered when she kicked it appeared to have somehow multiplied.

Reva's eyes slid up from the floor over the cramped space to her sister and mother, who were standing huddled together near the little microwave on the counter. The timer dinged, and Crystal opened the microwave and pulled out two steaming mugs. Darlene scooped instant coffee into each mug, humming as she did so. Reva had a sudden flash of her mother working in this same kitchen, years before, when it was clean and new. Reva and Crystal had always set the table while Darlene finished up dinner in the kitchen, humming along to whatever they had playing on the radio.

"Hey Darlene," Reva said, her voice hesitant. She watched Darlene as she dumped powdered creamer into her cup of instant coffee, her worn red tee shirt with a white sea shell pattern stretching over her rounded shoulders. Her grey-streaked blonde hair was loose and limp around her shoulders, her pale face puffy and bare. Darlene looked smaller than Reva remembered—well, shorter and rounder—but it had been a long time since Reva had seen her outside of her room, where she was usually tucked away in her bed or in her rocker when anyone visited, including her daughter.

Darlene finally turned and nodded hello in Reva's and Tommy's general direction, her gaze skittering everywhere but their faces.

Reva clapped her hands together and forced an enthusiastic smile. "Are y'all ready to get going? We can dig in right here, right now."

Darlene's eyes widened behind her glasses, and she turned to look up at Crystal, who dropped a slim, suntanned arm over her shoulders to give her a squeeze.

"Let us finish our coffee, and I need a smoke," she said. She looked at Reva, her eyes hard, dark. "Then we can get started. I'm sure you got us a list or something."

Reva spread her arms and looked pointedly around the room. "I don't know what good a list would do."

Crystal shrugged, moving toward the door. "Don't mean you won't draw us a picture anyway."

The screen door didn't have time to slam behind Crystal before Tommy was there, following her out. Reva shifted her weight from one foot to the other, studying the bright pink laces of her black cross trainers. She thought that she could pick up her left foot, then her right, then her left again, and cross the entire physical space between herself and Darlene. But she couldn't. She didn't know how, with the emotional divide threatening to swallow them whole.

"Mama, where should we start? Is in here good, or…" Reva trailed off, realizing that Darlene still hadn't looked at her or spoken. She took one step forward. "Mama?"

"What, baby?" Darlene said, looking at Reva as if she'd just realized she was there.

Reva blew a breath out slowly, fighting against the frustration bubbling up from her belly. "We have twenty-four days left to clean up the house, Mama. Do you remember?"

Darlene looked around the kitchen and began shaking her head. "But—we need to talk to them first. I was thinking that maybe you and me, we could come up with a plan and you could help with that."

"Talk to who?" Reva asked, her hands on her hips. "What kind of a plan?"

"The people at the county. I think if we can talk to them, explain to them that it's all stock for the store when I open it back up. If we tell them, they'll give us a little time, won't they? Maybe you and some of those lawyer friends of yours could explain it to them, that I need my things, and they can just cancel this whole thing." Darlene's expression turned from clueless to hopeful as she watched Reva for a reaction.

Reva closed her eyes and struggled to keep a hold on her temper. "Mama, no, they're not going to give us time. And they're not going to buy some cockamamie story about all this crap being stock for a nonexistent store." Reva pushed at a pile of plastic bags with her foot. "There is no store, and this isn't stock. It's just random—stuff."

"Just because the store's been closed for a while—"

"The store's been closed for almost twenty years," Reva said, her voice rising. "And it was a dress shop. She held her arms out again, turning in a circle. "I don't see dresses here, Darlene."

Darlene's chin quivered, and she searched for a clear spot on the counter to put her mug down. "I still got the dresses, but I don't want another dress shop. I've been getting together stock for a new shop. You'll see. This isn't all just random stuff. People like these things, just like me."

"Not many folks are in the market for other people's plastic grocery bags and old tabloid magazines. This needs to go in the trash." Reva bent to snatch up a handful of each.

"That's not trash!" Darlene yelled, shuffling forward and reaching for the tabloids.

Reva instinctively jerked her arm with the tabloids behind her back, turning to examine the one on top. "What exactly do you need a National Examiner from months ago for, Mama? Please tell me what makes this not trash?"

"I haven't looked through those yet." Darlene snatched at the stack in Reva's hand. It fell, scattering over other debris on the floor.

"Looked through them for what? A ridiculous story about Elvis and an alien having a baby? What do they even print in this things now?"

"There might be some ads in them. They have some of those good things you can order from collector place, things like that," Darlene said, grunting as she bent to gather up the papers. "It's nice stuff for when we get the shop up and running."

"Oh, dear Lord, I will not survive this," Reva said through gritted teeth. She took a deep breath and blew it out slowly between pursed lips. "Okay, Mama, let's look at these another way. You've already got all this stuff here at the house to use as stock, right? So, until you get yourself a place leased for whatever kind of shop you decide on, and get all this stuff set up in it, we don't need to be ordering more."

"But—"

"We don't need to be ordering more," Reva repeated, determined to continue. "Now, these old rags have outdated merchandise advertised in them, stuff customers likely won't be interested in, and you'd be buying it at retail price anyway, so you won't have any room to mark it up. You'd likely take a loss on anything you ordered from one of these."

Darlene shook her head furiously. "That ain't so. Those ceramics and collector things are valuable items. People want those to keep and pass down."

Reva took another deep breath. "All I'm saying is that maybe there's newer, more popular stuff to be collected now, and you can probably find it all on this wonderful thing we got called the Internet."

Darlene notched her chin up and blinked behind her glasses. "We got the Internet, Reva. And I got a PayPal. I can order online good as anybody."

Reva's stomach flipped with the horror of the thought of Darlene with access to Internet shopping and a credit card. But at least it proved her point about the tabloids. "Good, then that's all the more reason why we can toss out these old things. You can order the same stuff online."

"But I won't even know to look for what's in these here old ones if I don't go through them first. You ain't making me throw them away until I've looked at them."

"You know what? Fine. You want to look through all of these, then look through them, dammit," Reva said, scooping up all the tabloids she could see. She spun around, trying to find a place for Darlene to sit and work through them. "Where do you even sit down in here, Mama?"

Darlene worked her way to the little kitchen table in the corner of the room, pulled out the lone chair, and dropped into it. Reva eyed the stacks of paper products and mail in front of her until Darlene sighed and started piling them on top of each other to make room. When she'd cleared enough space, Reva dropped the pile she was holding on the table.

"I'd say you can flip through these in the next thirty minutes and pull out whatever you decide to keep," Reva said, scouting around the kitchen for trash bags. Coming up empty, she settled on pulling the trash can itself over by Darlene. "Throw them in here after you've gone through."

Darlene whimpered.

"Mama, you have to do this."

"Thirty minutes isn't very long is all."

"It is when we have less than thirty days to get through the entire house. Now, where's Willie?"

Darlene nodded toward the back yard.

"Okay," Reva said starting toward the door. She turned back before stepping outside. "You can do this. I know you can."

When Reva stepped out under the tin-roofed carport, Crystal and Tommy were huddled near the front of the house, smoking and whispering. She let the door slam behind her. Crystal startled at the loud bang and whipped her head around, her ponytail fanning over her shoulder.

"Damn, Reva," she said. "You scared the shit outta me."

"Where do you want to get started? Your room?" Reva intended to keep to the business at hand—it was the only way she knew to make any sort of progress and keep out of conflict with her sister. "Or you can help Mama in the kitchen while I work on the living room. Your call."

Crystal made a show of taking a drag off her cigarette, then thumping it to the dirt right beyond the cement of the carport. "It'll go faster if we all work in the same room at the same time, if it's gonna go at all."

"I'm open to that, if you'd prefer it." Reva crossed her arms over her chest.

"Really?" Crystal raised an eyebrow and looked from Tommy to Reva.

"Long as we're making some progress, we're happy to pitch in wherever we're needed. And since you're here with Darlene and Willie, you might have a better idea of where it would be easier to start."

"Okay," Crystal started, her face suddenly earnest, like she was giving it real consideration. "I was thinking if we start in a room that would go faster, that ain't so bad, maybe seeing the results right quick will get Mama motivated, so long as you don't push her."

"That makes sense," Reva said, nodding her agreement. "Which room do you think would be best?"

Crystal pressed a hand to her forehead. "The bathroom, I guess. We keep it pretty straight. Daddy's funny about the plumbing."

"Okay, so we start in the bathroom and move on out to the hall, you think?"

Crystal nodded. "We can do that."

Reva peered through the pouring rain to the shop out back. "Tommy, why don't you run on back there and see if you can drag Willie inside."

"Oh, hell," Tommy muttered under his breath, looking across the saturated yard to the shop. "Spent the whole week soaked to the bone, what's one more day?" He trudged past Reva and dodged her attempt to pat his shoulder.

"Thanks," she called as he jogged out into the downpour. "Shall we?" she asked Crystal.

The sisters went back through the kitchen door. Darlene was sitting right where Reva had left her, the stack of tabloids still piled on the tabletop in front of her. It appeared that she was still looking though the first one, and had dog-eared several pages of it.

"How many did you get through, Mama?" Reva asked.

Darlene shrugged. "Just this one. I need some scissors."

Reva looked to Crystal. "Are there scissors somewhere?"

Crystal scanned the surfaces of the kitchen and sighed. "Sure, somewhere."

"What do you need scissors for?"

Darlene glanced up at Reva. "To cut out the ads for the things I'm going to order."

Crystal shook her head. "Ma, there ain't no tellin' how old those rags are. You can't order none of that stuff anymore."

"We already went through that," Reva said to Crystal. "She wants to go through all of them anyway."

"Can't you throw those out and get new ones?" Crystal stood beside the table and picked up one of the tabloids, flipping through it, her fingers harsh against the pages.

"The new ones won't have the same ads." Darlene closed the one she'd finally finished with and smoothed the cover with her chubby fingers.

Reva's eyes were drawn to her mother's nails, which were expertly polished a metallic burnt orange with bronzed tips. The nails of her ring fingers were painted with a contrasting crimson shade, with three perfectly placed dots of the bronze down their centers. Reva looked down at her own short, bare nails and wondered at how—or why—her mother would bother to maintain a perfect manicure and live in squalor. But she didn't dare ask that today.

"So, get new ones and order out of those, Ma. What are you gonna do with all that crap anyway?"

"I have an idea," Reva interjected as Darlene's chin began to tremble over the tabloids for the second time that day. "Instead of spending time trying to find scissors to cut these out or debating whether we should, let's take pictures of the things you think you might look up later." She pulled out her phone.

"But how will I get them?" Darlene peered over her glasses at Reva.

"I can email them to you from my phone, simple as pie," Reva said. "See, let me show you." She flipped open the tabloid Darlene had dog-eared to the first page she marked, accessed the camera on her phone, and took a picture of the page. "I took this picture," she said, holding the phone so Darlene could see as she walked through the process, "and now I'll open my email account, right here. What's your email address?"

"RevaNCrys@ai.co."

Reva's heart squeezed at the unexpected nod to her daughters from Darlene, but she set that aside in the interest of forward progress. "Okay, so I can attach the picture to the email, like this, and then I send it to you, and you'll have it on the computer when you open your email again. Neat, right?"

Darlene gave Reva an uncertain glance. "But what if something happens to the computer?"

"We'll back it up."

Darlene heaved a sigh. "Still, something could happen."

"I'll keep them, too, in my phone and as the email attachments. I promise they won't be lost, Mama," Reva said, slipping into the reassuring voice and posture she used with nervous clients at the office before depositions.

"Well, if you really think it'll be alright," Darlene said, her voice barely above a whisper.

"It will be," Reva reassured her. She pulled a chair up beside her mother's, flipped to the next dog-eared page, and snapped a picture. "I'll get these, and then we can go through the next one together. It'll move faster that way."

Three hours, twenty-two minutes, and nine hundred eighty-three photos later, Reva closed the last of the stack of tabloids with a groan.

"Are you sure they're all saved?" Darlene leaned over to look at Reva's phone.

"Yes, they're all saved. But there are way too many for me to email to you all at once, so I'm going to get a thumb drive and pull them down for you from my cloud drive," Reva explained. "They're all already backed up, though, so you don't need to worry."

Darlene pressed both hands on top of the stack of tabloids. "But you said you'd send them all today, to my email."

Reva laid a hand on Darlene's arm. "It'll go way faster if we use the thumb drive, and you can move them all onto your computer, just the same, okay? And we'll have the thumb drive, too, as an extra backup."

"Okay, then we should go ahead and do that," Darlene said with an authoritative nod of her head.

Reva looked at her watch. "It's already close to two o'clock, and I really think we should move on to something else, maybe clearing the rest of this corner where the table is. Let's take a thirty-minute break for some lunch, then get back to it, okay? I'll get the thumb drive squared away tonight and bring it to you tomorrow."

As Reva reached to try and gather the stack of tabloids to throw in the trash, Darlene stretched her arms around them, a noise rising from her throat somewhere between a sob and a growl. She shook her head furiously, her eyes closed tight. "You can't take them until I see them on the computer."

Reva pulled her hands back as if she'd been stung. "Are you

serious? I showed you that they're already backed up, Darlene. I'm not going to lose them. These paper copies can go now."

"Not until they're on my computer."

Crystal stuck her head in from the hallway and took in the scene. "Are y'all ready for a break? I'm starving, and the guys are, too. They have everything cleared and boxed from the bathroom. There ain't really anything here to eat. Reva, why don't we go pick up something and get one of them thumb drives on the way back. You can take care of it right here, today, and we can be done with that."

"Okay, fine," Reva said, rolling her eyes. "Darlene, would you like to ride with us to the store? You don't have to get out."

"No, no," Darlene said, not moving from her guarding position. "Y'all go ahead. I need a little rest. But I'm gonna want to go through those boxes from the bathroom and the hall, Crystal. Y'all don't try and get rid of those before I see."

"Okay, Mama, we won't. What do you want to eat?" Crystal asked.

"Maybe some chicken and a biscuit, and a sweet tea."

"We'll get a picnic bucket of chicken and a gallon of tea, take it out back to the shop to eat," Reva said. "Maybe after we've all had a break and some food, we can work together some more and make a bigger dent."

Tommy nodded, coming through with Willie. "We're going out back to wait. I need outta here for a bit."

Reva gave him a look. "I hear you. Y'all listen out for her."

He nodded again but didn't respond. Reva owed him for the day, she knew.

As Reva led the way to the car, Crystal snorted. "This is never gonna work, you know."

Slamming the door, Reva waited for her sister to settle in before backing out. "Do you have any better ideas?"

Crystal stared back at the house as she answered. "She'll be hiding when we get back, watch and see."

"Maybe, but maybe not. She seemed okay."

"Just wait and see," Crystal said again, rolling her eyes.

Reva tried to ignore the sinking feeling in her gut. This time, she knew Crystal was probably right, and she was getting it all wrong.

CHAPTER 10

"Funny, isn't it?" Crystal asked.

"What's that?"

Reva and Crystal hadn't spoken another word to each other in the car until then, as they passed Blossom Hill. The old farmhouse was a standout, even on a dark, rainy day like this one. The yard was perfectly manicured, the flowerbeds planted with butterfly bushes, daisies, and lantana, and ferns nearly bursting from their baskets hanging on the wide front porch. And now you could just see Bay and Scott's place a little further down the driveway, by the pond. It would make a wonderful place to raise a new family, Reva thought.

"How some people always get exactly what they want, all the time, and other people never get one damn thing they wish for."

"Still not letting you smoke in my car," Reva said, half smiling at her sister.

"Ha!" Crystal turned to face Reva.

"Where'd that come from?" Reva asked.

"Just thinking about Bay LaFleur, Mrs. Murphy."

"Ramirez," Reva reminded Crystal. Scott Murphy had taken his biological father's name last year after finding out who he was.

"Yeah, her. She's got such a perfect little life. Grew up in that fancy house on the Hill, perfect parents, hot brother—I'm still trying to figure out how our cousin scored Ethan LaFleur—hot husband…"

"Crys, you do realize that Bay's twin sister died when we were kids, and Scott was held by the Taliban and almost didn't make it home from Afghanistan, right? He's struggling with that still. And her music career was kind of a disaster. That's not exactly a perfect little life."

69

"Well, look at her now, married to the hot hero, having a baby, living in a brand new house, writing hit songs…doesn't sound like such a bad outcome to me."

Reva could see Crystal's point, but still, she felt the need to defend her friend. Bay had been through so much that neither of them could imagine. "I'm just saying, she's seen her fair share of heartache and trials. She's done her work to get where she is. You can't fault her for that."

Crystal tapped her pack of cigarettes against her knee, which had begun to bounce. "Yeah, well, I can fault her for being such a snotty bee to us growing up."

"She was not." Reva said firmly as she pulled into the restaurant parking lot.

"Then why were we never invited to any of those parties at the barn, or the bonfires?"

Reva's nose crinkled. "What do you mean? I was always invited."

Crystal huffed. "No, Tommy was always invited, and he took you with him. There's a difference, Sis."

Reva rolled her eyes. "I was invited."

"Oh, I see. Perfect little Reva was included, but I got left behind, like always."

"Whatever, let's just get the food and go. Today's not the day for this fight."

The sisters were quiet as they drove back to the house. As soon as they parked in the driveway, Crystal was out of the car without offering any help with the food, a cigarette already perched between her lips waiting for the lighter.

"Fine, pout if you need to," Reva mumbled as she snatched the bags from the back seat and struggled up the steps.

"Mama," Reva called from the kitchen door, "we're back! Come on out and eat with us."

She waited for a response, but not hearing one, she stepped through the kitchen and hall to tap on Darlene's door. "We've got lunch out in the shop, if you want to come out and eat with us."

When there was no answer after several long minutes, Reva tapped the door with her knuckles again.

"She won't come back out today, Reva." Crystal stood in the kitchen doorway, shaking her head. "This is what I was afraid of after this morning."

Reva followed Crystal back into the kitchen. "But we barely did anything this morning. We struggled to get through this pile of..."

The stack of tabloids was gone from the table. Reva checked the trash, but knew she wouldn't find them there.

Crystal sighed. "See, that's what she does."

"Where did she put them?" Reva asked Crystal.

Crystal shrugged. "Who knows. If you try to get rid of something she isn't keen to part with, she'll hide it. I got no clue where she hides it, but...well, she hides it."

"But why would she hide those when she knew I was going to get the thumb drive for the pictures? She'd have them on the computer today."

"Who knows why she does what she does? But if she's in that room with the door locked, you ain't gettin' those things back today," Crystal said, looking all too pleased with herself for having been right.

Reva threw herself down into the lone kitchen chair with a grunt. "She's gotta come out of there at some point, at least to eat or pee. And when she does—"

"Don't kid yourself. She's in that room for days on end sometimes, with a stash of junk food and God knows what else. Long as she knows you're here and trying to throw out stuff she's not interested in partin' ways with, she'll wait you out."

"Why do y'all let her behave like this?" Reva asked, disgust twisting her face.

Crystal two took long steps and bent at the waist to get in Reva's face so fast it seemed she'd been waiting for the opportunity. "That's easy for you to say, sittin' pretty over there at Gran's house pretending your people over here don't even exist. Why do we let her, Reva? What in the hell do you suggest we do about it?"

Reva sprung to her feet and pushed past her sister. "I suggest you wash a dish or two," she said, waving an arm toward the sink, "or get some of this crap off the counters away, or better yet, in the trash. If Darlene's spending most of her time shut up in her room snacking on cheese puffs, why don't you haul some shit right on out of here? Not like she'd notice."

Crystal's eyes flashed with anger when she met Reva's gaze. "You don't think she'd notice?" Crystal picked up a stack of one-use storage containers from the counter and threw them at Reva, scattering the clear plastic bottoms and flimsy blue lids over the floor. "Take those to the trash out there today and see where they are tomorrow morning. She'll dig through the trash cans at night while we're sleeping like a damn scavenger and put back whatever we took. You could take two of the ten, and I promise you she'd know two were missing and go pull them back out, or find ones to replace 'em. And after all that time she spent lovin' on those magazines with you today, you can rest assured that you'll have to take them over her dead body. You think you're gonna come in here all logical and level-headed and tell her she's got to clean up overnight?"

"Crystal, we have less than a month to clean out the entire house," Reva said, her voice rising with frustration. "We don't have time to drag our heels over a pile of stupid tabloid magazines. God, we wasted hours on them today already."

Crystal plopped down in the chair Reva had exited and started chewing on the side of her thumb. "Still, Reva, you can't just steamroll over her."

Reva blew out a long breath, then leaned against the counter, defeated. "This may be more than we can handle by ourselves after all. Maybe I should call one of those people the fire marshal recommended."

Crystal laughed. "Mama or Daddy neither one'll let them county folks back in here without a fight."

"In twenty-four days, those county folks aren't going to ask when they show up. I'll call one of those cleanup guys they suggested. We can't do this without help, obviously."

"Let me do it."

Reva cocked a brow at her sister. "Let you do what?"

"Let me call the cleanup guys. I'm living here, so I can be here to meet with them and help easier than you. And I reckon it's the least I can do, since I moved back in rent free and all, as you keep pointin' out."

"Listen, I know sometimes I say things in frustration…"

Crystal held a hand up to stop her. "Nah, it's okay. I can do more to help out, and I'll start with this."

"Okay," Reva said, eyeing Crystal cautiously. "Will you let me know how it goes when you talk to them?"

Crystal nodded. Reva could see the wheels turning in her sister's head, and it tweaked her nerves.

"You sure?"

"Yeah, I got it," Crystal said, rolling her eyes. "Trust me."

Checking the time, Reva grimaced. "I guess today is a bust, if Darlene won't even come back out of the bedroom. I'll go round up Tommy and go home. I need a long, hot shower and a glass of wine after this day."

"I'll go get Tommy for you," Crystal said, getting to her feet. "I need a smoke, anyway."

"Tell him to bring some of that chicken. I don't feel much like cooking."

Left alone at the kitchen table where she'd spent much of the day with Darlene, she sat back down at the table and let her shoulders slump and her head tip forward. She examined the stacks that remained on the table: random unsorted mail, several packages of holiday-themed paper plates and napkins, a few partially-burned scented candles, a pile of dish towels that could have been clean or dirty.

As she stood to leave, she noticed a lone tabloid left on the floor under the table. Bending to grab it, she balled it up in her hands and fought back tears of frustration. She wanted to hope that somehow the house would be salvageable, that Crystal would make that phone call and whoever came out to help their parents would somehow get Darlene on board with the cleanup, but the outcome of the day's work hadn't left her much hope to cling to at all.

GINA HERON

CHAPTER 11

"Hey Reva, did you lock up?"

"Gimme a minute," Reva called to Macon, glancing at the clock. It was three past noon on a Wednesday, file review day, when they closed up shop promptly at noon. Reva would make a run to pick up lunch, and they'd eat while reviewing the active case files, then Reva would set up any new files while Macon reviewed the comprehensive case log for any missed follow-ups. There rarely were any, given that the one thing he and Reva had in common seemed to be an obsession with organization.

She saved the file she was working on and went to the lobby to lock the front door. Macon stood in the threshold of his office, arms crossed, and laughed as he watched her. "You wear a lot of black, don't you?"

Reva furrowed her brow and glanced back at him. "I guess I like to keep things like my wardrobe simple," she replied. "I assume it's appropriate."

"Oh, sure," he said, shrugging. "Just realizing I don't think I've ever seen you wear much color."

"I... wouldn't have guessed you'd notice."

"Thankfully quiet, this morning, right?" he asked, still watching her as she moved around the office.

"Yep. What are you feeling up to today?" she asked, holding out the binder of alphabetized menus she'd grabbed from her drawer.

Macon didn't move to take the binder from her hands. "Let's go out somewhere today."

"Macon—" Reva started to object, but he cut her off.

"We haven't been out to lunch in ages, and you've been eating at your desk every day lately. C'mon."

"Well, okay, but remember I have an appointment at three, so I won't be here all day."

"Oh, that's right," Macon said, a hint of curiosity in his eyes. He'd asked earlier where she was off to, and she changed the subject without answering. Sometimes that was enough with Macon. Other times, he seemed to think he was entitled to keep tabs on her every move. "Somewhere close then, and we'll bring a couple of the new case files along for review, if you've got them set up."

Reva grabbed the fresh stack from the corner of her desk. "Sure do. Want to walk over to Debbie's?"

"Works for me," he answered.

Reva hurried ahead of him as he locked up the back door. She carried the new files as they crossed the side street to the little diner on the corner of the main road.

"Still so muggy, but at least the rain's holding off today," Macon said, making small talk along the way. It had been a rare dry day so far.

"Mmhmm," Reva murmured, glancing up at Macon and thinking about her law school acceptance letter, tucked between the fourth and last files in the neat stack. Since she hadn't asked him for a reference letter, Macon wasn't aware yet of her application, so she knew the acceptance would be a surprise. She hoped he would be happy for her, even if it meant she wouldn't be able to work at the office in New Hope once school started. But she needed to talk to him about nominating her for the firm's yearly grant. After seven years of hard work, graduating with honors and blowing the LSAT out of the water, she hoped she'd be a shoe-in.

She had to rely on Macon at this point to push through her nomination. Her stomach rolled every time she thought about that fact.

Sliding into a booth by one of the big front windows of Debbie's, Macon and Reva spread the files she'd brought over between them.

"Two specials, Macon?" Debbie called from behind the counter.

"Two specials," Reva called back, smiling up at the regular waitress, Hailey, as she sat down two glasses of the best sweet tea in the county.

Hailey smiled back at Reva before turning her full attention to

Macon. "Hi, Mr. McKinley," she said, tugging at the hem of her snug tee shirt with one hand and flipping her long, blonde-streaked hair over her shoulder with the other.

"Hailey," Macon answered with a nod and a wink. "Good to see you again. Gearing up for school?"

"Yeah, I guess I am." Hailey leaned a trim hip against the edge of the table. "My schedule's gonna get crazy in the next few weeks. Nothing like a bigshot lawyer's, though," she teased, cutting her eyes playfully at Macon.

"Especially a bigshot lawyer with a beautiful wife and toddler at home," Reva interjected. She wasn't exactly sure what kind of dance she was witnessing between her boss and the waitress, but it made her uncomfortable enough to point the girl's attention to the ring on his finger, even though she knew that didn't matter as much to some as it did others.

"Well, I guess I better get back there and make sure your order's out on time," Hailey called over her shoulder as she walked away.

Macon turned his attention back to Reva, grinning.

"What have you got for me?" he asked before taking a sip from his cup.

Reva took a deep breath and shoved down her irritation.

"I've got three new accident cases, boiler plate pleadings drafted for you, and I've got a pro bono from DSS," she said, tapping each file with her pen.

Macon rolled his eyes and slumped in the booth. "Schedule something to get me out of the pro bono."

"No can do," Reva said, shaking her head. "You've passed on the last two. The judge'll have your hide if you try to get out of a third."

"You're probably right."

"Anyway, I've got everything pretty well together for it to get you started. You can look these over while I'm out this afternoon and I'll get everything filed in the morning."

Macon studied Reva across the table, one brow cocked and a slight smile lifting a corner of his mouth.

"What?"

"You're really good at your job, Reva. I was thinking, maybe you should look into expanding your horizons a bit."

"Funny you should mention that," Reva said, a smile of her own blooming across her face. "I've been thinking the same thing." She pulled the thin file that held her law school acceptance letter out from the stack.

"Wait a minute," Macon said, laughing, "is that an application? Don't tell me we had the same brilliant idea."

"Well, I may have had it a little ahead of you," Reva beamed. "This isn't an application. It's my acceptance letter." She handed the folder over to Macon and watched his eyes go wide as he read the letter.

"I wasn't—" he began, then shook his head. "Reva, I was going to suggest you apply to paralegal school."

"Oh," Reva said, shrugging. "Well, I did one better, I guess. Can you believe it? Early acceptance, even. I can start in the spring semester."

"I see that," Macon said, studying the letter. His mouth twisted into something less than a smile.

"What?"

He shook his head. "Nothing, I—no, this is great. Really, congratulations."

Reva squared her shoulders and pressed her back into the booth cushions. She took a steadying breath. "You seem less than enthused."

"You caught me off guard is all," Macon said. "When did you decide you were interested in law school? You never mentioned it to me before."

"I didn't want to bring it up if there didn't turn out to be any reason to bring it up."

Macon nodded. "You didn't think you'd get in."

Reva watched a group of four silver-haired ladies shuffle past the window toward the door. "I wasn't sure. It could have gone either way."

"Didn't you need any references?" he asked

"Kevin Payne wrote one for me, and Judge Hawke. A couple of the other attorneys I've worked with at the firm."

Macon sat back further in his seat, eyes wide. "Judge Hawke? Really? How'd you swing a reference from him?"

Reva nodded, sipping her tea. "I did research for him right after I graduated from college, part-time. He told me then I'd make a brilliant lawyer, if only…"

"If only?" Macon prodded.

"If only I hadn't married young and tied myself down in New Hope before it occurred to me that I might want more."

"Judge Hawke told you that you'd make a brilliant lawyer?"

"I believe those were his exact words," Reva said, smiling at the memory. It was one she'd held close to her heart for years.

"Wow. Judge Hawke doesn't like anyone, you know."

"He liked me just fine. You have to know how to handle him," Reva said, smiling sweetly.

"I won't ask," Macon said, rolling his eyes.

Reva nearly spit out her sweet tea. "Nothing out of the way, mind you," she said through her coughing fit. "I figured out how he liked things handled, and I handled them that way."

Macon studied her across the table, looking as if he was measuring his words carefully. "That's the thing about you, Reva. You're so good at the work you do now. Honestly, I wasn't even going to recommend a paralegal program because you need it, I'd like to see you have the title you already earn every day at the firm."

"Then don't you think it would stand to reason that I'd also be good at what you do?"

Macon sighed. "It's not that I don't think you'd be a good lawyer. You'd be a fine lawyer, I'm sure."

He paused as Debbie delivered their food to the table herself. Reva stared down at her plate, her appetite completely gone. She picked up her fork anyway, swirling gravy into the mashed potatoes with the tines. The tears she had to fight to hold back surprised her. She hadn't realized how much she'd been counting on Macon's support until the moment it was clear she wouldn't have it. Even though their relationship was awkward, she'd hoped that it wouldn't be too difficult to get him on board.

"Hey," Macon started, leaning in, "I don't mean to take the wind out of your sails, okay? I'm thinking of the bigger picture. Your home is here, your husband and family—"

"We're not that far from Columbia, though. Plenty of people commute back and forth every day, or stay over a night or two during the week."

He nodded slowly. "That's true."

"Say what's on your mind, Macon. There's obviously something."

"Okay," he said on a sigh. "What does Tommy think about all of this?"

Reva shrugged. "He'll come around."

Macon huffed, leaning back in his chair. "I assume he didn't know what you were up to, either?"

"You say that like I was doing something nefarious," Reva clipped.

"Well, going off behind your husband's back on something as huge has applying to a law school, hours away from home... not to mention the expense of it."

"It's a couple of hours away, that's all. I can make that work. I could maybe stay on at the firm's Columbia office part-time. And, I was thinking," Reva paused, took a steadying breath. "Maybe you could put my name forward for the firm's grant?"

Macon dropped his hands on the table and stared out of the window. "Let's see what you end up deciding, okay? Don't get ahead of yourself, especially if you haven't even sorted it through with Tommy."

Reva shifted her weight and fumbled with the files that she'd restacked on the table. "You know, Macon, this isn't 1950. Tommy doesn't make my decisions for me. I don't need his permission."

"Reva, he's your husband, for God's sake. Whatever happened to 'love, honor, and obey?'"

"The obey part wasn't in my vows," Reva said through gritted teeth.

Standing up and gathering the files and her purse, Reva called over to Hailey. "Would you box up our lunches, please? I lost track of time and have to get to an appointment. Macon'll take them back to the office."

"Reva, I didn't mean—"

"Don't worry about it, Macon. I got other things to do today. We'll talk about it another time."

"Let me know..." he started as she walked to the door.

Reva didn't stop to acknowledge his request. She couldn't afford to—couldn't afford the tears that still threatened to spill. She might need them later.

CHAPTER 12

"Are you kidding me?" Reva muttered under her breath as she walked into the waiting area of her OB/GYN's office. She almost stumbled as she scanned the room and her eyes landed first on her husband, who she'd been certain wouldn't take time out of his day for this appointment, and then on her mother-in-law sitting beside him.

Reva glared at Tommy when he met her gaze, then walked to the check-in window, her hand shaking as she scribbled her information on the pink paper form provided: name, time of appointment, time of arrival, doctor, change of address since last visit (no), change in insurance coverage since last visit (no).

When she tore off the top slip of paper and held it up to the window, the receptionist, Tina, finally looked up at her. She smiled and pushed open the glass. "Reva, hey. How are you?"

Reva shrugged, the anxious churning in her gut making it difficult to hide her unease. Tina's gaze softened with compassion. Doctor Keller's staff knew Reva, knew her case. Sometimes, their kindness leaned too far into sympathy and chaffed. Today, though, she figured she'd use that sympathy for a little extra buffer.

"Tina, if Tommy and Amelia try to come back with me, do me a favor and tell them Doctor Keller needs to see me on my own?" Reva whispered.

Tina nodded her understanding. "Sure, sweetie. Whatever you want—that's always your decision."

"Thanks, I know. It'll be easier for me if it's coming from him."

Tina nodded again. "I got you."

Reva turned and walked slowly to the bank of chairs where Tommy and Amelia sat, both looking sheepish. She sat down next to Tommy without speaking, placing him between his wife and his mother, a familiar position for him the last decade.

"I know you said not to come…" Tommy started, trailing off before reaching over to squeeze Reva's knee.

"Yes, I did," she said, bristling at his touch. "This is just a checkup, like I said."

Amelia leaned forward to peer around Tommy at Reva. "I hope you don't mind, when Tommy told me you had an appointment today—well, I thought maybe you could use a little extra moral support is all."

Reva took a deep, steadying breath and tried at a smile for Amelia. She knew in her heart that Amelia's reason for being there was sincere. She wanted to support Reva—that is, she wanted to support Reva if what Reva wanted was the same thing that Tommy wanted.

And what Tommy wanted was for Reva to try for another baby.

Her stomach churned at the thought. "Thanks for that," Reva said, "but it's really just a regular checkup."

"Still," Amelia said, "we want to be here for you, honey, for the whole process, whatever it might be." She reached across Tommy to squeeze Reva's hand. Reva tried not to tense at the gesture.

"Reva, you can come on back."

Tina's voice startled Reva from her seat. Tommy started to stand up, but Reva held her hand up to stop him. "They'll call you back after the exam," She said.

Tina nodded. "Just Reva for now, y'all."

Reva mumbled her thanks to Tina as they walked side by side down the hall, and Tina bumped her shoulder into Reva's in silent solidarity. They bypassed the second waiting area and went straight in for vitals before Tina led Reva into a room for her exam.

As she sat with her thin hospital gown tucked tight around her, the paper over the exam table crinkling beneath her legs, she knew she wouldn't have to wait very long, which was usually a relief. But today, with Tommy and Amelia sitting out in the lobby waiting for her, dragging it out a bit didn't seem like the worst idea.

She wouldn't have much time when the exam was over to get her story together. And if either of them insisted on coming back, on talking with Doctor Keller, she'd have some explaining to do.

Reva could always refuse, but she also knew how suspicious it would be if she did. Doctor Keller would likely say the same thing today that he had at her last two appointments, and she wasn't ready to share that with Tommy, or with Amelia. Not yet.

Tensing at the gentle tap of knuckles against the door, Reva thought that she probably never would be ready again.

Dr. Keller gave Reva a cautious smile as he joined her in his office after her ultrasound and exam.

"So, what's the verdict?" she asked when he was settled into the chair behind his massive mahogany desk.

"Getting right to the point," he said, taking his glasses off, "there's no reason why you and Tommy can't try for another baby. Everything on your ultrasound and from your examination looks normal. Unless something surprises me in your lab results, you're all set."

Reva swallowed hard. "So, no reason?"

"None that I can see, from a strictly medical perspective." He returned his glasses to his nose and flipped through her chart again. "So, if you're ready this time, I won't write you another prescription for your—"

"No," Reva broke in, leaning forward and holding out a hand. She suddenly felt flushed. A trickle of sweat ran down her spine. "No, I'd like to wait a little while longer."

The sympathy in Dr. Keller's eyes had her swallowing against the lump in her throat again. "That's your call, of course."

"I mean, I'd like to be sure, you know? I got accepted to law school, and Tommy's business keeps him so busy…"

"Reva, I know that you've been through a lot of challenges, and there are things to consider besides your physical ability to carry a child. I can't speak to any of the other reasons you might have for waiting, but…"

"But you know better than anybody how scared I am to do this again."

Reva tried not to think about the day she'd lost Tee Jae two years earlier. Ever. She'd considered changing doctors altogether afterward, starting over with a new OB/GYN, even though she loved Dr. Keller. Amelia had convinced her to reconsider, and Reva knew she'd been right.

Still, it was hard to sit across the desk from him and keep her composure during these conversations. He'd been the one there coaching her through the delivery of her stillborn son, with tears in his own eyes as he tried to comfort her. He'd held her hand afterward as she said goodbye. Tommy hadn't been there in the room with her. He couldn't hold it together. So, it was Dr. Keller. He understood.

There was a long silence before Dr. Keller responded. "There are other things for you to consider going forward, Reva. You're not quite thirty yet, and there's still plenty of time for you to conceive, if you'd like a family, but take that into consideration as you make plans."

"What about my eggs?" Reva blurted, the thought that had been bubbling in the back of her mind surfacing quickly. "Can we freeze my eggs?"

"That's an option to consider if the time comes," Dr. Keller responded, nodding.

"Let's do that. I want to do that."

"One thing at a time, okay?" Dr. Keller said, his kind smile returning.

Reva dabbed at her eyes with the backs of her hands and nodded.

"This is all good news, you know. You don't have to make any decisions today. I'll get that prescription in for you. It'll be at the checkout window." Dr. Keller came around the desk and squeezed her shoulder. "Take a few minutes before you go if you need to. No rush. On any of this, okay? Take your time and make sure you do what's best for you."

"Thank you," she whispered.

Left alone in the office, she pulled out her phone and considered texting Tommy that she'd be out in a minute, but thought better of it. She didn't want to give him a chance to talk with Dr. Keller if she could help it.

So, instead of exiting through the lobby, once she'd checked out, she headed down the stairs and outside. Then she sent Tommy a text telling him to come down with Amelia and meet her outside the main entrance of the women's center.

As she waited, she paced a little, slapping her hands against her cheeks lightly. She started to sweat immediately in the mid-afternoon humidity, both from the heat and her nerves jangling through her body. These trips to Dr. Keller were enough to provoke her anxiety, but adding Tommy and Amelia to the mix, the questions she knew would be coming, sent her spinning.

"Reva, what's going on?"

She turned at the sound of Tommy's voice. Amelia took in Reva's sweaty, disheveled appearance, and her forehead crinkled with concern. She took Reva by the elbow and led her into the shade of the building.

"Honey, what happened? Amelia asked. "Are you okay?"

Reva shook her head no, but said, "Yeah, I'm—I'm okay. I needed to get some air."

"No small feat in this heat," Amelia said, fanning her face with a hand. "What did the doctor say?"

"Mama—" Tommy started.

"I'm sorry, but—well, Reva, you're obviously upset. I'm concerned about you is all."

"I know, Amelia," Reva said. "Everything is the same. It's not time yet."

Amelia nodded slowly, looking to Tommy.

"What else did he say?" Tommy asked.

"Nothing new, really. We talked about freezing some eggs."

Tommy rolled his eyes and groaned.

"I told him we're not ready to consider that yet. Listen," Reva said, taking a step back from the united front of her husband and his mother, "I'm a little overwhelmed here. I need a little quiet time to process, and then I can fill in the details, okay?"

"Of course," Amelia said. "We wanted to be here for support if you needed it. You have so much on your plate right now with work, and your folks, and now Tommy tells me you're actually thinking about going back to school…"

Amelia trailed off as Reva's eyes narrowed, cutting to Tommy.

"She was gonna have to find out sometime, if you're not going to be taking on more at the Roost like we planned," Tommy said, raising his shoulders in a shrug.

"Thanks, really," Reva said, crossing her arms over her chest. "I'll see y'all later."

With that, Reva turned away and hurried to the garage where she'd parked on the second floor, jogged up the stairs, and retreated to the solitude of her car.

She considered for a moment whether she should go back to work for a couple of hours, but she didn't feel like risking any more awkward interactions with Macon, especially not after their conversation over lunch. She drove home on autopilot. A sense of relief settled around her heart as she approached the one place she'd consistently felt at ease her whole life. But fresh tears sprang to her eyes at the thought of never filling that house with a new generation of children to feel the warmth and love built into its bones.

What she was doing to Tommy was wrong, keeping the truth from him. She knew that. But she also knew that, as much as she'd always dreamed of having a family with him, she wasn't ready to take a chance on a fresh wave of grief after the losses she'd already suffered. Her body might be ready, but her heart wasn't.

And, if she was completely honest with herself, she didn't know if it ever would be.

Reva walked to the edge of the water behind the house. She knelt in the grass, the weight of her confusion too heavy on her shoulders to move forward. Closing her eyes, she whispered into the wind that swirled around her, feeling the moisture from the earth seep through at her knees as the heavy clouds above her finally broke. She couldn't have followed her own thoughts in those moments if she'd tried, but from somewhere inside her came a plea for help, for direction, for a sense of family she'd lost when Gran passed, for any little bit of peace, for something in her life to fall into its proper place.

When she opened her eyes, Lucille had drawn near her, the lone witness to the pain dripping from her cheeks. The bird kept her eyes trained on the water, as if to respect the privacy of the moment yet still be there. So much like what Gran would have done.

"You can't always have the thing you want most, Lucille," Reva whispered. "Sometimes, you don't even know what it is you want most. Maybe that's the truest thing I know."

CHAPTER 13

Reva felt the vibrations from her cell phone, which was stowed away in her top desk drawer, for the third time in twelve minutes. She shook her head and continued with her transcription, finishing up Macon's sixth recording of the day. She checked the display on her machine to see how much was left to get through.

"Four more already? Ugh. What's naggin' his ass this morning, I wonder. Doesn't he know it's Friday?" she said under her breath.

It wasn't lost on Reva that Macon had been keeping to himself since their conversation at Debbie's two days earlier. He hadn't asked about her appointment, nor had he mentioned putting her name forward for the firm's grant, like she'd asked. She had to admit feeling a little rattled that he might be that convinced that law school would be the wrong choice for her. And a little disappointed that he would sell her short.

She printed the letter she'd just finished, added it to the stack she was making for Macon's review and signature, then grabbed her phone from the drawer to see who'd been calling.

"Caprice?"

Reva's heart fluttered at seeing the three missed calls from the girl. She dialed her back and waited impatiently for an answer, tapping her foot against the plastic mat beneath her office chair, watching Macon's closed door and hoping he wouldn't decide to open it in time to find her on her cell phone.

Not that it had ever mattered before. But Macon had been in a mood, no denying it. She didn't want to stir the pot.

"Miss Reva, thank the Lord," Caprice picked up on the third ring, breathless.

"Hey Caprice. What's going on?"

There was a heavy pause on the other end of the line, completely out of character for the chatty teenager. "You better come see for yourself. I ain't seen the likes of this before."

"The likes of what?" Reva asked, her voice rising.

"There's all kinds of vans outside, TV vans, and your folks' place is crawling with people."

Reva jumped to her feet, fumbled with the office phone to set it to go to the voice mail system, then snatched her purse from beneath the desk. "On the way," she said, hanging up without waiting for a response.

It wasn't quite eleven o'clock yet—way too early for her actual lunch break—so, rather than having to talk to Macon in his present state, she shot him a text message:

Have a little family emergency to deal with. Taking lunch early. Phone is rolled to VM. Be back ASAP.

And with that she dropped her phone into her purse and willed herself not to worry about the fallout. Considering the implications of Caprice's call to her, she had a bigger fire to fight than whatever was going on with Macon.

Driving like the hounds of hell were on her heels and checking the rear view every half minute, sure that a police cruiser would fly up behind her and ruin her perfect driving record, Reva tried to keep her mind from spinning out to worst-case scenarios. There was no chance of her coming up with a likely reason there would be TV vans out front of her parents' house, so there was really no use trying. The closer she got, though, the faster her heart fluttered in her chest. Being summonsed like this for a second time in as many weeks left her wondering how close her entire family was to imploding.

When she took the right onto her parents' street, she could see the vans Caprice mentioned, and Caprice herself leaning against her mother's mailbox, not even attempting to hide her interest in the scene. Reva pulled off the road and threw the car in park, barely hesitating to take the keys and slam the door before jogging to Caprice's perch.

"I ain't seen nothin' like this in all my days," Caprice said, shaking her head as Reva reached her side, in a tone that would have been better suited to a seventy-year-old. Reva had to wonder where she picked up the dramatic flair.

Reva rested a hand on Caprice's shoulder. "What exactly is this? Surely you got it all figured out by now."

"Little while ago, them two vans pulled up in the driveway over here. Or I reckon it was a little while ago—I didn't see 'em pull up, just saw 'em when I was coming out to sit on the stoop, you know? Figured they was here to help with cleaning up and whatnot."

Reva nodded, studying the vans. "Maybe Crystal actually managed to call in some help without me having to step in. If so, that's a first."

"Well, she's over there, for sure. She came bustin' out the door and down the steps, teeterin' around on red high heel shoes—who wears those things at home, anyways?—so she must have been waiting on them, I figured. Met them right out in the driveway before they could even get themselves out of their vans." Caprice paused for a good giggle. "And those heels sunk dead in the dirt every step she took. Anyway, there's five of them that was in the vans that piled out. The guy with the bigger camera is under the carport, I think. He went inside for a minute, but then they sent him right on back out."

"Guy with a big camera?" Reva asked, straining to see past the vans without being seen.

"Like one of them they use for TV," Caprice said.

Reva's heart lurched in her chest. "Oh no," she whispered, stepping closer to study the side of the van, the emblem splashed there suddenly ringing all sorts of bells in her head. "It's not—it can't be—"

"I think it is," Caprice said, cocking a brow.

Reva jogged across the street toward the two vans and ducked in between them, catching a glimpse of a lanky black guy in a polo shirt standing casually beneath the carport, playing with his cell phone.

"Hi," Reva said, emerging in front of him. He looked up at her and then to the side door as she extended a hand. "I'm Reva Patterson. This is my parents' home."

"Hey, I'm Terrance," the man took her hand, half his mouth curling into a smile.

"What?" Reva asked, sensing his scrutiny.

He shook his head. "There's always one, in every one of these families."

"One what?" She scrunched her face.

"One who doesn't fit with the rest. I was hoping you'd show up soon, see if maybe you could convince your mother to let the big black guy in."

Reva covered her face with her hands. "Oh no…oh, she didn't. I'm so, so sorry—"

Terrance shrugged a shoulder. "At least she didn't shoot at me. Yet."

The color drained from Reva's face as she struggled to find words to express her embarrassment, and to explain Darlene's inexplicable behavior. It was another of the things Reva could point to as a shift after her mother's illness. She could never recall Darlene being rude or averse to anyone before she fell ill, but after, she'd turned skittish, particularly with men, and most particularly with black men.

"Why are you here? I mean, not you specifically, but—" Reva paused and pointed to the vans in the driveway.

"We're filming an episode here. Or at least we're supposed to be filming. I'm part of the camera crew for Help with Hoarding."

"How—but why are you here? I mean the show."

Terrance answered with a lift of his brow and a nod toward the house.

"Well, yeah, I know, hoarding. But—did someone call you? Who called you?"

"All I can tell you is what we got in the briefing on the way. The call came in from the daughter residing in the Tucker residence with her parents—and I gather that would be your sister and not you—who said the family has less than thirty days to clean out the hoard or have the home deemed unlivable and scheduled for demo by the county." He raised a hand and started a countdown. "We have an unstable, possibly mentally ill mother, a father who is an enabler, one daughter who's sacrificed her independence to stay home and care for her parents, and another daughter who washed her hands of the situation and never visits."

Reva's face twisted with disbelief, which got a laugh out of Terrance. "I cannot believe the nerve—my sister has spent most of the last ten years in and out of rehab and her multitude of boyfriends' houses. I did not wash my hands—oh, nevermind." She stomped to the stoop at the back door, stopped and turned back to Terrance. "I am truly sorry that we've bothered you all with this mess, but we won't be needing a TV show filming out here. The absentee daughter will handle it."

Terrance held up his hands. "The contracts aren't my department. You'll have to take that up with the producers. They'll need you to sign a waiver for the filming, too."

"Contracts?" Reva muttered curses under her breath as she picked her way through the kitchen, toward Darlene's room, where a little crowd was gathered around her mama's chair.

"So, Mrs. Tucker, how would you feel about parting with any of this stack of papers?"

Reva couldn't suppress a laugh at the irony of the petite blonde woman's question to Darlene as she slipped into the room behind Willie. Heads turned toward her, but her focus at the moment was drawn to Crystal. Caprice had been right—her sister looked ridiculous standing on precariously high red heels in a denim skirt short enough to skim her ass cheeks and a bedazzled red tank top, black lace bra showing through for the world to see.

"I was baffled outside as to why you would have called in a whole damn circus to humiliate your own family, Crystal," she said, letting her eyes drift from her sister's overdone hair to her ridiculous shoes, "but I can see now that you're finally fulfilling your dream of playing a hooker on TV."

Crystal crossed her arms over her padded chest, popped a hip, and jutted out her chin. "Whatever, Reva. At least I'm doing something to help. What are you doin'? Coming over here one day a weekend begging Mama to throw out newspapers she scrambles off with and hides elsewhere? We ain't got time for that nonsense. We needed some professional help."

"There is professional help to be had that doesn't come with a camera crew," Reva said, a little too loud.

The blonde woman, forming a sharp contrast to Crystal with her dark slacks, dress shirt, blazer, and sneakers, moved between the sisters and extended her hand. "You must be Reva. I'm Lindsay Close, clinical psychologist specializing in anxiety disorders and hoarding."

Reva studied Lindsay's hand, the pale skin a bit pink, blue veins standing out against it, clean unpolished nails. She'd bet Lindsay scrubbed those hands damn near bloody after a day in a house like this. She finally reached out her own hand to shake

Lindsay's. "That's me, the one who has apparently abandoned the family and left them to live in squalor."

Lindsay's soft expression faltered a little, a hard line forming in her forehead. "We're not here to take sides between you and your sister, Reva. We'll do the best we can to help your parents save this house. We hope you'll help with that, as well."

Reva nodded slowly, appreciative of Lindsay's bluntness, at least. "Of course, I want to help my parents. But I'm not thrilled about doing it with cameras rolling." Reva glanced to the corner, where a second cameraman—a white one—stood filming. "Can you quit it, please?"

Lindsay nodded at the man, who pressed some buttons and lowered the camera from his shoulder. Another man who stood holding a microphone on a pole lowered it, too, and moved closer to the cameraman to chat.

"Let's step outside and talk this through, shall we?" Lindsay walked around Reva, past Willie, and through the kitchen without looking back to see who followed. Reva sensed the other woman was accustomed to being in charge, smoothing things over, and getting people to see things her way. She'd be useful given the situation they faced with Darlene, Reva could admit, but did she have to come with the camera crew?

Lindsay gave Terrance's arm a squeeze and stood beside him when they reached the carport. Crystal stood away from the group and lit a cigarette.

"I told you I'd take care of getting help in here, and that's what I did," Crystal started in, narrowing her eyes at Reva. "I don't see what the problem is, except maybe for once everybody ain't going along with your way."

"You had a list of numbers for agencies that could come help with cleanup, Crystal. I'm pretty sure no TV shows were on the list."

"Well, you know what those agencies aren't, Reva? Free. And this TV show is."

"How much would they charge?" Reva asked, knowing her parents likely couldn't pay whatever the fee might be, and that Crystal had nothing to contribute. But Reva could find a way, if it meant avoiding the humiliation of having their family's shame broadcast for the entire world to see. She thought of Tommy's family, the Pattersons, of Amelia and the Pearl Girls sitting around at their beach house on Edisto, swigging their spiked sweet tea or mint juleps, watching a full hour episode of Help for Hoarders featuring Reva's own family, congratulating themselves for having the good sense to shut her out when she married Tommy. Surely someone who came from a family like hers, from a mess like this, didn't belong in their midst. Her face flushed at the thought.

She'd find the money for a service. She had to.

"The cheapest one estimated eight thousand dollars," Crystal said, her expression smug as she watched Reva's mouth go slack.

"Eight thousand?"

"Yeah, big sister. You got that stashed somewhere? We sure as shit don't have it over here."

"The cost of the services is out of reach for most families of hoarders, unfortunately," Lindsay broke in. She directed her attention to Reva. "I'm truly sorry that you feel blindsided by our involvement, but let me assure you that we will get the job done for you and your family. Our understanding was that you weren't interested in participating with the cleanup, but I can see that's not the case."

Lindsay glanced in Crystal's direction. "I regret that we were misinformed. But we're here now, all of the contracts are in order, and frankly, your parents are running out of time if they're going to keep their home. If you really want to spend time considering other options, I'd ask that you do so quickly. There are other families in line behind yours who'd welcome the opportunity for our assistance."

Reva's heart pounded against her ribs. She hated feeling backed into a corner, and she didn't know what to do. If she sent Lindsay and her crew away, would she be able to find the time, money, and assistance her parents needed in less than a month? On the other hand, could she live with the humiliation of this ultimate exposure of her family's dirty secret?

"I wish—I don't—"

"You're worried about this being so public, right?" Lindsay laid a gentle hand on Reva's shoulder. "Believe it or not, having this out in the open, and actually dealing with the hoard and the underlying issues that have contributed to your mother's disorder, it will remove a huge burden for all of you. And, in the process of cleaning this out, we can start your mother down the path to wellness. Your parents can have a fresh start. You all can. I'd encourage you to see this as an opportunity for your family, rather than an embarrassment."

An opportunity, rather than an embarrassment.

Or an opportunity *and* an embarrassment. It didn't really matter at this point. Her parents were about to lose their home. Reva had already tried once and failed with her mother at making the smallest of dents in the hoard.

She studied Lindsay for a long moment. The slight, austere woman didn't look one bit up to such a challenge, not in stature. But the way she held her poise under Reva's severe scrutiny, the square set of her narrow shoulders, the quiet determination of her pretty features—competence oozed from her pores.

"Okay."

Lindsay gave Reva a slightly victorious smile. "Okay. Let's get started. Reva, I have some things I'll need you to sign."

"Excuse me," Terrance said, "but am I going to get to work for my pay today?"

"Yes, you are. I'll deal with Darlene," Reva said. "If we're going to tackle the issues, let's tackle them."

Crystal huffed out smoke and put out her cigarette under her shoe. "Great. Come on in and take over, like usual."

"With pleasure," Reva replied, giving her sister a cold stare. "Just remember, you chose this. Now pick up that cigarette butt, would you? No time like the present to get started."

"Indeed," Lindsay said, following Reva now. "Terrance, I'd like for you to start with Reva on a tour, since she can handle the...situation...with her mother. Does that work for you?"

"Sure thing, boss," Terrance said. "That okay with you, Reva? Think you can get her to work with me?"

"Terrance, you don't even need to ask. If I have to go along with this, Darlene's going to go along with you. Her behavior is unacceptable on a lot of levels."

"You're right, but...well, I imagine there's a trigger of some sort there, right Lindsay?"

Lindsay nodded. "We'll explore that, definitely. But what I'd like to do now," she said, holding on to Reva's arm to stop her in the hallway, "is explore a little with you."

"This is about Darlene, about her hoarding, fixing this," Reva said, holding out her hands to indicate the mess around her. "It's not about me."

"It's about all of you, Reva, whether you realize it or not," Lindsay said. "The family system is always a large part of both what sustains the hoarding issue, and what resolves it. And, if you look deep enough, you may have carried some issues of your own forward, growing up with a parent who hoards."

Lindsay paused, as if for effect. "Your involvement, your healing, will not only be a help to you. It will be a help to your family as well."

Reva nodded. "Okay. What is it you need me to do?"

Lindsay looked up and down the hall from where they stood in the threshold of the kitchen. "Which one was your room?"

"Oh, no," Reva said, her eyes wide.

Lindsay stood patiently watching her, waiting for Reva to move to the right door.

"Really?"

"Since we're going to spend a little one-on-one time, I think it will be the best place to start. I imagine it's the room where you spent most of your time after Darlene's illness?"

"I guess. As much as I could, when I wasn't at school or at Tommy's. A lot of my time here was spent trying to keep up with meals for everyone and making sure we had clean clothes to wear. I haven't set foot in that room since I got married," Reva said, her voice barely above a whisper. She'd turned her head to look at the door to her childhood bedroom, but she caught the slight nod of Lindsay's head in her peripheral vision, Terrance lifting the camera to his shoulder.

"Lead the way," Lindsay said, stepping forward to place her hand on Reva's shoulder, a show of silent, affected support for the camera, she was sure. It was a comfort, all the same.

Reva stepped gingerly between piles of God-knows-what on her way down the hall and stopped in front of her old bedroom door. She grasped the knob and, without allowing herself to hesitate, turned and pushed. The door met fierce resistance on the other side, and through the inches-wide crack she managed, the reason why was devastatingly clear. She let go and let the door shut.

"We can't get in there."

"Willie, can you help us, please?" Lindsay called from where she stood behind Reva.

Willie stepped out of Darlene's room, the scowl on his face a clear indicator of how happy he was to help with any of this.

"We're not going to be able to push it in further," Reva said.

"We'll need to take this door off the hinges," Lindsay said to Willie, who rolled his eyes in response.

"I guess that's one way to handle it," Reva said, closer to smiling than she'd been since she arrived.

"And any others that won't open, Willie," Lindsay said. "Please."

"Why did we call you people in to save the house if we're going to have to tear it down to do it?" Willie grumbled as he went for his toolbox.

Reva grabbed his hand and squeezed it as he walked by. "It's okay, Willie. Let's just get this done," she encouraged.

Reva stepped back when Willie returned and went to work unhinging her bedroom door. Leaning against the far wall, she closed her eyes and recalled the room as she'd left it the morning she moved out, the last time she'd seen the door open. The room wasn't very big—none of the bedrooms in their little shotgun house were—but she'd made the most of the space, pushing her twin bed all the way against the back wall. And it was dark, faux wood paneling, so she'd taken down the curtains from the one window to maximize the light. She'd nearly papered the walls with pictures torn from magazines, places she'd like to visit, houses she dreamed of building, gardens she planned to plant, people she wanted to be…it had been a means of escape, she imagined, from the chaos around her.

Had Tommy been the same? An escape? The thought bubbled up to the surface before she could tamp it down. She remembered the feeling, the heady rush of being loved by someone like Tommy. Reva had grabbed hold of that love, and she'd never looked back.

Willie grunted as he pulled the bedroom door loose and moved with it sideways down the wall, almost toppling Lindsay over in the process. Reva peered into the nearly dark room—stuff was piled up so high the window was nearly covered—and recognized nothing. Lindsay reached in, searching with a tentative hand for the light switch. She found it and flipped it on, and the one lone bulb mounted in the center of the ceiling buzzed as it came it to life.

Reva's breath caught in her throat. The room was under the piles of—what was even piled everywhere? She could see snatches of her former space: the pictures taped high up on the wall, the top half of the mirror over her dresser.

"Can you get in at all?" Lindsay asked, peering around her.

Reva shook her head. "Maybe if we go up and over."

Lindsay tugged at Reva's arm so that she faced her—so that Terrance had a better angle with the camera—and turned sympathetic eyes up to Reva's.

"How do you feel, seeing your old room like this?"

A laugh bubbled up from Reva's core, even though she couldn't find one damn thing funny about the situation. "I—I mean, it's not like I haven't known it would be like this. I haven't—it—"

"You've put it out of your mind, right? Avoided it?"

Reva reached into the room and grabbed a bag from the heap of crap blocking the door. "What else can you do?" she asked, holding up the bag. "I mean, look at these. They're page-a-day calendars from two years ago." She sat that bag at her feet and grabbed another, holding it out for Lindsay again. "More of the same. These are three years ago."

"Why do you think your mother would be keeping these?"

"How would I know?" Reva tossed another bag at her feet, pulled another from the pile in front of her. "This is literally a pile of old calendars. Bags and bags full of page-a-day calendars. For what?"

A crash from down the hall distracted Reva from the cluttered room in front of her, and she turned just in time to see her father falling to the floor with a door on top of him. Terrance put his camera down and ran to his aid, Lindsay and Reva close on his heels.

"Willie, are you alright?"

Terrance lifted the door and walked it out through the kitchen while Willie sat up muttering under his breath. Reva and Lindsay helped him to his feet. "I'm fine, I'm fine," he said, shooing them off.

"Are you sure?" Lindsay asked.

Willie's eyes met Reva's, and she could see it was all he could do to hold back his tears. "I wish it hadn't come to this, baby girl. I'm sorry I didn't do something about it sooner."

Reva watched Willie stomp down the hall, heard him make his way outside through the kitchen.

"Willie, wait—" Reva said, starting after him.

"Let's give him a little space, let him process," Lindsay said, grabbing Reva's arm. "It's an upheaval for him as much as it is for your mother."

Reva sighed. "I'm not entirely on board with this, just so you know. But, right now, I need to head back to work. I had no idea this was coming, so I haven't planned for it. I didn't have the time off today."

"I'm sorry about that," Lindsay nodded.

"Not your fault. What's happening here the rest of the day?"

"I'll work a little more with Darlene and Willie, see if I can get a feel for your mother's level of hoarding behavior, what we need to do. There's not much more to film for today. First thing next Friday morning, we'll have a meeting to plan the cleanup with the family and the cleaning team. Cleanup will begin then and run through the entire weekend. I hope you can be here next Friday?"

Reva nodded. "I'll make it work. I guess I'll see you later."

Reva went back to her room and peered in one last time, shaking her head, then snatched the bags of calendars from the floor before heading outside.

Caprice was lurking near Reva's car and gave her a bright smile as she approached.

"Hey Miss Reva," They leaned against the trunk of Reva's car in the driveway, side by side, surveying the front of Willie and Darlene's house. "So, are y'all doing a TV show? Is that what this is all about?"

Reva nodded. "It would appear we are, whether I like it or not."

"Why wouldn't you like it? Y'all are gonna be on TV! Man, that would be so cool. Y'all might be reality TV stars or something after this."

Reva laughed. "Don't give Crystal any ideas, okay? I'm afraid she's already got stars in her eyes. Lord have mercy, she was dressed for…well, that's not for tender ears like yours, is it? But you were right about the heels." Reva nudged Caprice.

"No offense, she's your sister and all, but she too old for them mini-skirts. I 'bout nearly saw every bit of her goodies when she hopped up in Mr. Tommy's truck when he came by here the other day."

At the mention of Tommy, of Crystal getting into Tommy's truck, Reva felt her heart do a funny lurch. "When did you see her getting into Tommy's truck?"

"It was earlier this week, Tuesday I believe. Remember my desk with my computer is right in there under the window? I was watching some videos, and then there they were."

"Yeah, I do remember you telling me about your desk," Reva said, trying to keep her expression neutral. "You sure it was Tommy's truck? Crystal's likely had a boyfriend or two around since she's been back. It wasn't maybe one of them?"

Caprice shook her head firmly. "No, I know it was Mr. Tommy because his truck has that tree service logo thing on it, that magnet. Anyway, I was inside messin' on the computer, like I said. I was still trying to keep an eye out, you know, because you asked me to. It was quiet 'til I heard the truck come up. When I peeked out, I saw it was Mr. Tommy. I figured at first maybe you were with him, and y'all had to come back over for something or other. But then Miss Crystal ran out, and in them same heels. Hopped right on up in the truck and they drove off."

Reva swallowed hard. "Did you notice when they came back?"

"It was over an hour later they came back. She hopped back out the truck in her bare feet. I reckon she didn't want to get more mud on 'em. All this rain, it's so muddy everywhere."

"Interesting," Reva said, her eyes narrowed as she stared down the road, trying to make sense of what her husband and her sister might have been doing together. And why neither of them had mentioned it to her.

"I didn't know if it was a good idea to call you about that one, but I thought you ought to know," Caprice said.

"You did the right thing, sweetie. Thanks," Reva said.

Reva threw herself into the driver's seat of her car and tossed the calendars she still held in the back seat. She started the engine and sat for a moment, uncertain of where to go or what to do, her thoughts spinning out of control.

Was something happening between her husband and her sister, in the middle of this now all-too-public fiasco with her parents? Would Tommy—no, he wouldn't.

Would Crystal? No. Her sister had crossed a lot of lines in her life, but surely she wouldn't cross this one.

Something twisted in Reva's gut anyway. So, she shifted the car into drive and let it take her toward an answer to the new questions forming in her mind.

CHAPTER 14

Reva sat in her car for a while after pulling up to Tommy's job site. He'd been working the last few weeks in New Hope, clearing a lot on the old Murphy farm where Scott's grandfather Ramirez would be building a little place for himself. It wasn't a big enough job for Tommy's full crew, so he had most of his guys over on a logging site near Bluffton. Over here, it was just Tommy and one of his foremen, Jeremy. He was so engrossed in the work that he didn't notice she was there. Either that, or he couldn't really see her car behind the trucks.

So, while she tried to order her thoughts and calm the pounding of her heart, she watched him. Tommy may have had his faults, but lack of work ethic wasn't one of them. And, while it was hard, manual labor he did, he made it look like an art, both in the outcome and in the way he operated on a site, the way he moved. Tommy was working his way through underbrush with a chainsaw, stopping from time to time to move what he cleared into a small fire burning at the back of the property. Finally, he stood at the front of the lot, taking in the progress. Jeremy got off the cutter and came over to stand beside him, and while they talked, Tommy swept his hands this direction and that. Reva knew he had a picture in his mind, a concept, and he was sharing it with Jeremy, making sure he understood the aesthetic that he wanted, that they cleared everything just so, and left a canvas for the landscapers to come in behind them and make a beautiful yard for Mr. Ramirez, a perfect backdrop for the home he planned there.

This, Reva thought, was art for him. This was his passion, and she respected it. She'd never have asked him to pursue anything different, no matter how many greasy uniforms ruined her clothes in the wash, or how many of their good towels wound up stained from the grease and grime he was never entirely free of, the trails of dirt he tracked in on his work boots, which he never seemed to remember to shed before he got to his chair. She smiled at the thought of that ruined chair. No one else would ever sit in it.

None of it mattered, though, because he was doing the thing he loved. She wished he could look at her dreams the same way. Reva didn't have the luxury of having settled into the thing she loved right away. She'd had to work her way into it—into believing that it was a thing she could achieve.

And now that she'd gotten in to law school, after everything she'd lost, deferred, given away…how could she walk away from something she wanted so badly, now that she knew she could have it?

Finally, Reva stepped out of the car.

"Hey guys," she called, getting Tommy's and Jeremy's attention as she picked her way around the soggier spots of the lot. "It's looking great over here."

"Hey hon," Tommy said, offering her a quick kiss on the cheek without brushing up against her clean clothes. "Why aren't you at work?"

"Hey Jeremy," Reva said, "How's it going?"

"Good, good," he answered, grinning at Reva. "'Bout to starve, though."

"Y'all didn't stop for lunch? I sent enough leftovers with Tommy this morning to feed both of y'all."

"Trying to wrap up over here soon as we can, before any more of this rain comes through." Tommy looked up at the bright afternoon sky as if he could warn off the storm clouds that kept popping up in the late afternoons.

"Thanks, ma'am," Jeremy said, smiling. "I'll set that up at the truck for us, bossman, if that's okay?"

Tommy nodded and Jeremy left them alone to talk.

"Tommy, you're not going to believe this shit when I tell you."

He laughed. "Try me."

Reva broke down the day for him, from Caprice's call to the scene at her parents' house, and the contract they'd already signed with Help for Hoarders.

"I thought there was some services the county told y'all about that could come in and help. Why not do it that way instead of on TV? I mean, why would y'all want to put your parents' mess out there for the whole world to see?"

"First off, because my sister really wants to be on TV. Second off, because those services cost money and the TV show does not."

"How much money?" Tommy asked.

"We are not asking your family for any money, Tommy." Reva said.

"We could borrow some against the house, Reva. It can't be that much."

"Oh, no, we are not. I promised Gran. She and Pops owned that house outright—"

"And he built it with his own two hands, blah blah blah. I know."

"It's already done anyway, and frankly, we don't have time to change course at this point."

"So, what does this mean? What happens now?"

"Next Friday the cleanup starts and runs straight through the weekend. Full family participation required."

Tommy shook his head. "I'm staying out of this, Reva. Far out of it. I got enough on my plate with the two jobs going right now, and I'm not gonna be over there with cameras and all that going on."

"Don't worry about it, I'll manage it. I wish…"

Reva looked down at her shoes, at Tommy's muddy boots. She didn't know what to wish anymore.

Tommy walked her back to the truck where Jeremy sat on the tailgate eating a sandwich.

"This ham's really good, Reva," Jeremy said, unwrapping a second sandwich from the cooler. "Want one, bossman?"

"I'm good for now," Tommy said, lighting a cigarette. "I'm gonna run the cutter for a bit, let you get some beauty rest."

Jeremy laughed. "Yeah, it'll take more than an early lunch break to make me pretty." He rubbed the blonde stubble on his handsome chin. Jeremy couldn't be much older than twenty. He reminded Reva of Tommy when he was that age—all brute strength, charm, and testosterone. The one way he was unlike Tommy was that he had a different girl every other week.

Tommy had always been hers.

"So, how have things been going?" Reva asked, taking a

sandwich for herself and hopping up on the tailgate, the cooler between them.

Jeremy nodded as he chewed. "Things are good."

"You still enjoying the work?"

"Oh yeah, I can't imagine doing much else," he said, smiling at her. "And Tommy's a pretty good ol' boy to work for."

Reva laughed. "Yeah, I reckon. He's only occasionally moody. Mostly when it rains. Which is all the time right now."

Jeremy laughed with her. "That man hates the rain."

"He hates losing money. Between you and me," Reva started, leaning in and dropping her voice, even though Tommy couldn't hear them if he wanted to, "has he seemed okay lately?"

Jeremy shrugged his shoulder and turned to watch Tommy on the cutter. "Mostly. I reckon he's been a little distracted with what family stuff y'all have going on. Not that he's told me details or anything, but mainly it's that he's had to leave here and there for stuff. You already know that, though."

"Yeah, he's been a big help, especially with Crystal," Reva said, floating the bait to see if Jeremy would take it.

"I was wondering about that," he said.

"What were you wondering?" Reva asked.

"Why she was around here lately. But I'm glad he's helping her out. I know she's been through a lot, which means I guess you been through a lot with her."

And there it was.

"I don't know what we'd do without Tommy," she said, watching her husband in the cutter, seeing him in a totally different light than she had just moments before.

CHAPTER 15

Reva left Tommy and Jeremy with her mind racing, thoughts spinning out of control. Macon had texted her to say he was closing up the office, going out for a round of golf, so she didn't need to rush back.

She didn't realize she wasn't driving back to work, or toward home, that she'd even left New Hope and drifted toward Bluffton, until she realized her autopilot had led her to the banks of the Maye River.

She parked the car and sat on the little dock by the church where the river bends peacefully on its way to the sea. She brought the bag of calendars with her from the passenger seat of the car, intending to toss them one by one into the fast-moving water. But she couldn't pollute the river, which made her laugh, because her parents' house had been polluted with this crap for years. She poured out the boxed calendars beside her, noticing that they'd all been opened at some point. The little seals were broken, and some of the box ends were still open.

She plucked one from the pile and shook it from the box into her lap. The theme of the calendar was Crazy Cats.

"Who buys these things, anyway? Except my mother."

It looked brand new to Reva, except that the spine was broken in one spot. Flipping through the days with her thumb, she found a spot where one day was missing. It was clear the page had been removed.

"July 27...my birthday," Reva whispered. She crammed the cat calendar back in its box and picked up another one. This one featured popular office cartoons. She found an empty space in it, too, where July 27 should have been. The next she pulled was Zen wisdom quotes. July 27 was missing again. All eight that were in the bag were the same.

Were the rest of them in her old room similarly altered? Reva knew that Darlene was always buying stupid crap thinking she'd one day open another store and resell it all, but...

"Why would you buy up these calendars just to pull one day out of all of them? They're unusable. Of course, they're also all...old. Nobody would buy them anyway. But why rip out my birthday?"

Reva was well aware that her mother's illness had come on on her ninth birthday. It had been a bitter truth she'd had to swallow every birthday of her life since turning nine. They'd never celebrated it as a family again. Only Gran tried to make the day special for Reva somehow. And her dad would do something small for her the weekend after.

But Darlene acted as if July 27 literally didn't exist. Apparently, that's how she wanted it.

The sun had begun to dip over the wide river, dousing the surface of the water with pinks and oranges, deep reds and gold. There was always a breeze here near the water, tempering the heat of the day. Reva sat on the dock with her feet dangling over the water, the calendars piled haphazardly to her right. She wished that the quiet moment, the soothing flow of the river beneath her, could help calm the storms raging in her mind and heart.

The arrival of Help for Hoarders had caught Reva completely off guard. It had been embarrassing enough, imagining any strangers at all coming in to her parents' home to help with the cleanup, but she'd been coping with that idea a little better every day. What had Crystal been thinking, calling in a TV show?

She knew what Crystal had been thinking—she'd been thinking of herself, of being in the spotlight. Crystal had never been one to concern herself with the fallout of her actions, especially the impact they had on those around her.

But it was too late now to even concern herself with it. Contracts had been signed, and the crew was here, and ready to tackle the mess they were in. There was no time to scramble after other options. She'd have to hope that there weren't very many people around New Hope who watched hoarding shows.

Of course, there was the issue of the vans in the yard, and the trucks that were on the way to handle the hauling off of all the crap. Word would get out about the show. People would be watching.

"Damn it to hell," Reva muttered to herself.

"Fancy meeting you here."

Reva startled at the voice behind her. She turned to find Elizabeth McKinley studying her, her daughter, Amber, hanging on her hip. "Oh, hi Elizabeth. Sorry. I was just…"

What was she doing here, sitting on a dock in Bluffton in the middle of the afternoon? She couldn't very well tell Tommy's cousin—and her boss's wife—that she was sitting here lamenting her entire life.

"Yeah, me too," Elizabeth said, smiling in that Mona Lisa way she always did.

Reva relaxed a little, feeling let off the hook for the moment.

"May I sit?"

"Of course," Reva answered, glancing back up at Elizabeth and the little girl, Amber, she held in her arms. "Hi baby," she said, reaching out to touch Amber's pretty blonde head, which the girl promptly dropped to her mother's shoulder, hiding her face.

Elizabeth laughed. "This one's suddenly gotten a bashful streak."

"How old is she now?" Reva asked, knowing already. Remembering that her Tee Jae and Amber would have been the same age. She'd been pregnant at the same time as Elizabeth.

"She's two," Elizabeth said, then smashed a kiss into Amber's curls. "Are you okay?"

Reva's eyes stung in instinctual answer to Elizabeth's question. She knew if she tried to speak, the words would catch in her throat, but the tears would flow, so she shook her head instead and blinked hard.

"Me, either." Elizabeth leaned just enough to bump her shoulder into Reva's. "I'm a disaster. Macon says so all the time, so you probably already know that." She rocked a little as Amber reached down and picked up one of the calendars from the little pile between them, the one with the cats. "No, baby—"

"Oh, she can have it," Reva said quickly. "They were boxed—it's clean—they're—they're old calendars. I was throwing them away."

"Kit-cats," Amber said with a grin, holding the calendar high for her mother to see.

GINA HERON

Reva shrugged, sifting through the calendars. "Maybe she'll enjoy the pictures in some of these."

Elizabeth glanced over at Reva, concern and curiosity etching a line between her brows.

"We're cleaning some stuff out over at—anyway, what are you doing out here?" Reva asked, deflecting.

"Us? Macon's at work, and I was restless. Thought we'd take a walk, and I usually end up here when we do. It's beautiful today. I wish I had my paints. I wish I had time to paint. I miss it."

Reva recalled that Elizabeth used to paint, but she didn't know what she did now, aside from being Amber's mother, Macon's wife. She seemed to keep to herself for the most part. Amber leaned back and pulled at the pearl dangling around Elizabeth's neck, the large, creamy orb set in a bed of silver, like a perfectly round water droplet on a leaf.

"We missed you at Bay's baby shower," Reva said, remembering that Elizabeth hadn't been there.

"Sorry I couldn't make it for that. I still have her gift sitting on the dining room table. I guess I better get it to her before the baby's born, or at least before she graduates college."

The two women laughed quietly together.

"I guess I should," Reva finally said, the sun dipping closer to the tree line in the west.

"Us too," Elizabeth said.

"If it's not too much to ask, could you maybe...not mention seeing me to Macon?"

Elizabeth nodded. "Of course. Our secret."

"Hey, if you ever want to come out here and paint one evening, let me know. I'll watch Amber and let you work. You should be doing what you love."

Elizabeth almost smiled again. "Thanks, I'll keep it in mind. I'd like that, I think."

Reva walked back to her car, swinging the bag of calendars she couldn't wait to dispose of, feeling grateful to Elizabeth for keeping her secret from Macon, and for the brief moment of camaraderie between them. She'd spent the entire day feeling attacked on all fronts, by outsiders and insiders alike...by her own personal history, even.

As the day slipped away, she couldn't find any solace in the

108

knowledge that maybe she wasn't the only one who felt that way, but at least she knew she wasn't alone.

GINA HERON

CHAPTER 16

Reva took one last quick inventory of her desk and the front waiting area before she answered the knock at the back door of the office.

"Hi, Juliette." Reva smiled and held the door for Juliette Jones as she strode into the tiny kitchen, briefcase and pastry box in hand.

"How are ya, Reva?" Juliette grinned and placed the box and briefcase down on the table, not waiting for a response. "I brought your favorites from Sugar."

"You always do." Reva leaned in for the proper hug Juliette never failed to offer her when she visited from the main office in Charleston, along with the most delicious pastries Reva had ever sampled.

Juliette grabbed a mug from the cabinet and poured herself a cup of coffee. "I didn't see Macon's car outside," she said, stirring in a hefty dose of cream and sugar.

"He's not in yet this morning," Reva said, leaning against the counter. "I think he said Amber had a well visit, and he was going with Elizabeth."

Juliette nodded. "I'll get situated in the conference room. We have a solid hour before Tyler and his client get here."

"Short deposition or long today?"

"Likely short," Juliette answered. "Unless Tyler gets carried away. You know how he is."

"Sometimes it's like he thinks he's supposed to filibuster his way through a deposition instead of just asking the questions," Reva said, finishing with a sigh. "What else you got today?"

"Nothing else here, and I cleared my afternoon at the Charleston office just in case. We doing lunch?" Juliette asked.

"If you've got time, definitely. There's something I need to talk to you about," Reva said as they walked down to the conference room.

"Sounds intriguing," Juliette said with a sly grin.

"I hope you'll be excited about it. I am," Reva said. The front door opened and the court reporter waved through the glass partition at Reva. "I'll send Irene back."

"Can't wait to hear all about it," Julie winked.

Reva went back to the kitchen and snagged a couple of pastries from the box and a cup of coffee. She hummed quietly as she moved around the kitchen and walked to her desk.

Juliette was one of the partners in the firm and worked at the office in Charleston, and she'd become by far Reva's favorite visitor, and not just because she brought the pastries with her. When they'd first met years ago, Reva and Juliette had an easy, immediate rapport. Reva thought it unlikely that they'd be fast friends, given Reva's background and Juliette's Charleston prep school upbringing, but she'd been wrong. Juliette, for all of her privilege, was a pragmatic, down-to-earth, friendly woman who happened to be fierce in the courtroom. Sure, her pedigree may have helped her make her way into the ranks of the Charleston elite, but she'd left no doubt of her ability to earn her keep. Juliette was a top earner in the firm, and a favorite among the staff. She'd become a role model, mentor, and friend to Reva over the years. So, Reva couldn't wait to share the news that she'd been accepted to law school.

The morning flew by with Macon out of the office, and after Juliette's deposition wrapped up, the two women walked to The Red Caboose. It had become a tradition of sorts for them. Juliette loved the backwoods feel of the shack, and it could be argued that the barbeque was the best the state had to offer. She brought the pastries from Charleston, and Reva always sent her back home with a pound of the Shack's pulled pork and a jar of jelly—pepper, plum, strawberry, whatever she had handy—from her homemade stash. They never even really discussed it. It just…was.

"So, you have happy news to share?" Juliette asked, rubbing her hands together as she watched Reva with clear anticipation. Reva noticed when Juliette's gaze dropped to her waistline, taking in the blousy top she'd worn that day.

"Oh—oh no, I'm not pregnant."

Juliette's face fell, and her posture caved. Her gaze shifted from Reva's face to her hands in her lap. "I'm sorry—I thought—I assumed—"

"No, don't worry about it, Jules," Reva said, waving a hand dismissively. She took a long sip of her tea. Everyone assumed that Reva desperately wanted to have a baby, and she didn't have the energy to correct that assumption. Even though she'd come to expect the questions that came along with her history, the sting of it never went away. "I'm not so focused on that particular challenge at the moment."

"Okay," Juliette said, leaning in, eager to move the conversation to the next topic. "Tell me the news."

"I decided last spring that maybe I'd apply to law school. I'd already prepped for the LSAT twice, and so I took it."

"Reva, that's wonderful! How did you do?"

"I did good. I scored 168."

Juliette's eyes went wide. "Wow. Well, why am I acting surprised? Of course, you did. Where are you applying?"

"I already applied, actually. To the University of South Carolina. Already accepted, too." Reva took a long sip of tea, grinning into the styrofoam cup as Juliette's grin split her face.

"What? You didn't even tell me you were applying! Congratulations, Reva. I'm so proud of you." Juliette was on Reva's side of the table hugging her. "When do you start? What did Tommy say? You must be so excited!"

Reva nodded as Juliette fell back into her chair. "I didn't want to say anything to anyone about it until I saw how it turned out, you know? Anyway, I can start in spring, or wait until next fall semester. I have to figure that out still. Tommy...well, he's not exactly on board yet. He thinks things are fine the way they are. So, I'm as excited as I can be to have been accepted to a school I really can't afford, knowing that I will likely have to divorce my husband if I try to go."

"Reva, you have to go. Not going is not an option." Juliette tapped her index finger against the table to emphasize the statement.

"You think?" Reva asked, letting her uncertainty show with her friend.

"I can't think of a single person who'd make a better lawyer than you would. Hell, you're practically running this office for us as it stands. I mean, Macon's fine and all, but you do most of the real work. You're smart, and compassionate, fair-minded. And, if you don't mind my saying, you're due a dream come true, doll."

Reva let out a breath she didn't know she'd been holding. "Thank you for that, Jules. I've been second guessing everything since I told Tommy about it. He's totally against the whole idea. And Macon wasn't much more enthusiastic when I told him. Which means he wasn't even a little bit enthusiastic, like at all."

"Well, I can't imagine why." Juliette sat back in her chair and rolled her eyes. "Macon will be in a pickle with you at school. But you can work part-time at the office in Columbia. Hey! What about the grant from the firm?"

"I brought it up to Macon when I told him I'd gotten accepted to school. He thought I should wait and think through whether or not this was something I really want. Actually, it was more that I shouldn't do something that isn't what my husband really wants."

Juliette's expression shifted into her all business face. "Macon's a shit. Don't give it another thought. I'll take care of it."

"Well, I haven't decided—"

Juliette held up a hand and gave Reva a stare so cold it would ice over hell. "You have decided. And if you haven't, I'm deciding for you. Right now. You're going to law school, if it kills me. And I don't want to die."

Reva laughed. "In that case, I guess the news is that I'm going to law school. I'm going to law school."

Juliette laid some cash on the table and stood up. "See there, now you're starting to believe it yourself. Looks good on ya. Now, let's get back to the office so I can get things in the works."

Reva stood and pulled Juliette into a hug. "Thank you," she said quietly as Juliette hugged her back fiercely. "You have no idea how much it means to have someone on my side."

"Oh honey, you're welcome," Juliette said. "Always."

And Reva knew she meant it.

"Hey ladies, leisurely lunch hour, I take it?"

Macon was in his office when Juliette and Reva returned from lunch.

"We were celebrating, Macon," Juliette said, leaning against the door frame of his office.

He smiled, looking from her to Reva, who was settling in at her desk. "What are we celebrating?"

"C'mon, you already know—I can't believe she told you before me, whether you're the one she works for or not." She turned to give Reva a wink.

"Oh, yes, our Reva's been accepted to law school," Macon said, his voice flat.

"And at South Carolina, so we can keep her at the firm while she's there."

There was a long pause before Macon spoke. "Let's not push. Those are big decisions Reva needs to make for herself."

"I agree with you, Macon, one hundred percent," Juliette said. "And soon as she decides she's going, and when she's starting, we get her in the Columbia office."

Macon's laugh was forced, Reva could tell. There was something satisfying about having Jules bait him and it was amusing to watch, but Reva could sense the undercurrent of displeasure in his tone, and something in it disturbed her. Jules was having fun with him, but if there was fallout, it would turn out to be at Reva's expense.

"In all seriousness, if you don't mind, I'd like to take the lead submitting her for the firm's grant. I can't imagine anyone who deserves it more, or who would represent the firm any better at the school. I'll get you to sign on with me, of course, but it would be my honor to throw her name in the hat, as long as you don't mind."

Reva looked up to see Macon staring straight at her from his desk, his face stony. "Again, I'd say let's give Reva some time to figure out if this is the right direction for her. And if so, I'm happy to put her name forward. Soon as she's sure she's ready."

"Fair enough, fair enough," Juliette repeated. "Guess I'm going to pack it up and head back to the city."

"Come in and shut the door a minute before you do. I'd like to go over something with you," Macon said.

Reva tried not to notice how long Juliette was in with Macon, tried not to strain her hearing to see if she could catch any snatches of conversation, tried not to wonder what in the world they were talking about so long. Surely not her. Certainly not her.

When the door finally opened and Juliette emerged from

Macon's office, the smile she gave Reva looked half-hearted at best. Reva felt her own face scrunch, wanting to ask but knowing she couldn't.

"Need anything before you go?" she asked instead.

"No, just need to gather my things up from the conference room," Juliette said.

"Don't forget your box in the kitchen," Reva said, trying to act normal. To feel normal.

Then Juliette mouthed something to her, something like I'll call you later, and Reva blinked hard twice in response.

Juliette said her goodbyes and headed out. Reva braced herself for whatever might come from Macon, aware of the fact that he wouldn't be happy over her talk with Juliette, or Juliette's enthusiasm about her attending law school.

So, when he walked to his door and stood staring at her for a long moment, she froze beneath the scrutiny and waited.

But what he did next was the one thing she didn't see coming. He turned his back on her and shut the door.

CHAPTER 17

Reva slipped into the booth across from Tommy, where he was already swigging from a bottle of beer.

"Hey Reva," Maggie called on her way to the kitchen with another table's order. "Margarita?"

"Lord, yes," Reva called back to her, rubbing at her temples.

"Long one, eh?" he asked.

"You could say." Reva dropped her hands to the table, fidgeting with the silverware that was tightly knotted in a napkin in front of her.

"Me, too," Tommy said before draining his beer. "Me and Jeremy will be finished up on the Ramirez project by next week."

"Wow, that's great, babe. What's up next?"

Tommy shook his head, leaning back in the booth. "Not starting anything else until we finish up in Bluffton. I've been thinking, it might be a good time for me to slow things down a little, you know?"

Reva's eyes went wide. "You, slow down? That's—well, I guess I wasn't expecting that. I thought your plan was to keep expanding, maybe get another full crew together."

"I do plan to expand, eventually. But with everything else going on right now, I thought it might be better to pump the brakes on that until things settle down a bit."

Maggie came to the table with Reva's margarita and a basket of chips and took their order.

"This thing with my parents..."

"Yeah, that's definitely a big part of it. Getting their place cleaned up is one thing. Having it broadcast on TV is another one."

"I know, right?"

"Crys mentioned those shows when we were over there trying

to get a start on cleanup, but I didn't think she'd go on and call one in without even talking to you about it."

Reva took a deep sip of her margarita. "So, is that what you and Crys have been getting together about? Cleaning up my parents' place?"

She let her question land, then watched Tommy's face closely for a reaction. His mouth tightened for a split second, eyes narrowed a little further, but otherwise his expression was smooth as stone.

"I tried to talk some sense into her, but it didn't do any good, Reva. I'm sorry. I thought if maybe I could get her to see how this was gonna affect you, that you'd have to deal with the discomfort of my family seeing all this mess on TV, and people at the law firm...she didn't hear me on any of it. And anyway, it didn't sound like whatever contract your folks signed they could just get out of. It would take time, and I don't reckon y'all have any."

Reva was quiet for a moment as she thought about the timeline, the conversations—the frequent conversations—her husband had been having with her sister, behind her back. Things didn't quite line up, and she knew it.

"Listen," Tommy said, shifting in his seat as though the silence had stretched out too long for his comfort. "I know you don't think I've been stepping up to help much with this, and I thought I'd try and handle Crys, take some of the pressure off of you if I could. Maybe that wasn't the right thing to do, but I know how tense it gets between you two. I thought I might have a better chance talking sense to her if she felt like she could trust me not to run back to you, so I didn't."

"Hey, thanks for trying, babe," Reva said, reaching over to squeeze his hand. "I didn't realize you were so concerned about it that you'd reached out to Crystal. I guess it was worth a shot. We both know she doesn't listen to me."

"Nah, whatever you suggest she'll do the exact opposite of. I was hoping I might get a better result. And I wanted to see—"

"What's that?" Reva asked, keeping her gaze trained on his face. The fact that he wasn't meeting her gaze, wouldn't look directly into her eyes, unnerved her. Something was off with him.

"I was wondering how hard she's partying, what she'd get into when she got out of the house."

"And?"

"She's drinking too much, but I don't think she's on nothing."

"Okay," Reva said, nodding.

"Here ya go, friends," Maggie said, grinning as she sat their entrees in front of them. "Who needs another round?"

"Me, for sure," Tommy said, twirling his empty bottle.

"No more for me," Reva said. "As long as today was, tomorrow's going to be longer."

"Tough one at the office?" Tommy asked, changing the subject.

Reva nodded. "A little. Juliette was in today for some depositions. Macon's being an ass lately. Business as usual, I guess."

Tommy pushed his fajitas nachos around on his plate with his fork. "Hey, speaking of your job..."

"Yeah?" Reva braced herself, uncertain of where Tommy might be going with the topic.

"I want you to know, I'm proud of you. Getting accepted to law school, I know that's a big achievement for you, and something you always dreamed about doing."

Reva smiled, her shoulders relaxing a little under the unexpected compliment. "Thanks, Tommy. It means a lot to me for you to acknowledge that."

Tommy turned his lopsided grin on her, the one that always stirred the butterflies in her stomach. "It took me off guard, you going off and doing that without talking it over with me."

Reva crossed her arms over her chest. "Well, I had a pretty good idea what you'd say, so I figured it would be best to ask forgiveness instead of permission."

"That's what they say," he said, then took a swig from the fresh beer Maggie sat down in front of him. "Like I said, I'm proud of you, getting in and all, even if you can't go."

"What do you mean, I can't go?" Reva stared at him across the table, her features arranged in an open challenge.

"Because, Reva, how would we make that work, you in Columbia in school all week? You make a decent living as it is, we got health insurance and all that through the firm, your retirement...why rock the boat at this stage of the game?"

Reva curled her lip in disgust. "Because, Tommy, maybe I

don't like the way it feels sittin' in a docked boat that's meant for sailing."

"How are we gonna make ends meet with you in school for three years? Have you thought about that?"

"I can work part time, and there's this grant from the firm…and if not that—"

"Ohhh no," he said, shaking his head in a huff, "don't you dare say we can borrow it on the house now."

"I think Gran would approve if I was using the money for my education."

"If you needed any more education," Tommy said, frustration simmering in his tone. "And what about kids, Reva? If we're ever having any, it's likely we better start sometime this decade. What did the doctor really say the other day, anyway? Why aren't you ready to try again?"

"I'm—I—you know what I've been through, Tommy. What we've been through."

Tommy rolled his eyes. "And here we go with this again." He guzzled the rest of his beer down and held the bottle up as Maggie passed by.

"Don't drink too much to drive home, please."

"Don't make me."

It was Reva's turn to roll her eyes. "Do you want to know what the doctor said?"

"I'm pretty sure I know what he didn't say. Unless…"

"Obviously I'm not pregnant."

He reached across the table and took one of Reva's hands in his. "But we could do something about that. Or did the doctor say otherwise?"

Reva shook her head. "No, babe, he said everything is fine, physically."

"So, we could have a baby, if we wanted to?"

"I don't know if I can," Reva whispered, giving Tommy a pleading look. "And you're so busy with work, and me, too, and I could actually go to law school…"

"Just one more time, Reva, please? Let's give it one more chance. If Dr. Keller says everything's good to go, I mean, he'd tell you if there was a chance it could go wrong again."

"There's always a chance, Tommy. I can't, not yet. I'm sorry, but I can't lose another baby like we did Tee Jae."

"But what if we don't this time, Reva? One last time...I want to try one more time."

A long moment passed, then another.

Tommy called to Maggie for their check. "Scratch that beer. I'm going for a ride," he said, sliding from the booth. He glanced at Reva. "Don't wait up."

Reva sat in the booth a while, sipping on her margarita, twirling the plain gold wedding band and tiny diamond on her left hand.

What had happened to her and Tommy? They'd been so in love back then, when they were first married, she was sure of it. They'd wanted all the same things—a simple life in the small town where they'd grown up, their own land, a comfortable living made from their own business, a house full of kids. Right out of high school, neither one of them could have guessed how hard it would be to reach such seemingly ordinary dreams.

But things hadn't been simple for them, beginning right from their wedding day. On a day when they should have been focused on joining their lives together as one, on celebrating, Reva ended up feeling shut out at her own wedding.

All because of a little ol' pearl that wasn't hers in the first place. Still, everyone in New Hope knew the tradition of the Pearl Girls in Tommy's family. Even Reva's cousin, Leigh, when she'd married Ethan LaFleur, wore a family pearl around her neck for the ceremony. And Reva doubted she'd taken it off since, she had been so proud to marry into the LaFleur clan. Reva could admit she'd felt some of the same sense of pride, marrying up into the Patterson family. It wasn't lost on her that she didn't come from their kind of people, but Tommy's family had been kind enough to her. They weren't thrilled about their engagement, given that they were so young, but Tommy lacked much purpose in life at eighteen, and without Reva, she'd been fairly certain he would have lacked even the little he had.

Amelia, Tommy's mother, had done her part for the wedding, hosting a bridal shower for Reva, going with the bridal party to select dresses, hosting the rehearsal dinner. And she'd pitched in decorating the double wide they'd lived in behind the Patterson's brick house. She even planted flowers at the front stoop—butterfly bushes with bright orange and yellow flowers and gerbera daisies. Reva had felt welcome in Tommy's family, until their wedding day. She'd waited in the little dressing room at the back of the church, expecting her future mother-in-law to tap on the door any second, velvet jewelry box in hand, to offer up the prized pendant that would initiate Reva into the Pearl Girls.

But it was Reva's own mother and sister who came to her that day, alone. Darlene clasped a beaded choker—costume jewelry— around Reva's neck.

Reva and Tommy's wedding day was the first day she sensed Amelia looking at her, watching her, with less than kindness. During the ceremony, Reva had tried to forget it, the missing pearl, her missing place in the family she was joining. She focused on their vows, on Bay singing "Grow Old Along with Me," on Reverend Walden's prayers for them. At the small reception in the church social hall, Amelia stayed busy with the food—she and Violet had insisted on handling the catering themselves, a gesture Reva had believed proved that they were accepting of her—and seemed to avoid Reva at every turn.

Reva spent her wedding night in tears, after Tommy had fallen asleep, trying to sort out what had gone wrong. Had Amelia's kindnesses all been an act? Had she believed that maybe, in the eleventh hour before the wedding, Tommy would change his mind about marrying her?

In the end, Reva had been sorry she'd accepted her new in-laws' generosity...the way they'd insisted on helping pay for everything with the wedding, right up to Reva's dress, providing the catering, getting a family discount on the flowers...maybe all of that was just an attempt to at least save face, to keep Reva's family's inability to host the right kind of event from embarrassing the Pattersons.

Whatever it was, there had been a definite shift from before the wedding to after. She had not been honored on her wedding day as a Pearl Girl, and over the ten years since her marriage, had been completely and utterly shunned from the group's activities. Tommy's family had never been less than polite with her, but the warm welcome she'd hoped for—and even expected—had never come.

It hadn't stopped Reva from trying, though. She'd tried and

tried and tried some more to be what Tommy's family would consider worthy of him, worthy of that pearl she'd never received. She'd kept their little home, modest as it was, impeccably clean, so that if Amelia ever popped in, she'd be impressed. But she rarely ever stopped by. When they'd lived on the Patterson property, Tommy stopped to see his mama every night before he came home to his wife. So, Amelia didn't have much reason to stop in and visit with Reva.

Reva had tried in other ways, too. She'd gone to college after she and Tommy married, on scholarship even, and worked thirty hours a week all the while. And she credited the Pattersons with consistently offering up their cool, quiet support of her, vis a vis Tommy.

And then there was the long wait—and the losses—as Reva and Tommy tried for a family. Amelia had been there with food, help around the house, and her quiet way of showing emotional support. Leigh and Bay, Elizabeth and her sister, Caroline, Violet...it wasn't that they'd not been kind and concerned with Reva. But they were the Pearl Girls, and Reva, although she should have been one of them, was not.

But she'd held out hope. All these years, she'd tried to live up to whatever standard it was she'd failed to achieve on the day she'd married Tommy. She'd gotten smarter, thinner (then thicker), better educated, better dressed, more refined...

All that effort, for all those years, was about to be shot to hell in a one-hour fiasco featuring the very worst, the very dirtiest, of her family's secrets.

Did most folks around New Hope already know Darlene had gone off the deep end when Reva and Crystal were kids? Of course, they did. Did some of them suspect—even know—about the hoarding? Obviously.

But no one had ever seen it up close and personal. Amelia might feel sorry for Reva, but she'd likely die of embarrassment. Being exposed on TV would solidify Reva's position as the outcast.

Which was really unfortunate, because all she'd ever wanted was to be one of them.

Back at home, in the quiet of the empty house, Reva wrapped up in Gran's old sweater and settled in to find Help for Hoarders online. Curled up on the end of the sofa with her laptop resting on the arm, she scrolled through the available episodes and clicked on one to play it. She didn't bother to check her tears this time as they streamed down her cheeks. She watched one episode, then another, and another, completely losing track of time. Reva had known that these shows existed—her awareness of them was acute. But she had avoided watching even one of them, even avoided the commercials for them if it was possible. If she had the remote, she'd always turn the channel. It was too painful, watching these other families struggle, fixing the very thing that was so broken in her own family.

She would have to face it now, like these families she'd been watching for hours, exorcising their demons. And, also like them, her pain, her humiliation, would be on display. She wouldn't be able to hide this part of her history anymore, not from Tommy's family, or the firm, the town...

As Reva sat alone in the dark, she thought that maybe it would be a relief if she didn't have to work so hard to hide anymore.

CHAPTER 18

Pulling into the parking lot at work, Reva's stomach churned when she saw Macon's Jaguar already parked in its spot, which wasn't an actual parking spot. He always pulled it close to the building, where it would get the most shade and be protected from anything falling from the trees.

Reva swung into one of the marked spaces at the back of the lot, gathered her purse and her lunch bag, and hurried to the back door. Even though she knew the alarm was off, she still checked it, out of habit. She made quick work of flipping on the lights and stashing her lunch, feeling late even though she really wasn't. An eerie quiet filled the office. It somehow felt more still, emptier than it usually did when she was first to arrive.

She didn't understand the tension that had settled in between her and Macon over her acceptance to law school. After getting the office set for the day and starting coffee, she got to her desk, determined to settle in to her work like she would any other day. As she booted her computer, she checked the transcription machine to find eleven recordings waiting. Her eyes went wide at the number.

"How long has he been here?" she wondered out loud, staring at the closed door across the walkway from her desk. Was he even in there? She still sensed that uncomfortable edge in the air, the discomfort of things unsettled.

There were forty-three emails waiting in her Inbox. She took a deep breath and let it out as she slowly scrolled up through the list, checking the oldest first, and looking for anything urgent that required her immediate attention.

And then she saw an email from Jules to the firm's partners, one with her name in the subject line. Jules had texted to tell her not to worry about Macon, that she'd handle the grant, and with everything else going on, Reva had put it out of her mind for the moment. She quickly clicked into it and began to read, blinking to clear her eyes several times as she did.

Team,

I was in the New Hope office earlier this week, and got the wonderful news that our very own Reva Patterson has been accepted to the University of South Carolina School of Law!

As you all know, Reva is one of our most tenured employees, and has provided excellent support to our entire staff during her years in the New Hope office. As such, I think it's vitally important that we support her in every way possible as she pursues her dream of obtaining her juris doctorate in Columbia.

That said, I'd like to extend my personal support to Reva and offer to sponsor her application for the firm's law school grant for the upcoming admissions year. While we've traditionally offered the grant to rising seniors in college, Reva is an excellent internal candidate and deserves our consideration for this assistance.

Macon, I know I'm likely beating you to the punch here, and am happy to co-sponsor Reva's application with you.

Reva, again, congratulations on your acceptance. I look forward to seeing the great things you do on your journey!

Reva pressed a hand over her pounding heart as she scanned up the list of emails and found many others with her name as the subject line. She sorted the email list by subject and read through each one, slowly, then once more to savor them, to let the congratulations and praise soak in.

The wide grin on her face was starting to make her cheeks hurt by the time she noticed Macon had opened his door and was standing there watching her.

"Oh," Reva said, her smile faltering a bit, "good morning."

Macon took a sip from the to-go mug of coffee he always brought in from home.

"The coffee's on. Should be ready by now, if you need a refill."

"I do. Make sure you get plenty for yourself, too. There's a lot of work to catch up on." He stared pointedly at the empty basket on the corner of her desk, where he'd pick up the dictation she'd finished for review. "When do you think you'll get started?"

Reva fought to keep the remains of her smile on her face. "I'm getting started right now," she said, glancing up at the clock on the wall, "approximately eight minutes before the official start of my work day. What brought you in so early this morning, anyway?

"I was sick of being at home," Macon answered.

Reva watched as Macon stomped down the hall, making a mental note not to spar with him all day.

She turned back to her computer and quickly drafted a thank you message to the partners, especially Jules, for the congratulations and support.

As she prepared her email, she realized that the one partner who had failed to respond to Jules' initial message was Macon. She couldn't imagine why he was being so unsupportive of her pursuing her law degree. Sure, they'd have to hire someone else in to work for him, and the transition would take time, but at least they'd have plenty of it.

She'd always thought they were friendly. It was hard to understand why he wouldn't want to see her succeed.

She hit Send on the email and shook her head, determined to clear all the questions and concerns swirling in her mind and focus on the workday ahead.

Nine dictations and three hours into the day, the back doorbell rang, and the security camera feed popped up on Reva's screen. Elizabeth stood beneath it, looking sad and awkward.

Reva glanced at Macon's closed door and back at the screen, wondering what was going on between the couple. She clicked the icon to unlock the door, then typed a quick instant message to Macon:

Elizabeth here

"Hey Elizabeth," Reva said, just as Macon opened his door.

"Hey there," Elizabeth said, one corner of her mouth raising in a half-hearted smile. "Macon," she said, looking up at her husband from beneath her lashes, "I was hoping you might have time for lunch."

"We're having a pretty busy day here, Liza. I wish you would have called." Macon crossed his arms over his chest, a smirk on his handsome face.

"I wish you wouldn't have left the way you did this morning," Elizabeth replied, keeping her voice so quiet that it was hard for

Reva to hear.

Macon shrugged. "Okay, fine. Reva, do you mind waiting for lunch until we get back? Or do you have plans to celebrate the big announcement?"

"No, I—it's fine—"

"Big announcement?" Elizabeth looked from Macon to Reva. "Oh my God, Reva, are you expecting?"

As Elizabeth's face broke into a grin, Reva's fell into a frown. "No, it's not that."

Elizabeth clamped a hand over her mouth, the transition from joy to horror twisting her face into an awkward mess of emotion.

"It's okay," Reva said, recovering. "I do have some great news. I was accepted to the University of South Carolina School of Law. And Juliette's nominating me for the firm's annual grant, so I may actually be able to swing it."

"That's amazing!" Elizabeth stepped around Reva's desk and wrapped her into a hug. "You must be so excited. I'm so excited for you!"

"It's starting to sink in," Reva said, laughing. "Honestly, until I saw the email from Jules this morning, I still didn't see a way to make it work."

"Well, let's not get ahead of ourselves yet," Macon said. "There are other candidates for the grant. It's always a great pool—"

"Macon," Elizabeth said, swatting a hand at him, "why do you have to do that? Give her a minute to be excited."

"I don't want to see her disappointed is all," Macon said.

"Well, I think maybe she's not going to be disappointed," Elizabeth said, giving Reva a confident smile. "Everyone knows how smart Reva is. You go on and on all the time about how you wouldn't be able to run this place without her."

Reva cocked a brow at Macon. "Is that so?"

Macon blinked slowly. "You're a great legal assistant, Reva. As I've pointed out to you."

"It's amazing that you're following your dream, Reva," Elizabeth said, her expression wistful. "You know, I studied art at UGA, and I thought maybe I'd do the graduate program at SCAD, but after Macon and I got married and, well, I can't tell you the last time I picked up a brush. Maybe I should look into it again."

"Yeah, that would work out so well, you going to back to school to pursue a hobby while our kid's in diapers," Macon said, his voice dripping with contempt.

"Macon, that's not—"

"It's okay, Reva," Elizabeth said, halting Reva's defense of her. "I know how Macon feels about it. And anyway, this is about you, pursuing your dreams. You should absolutely positively go for it."

"Thank you, Elizabeth." Reva stood up and hugged Elizabeth again, squeezing her tightly. "Don't give up on your dreams, either, ever," she whispered close to Elizabeth's ear.

"Okay, enough of the love fest, ladies," Macon said, ambling away. "Liza, let's go if we're going."

Elizabeth squeezed Reva's hand and mouthed a thank you.

With Macon and Elizabeth out of the office for a while, Reva printed off all the emails from the partners congratulating her, crammed them into an envelope, and placed it in her purse. She didn't know if anything would come of it. Macon was right, at least about the other candidates for the grant. They would be bright, young, determined, and as hungry for the financial boost as Reva.

She didn't know what she wanted. For the first time in her adult life, she felt completely unsure of herself.

But for now, for today, she would let herself be excited. With the current state of affairs in other areas of her life, it was good to have this one thing to hold on to.

GINA HERON

CHAPTER 19

When Reva arrived at her parents' house that Friday for a family meeting Help for Hoarders required ahead of the cleanup, she found Terrance back under the carport, sitting on the steps.

"Again?" she asked, hands on her hips.

"Nah, all's well, Reva. Good to see you again. Lindsay and the team are out back in Willie's shop with the family. They're just setting up. I had to take a phone call. My baby girl's having a baby herself any day now, so whenever the phone rings, I have to check in."

Reva smiled. "I understand. Congratulations."

Terrance nodded his thanks and started back toward the shop.

"Wait. What happens today? Prep me," Reva asked Terrance, plopping down on the steps, leaving him enough room to sit again.

"Usually, Lindsay and the cleanup crew manager walk the family through the plan for cleanup, how it'll work. And then you'll talk about the hoarding," he answered.

"Like what about the hoarding?"

"Things like when it began, what might have triggered it, if it's just your mama hoarding, or if Willie's involved, either hoarding himself or enabling, that kind of thing."

"Well, he's definitely enabling. I guess we all are." Reva shook her head. "This is so humiliating."

"Try not to think like that about it. All families have something, you know? The hoarding happens to be your family's something."

Reva laughed. "The hoarding, my sister's addiction, my—"

She stopped short of putting her own something into words. Her something felt like everything.

Terrance nodded. "Like I said, we've all got something we think we gotta have. I'm not the doctor here, but I've seen a lot with hoarders by now, and what I can tell you is that there's always

131

GINA HERON

a problem the hoarder in the family is hiding from. It's not so much that they're hiding something as much as they're running from something. You get what I mean?"

"You mean Darlene is burying herself in a pile of stuff because she's afraid?"

Terrance nodded. "Think that through. What's she so afraid of? I think you'll find some answers if you spend some time with that question. But let Lindsay help guide you through that. She knows what she's doing."

"So, I should get back there," Reva said with a sigh.

"Yes, you should," Terrance said, laughing. "Good luck."

Reva stepped inside Willie's neat little shop, where the group gathered inside had formed a circle of camping chairs. Lindsay greeted Reva when she came in and invited her to sit down on one side of Darlene, with Crystal on the other side.

"This is Dean, who'll be managing the cleanup crew on this project. His company works locally and can be available to assist after the show is done as well."

Dean gave Reva a warm smile and a firm handshake. His salt and pepper hair was covered with a red bandana, and he wore overalls and work boots, as if he stayed ready to jump into a job at a moment's notice.

The six of them sat down together while the cameramen took positions and started to film. Reva noticed that Terrance sat to the side facing Willie, Dean, and her, rather than facing Darlene.

"Okay, Darlene, we're together today to talk about what we've observed walking through the house, and how we're going to approach the cleanup process with Dean and his crew."

Darlene nodded and sat up a little straighter in her chair.

"What I'd like to start with is determining what areas the crew can work in with Crystal, Reva, and Willie, areas you'll feel comfortable with them sorting through things that can go and things that can stay without you having to sign off, so to speak?"

"Umm," Darlene looked around the circle, shaking her head. "I'll need to see what's being taken away. I mean, I don't think there's any one room I can say you could do without me. There might be things I can use for the store, all through the house. We've been saving things up for a long time now."

"What about the kitchen, Darlene?" Reva offered. "Crystal and

132

I know what dishes you use, and we could sort whatever mail and whatnot is in there for you to look through. We could go through the food and the things on the counter and—"

"No, no, you'd throw things away that I didn't get a chance to see, though."

"If things have been in there all this time you haven't seen, will it matter?" Crystal asked.

"It will matter," Darlene said, a sharp edge in her voice. "There might be something I need to see."

"Can we agree on certain kinds of things that they can go through and make decisions on?" Lindsay asked. "Like expired foods, empty bags, obvious trash?"

"How do I know that they won't just mix in some good things or things I need to see?" Darlene asked, folding and unfolding a tissue she held between her fingers.

Lindsay laid a gentle hand on Darlene's arm. "You'll know because your family loves you enough to be here supporting you through this process. You need to trust that your husband and your daughters want the best for you, and won't get rid of anything they know you'd like to make the decision on."

"But they can't get rid of things that I might be able to use."

"Okay, but do you think we can get rid of some of the things even you think of as junk, Darlene?"

Darlene lifted her gaze to the ceiling and shook her head, her body language posing direct opposition to the words she said. "Sure, we can get rid of the stuff I don't need for the shop, or things I can't use around the house. I could do that myself, though. I haven't felt up to it, you know? But I can do it."

Lindsay gave Darlene a kind smile. "Well, now you don't have to do it by yourself. You have a whole team here to help you, and won't it be great to get your house back where you can use every room?"

"That would be nice," Darlene said quietly, conceding.

"So, let's keep focused over the next three days, that this is the goal we're working toward. We want you and Willie to have a livable space that you can enjoy with your family, okay?"

"Okay," Darlene agreed, her hands folded in her lap, legs crossed at the ankle.

"Darlene, let's talk about when the hoarding started."

Reva watched her mother carefully after Lindsay's query, watched as her eyes closed and her face went slack, as Darlene retreated inside herself. She'd seen this happen so many times before when confronted with questions about what went wrong, what made her choose to live the way she was living, why she couldn't get rid of any little thing.

Maybe today was the day, with Lindsay's help that they could somehow get through to her, reach inside and pull her back out to face it.

Looking around the circle, Reva thought it was surely now or never.

"I remember when it started—or, more to the point, I remember right before it all started, I think," Reva offered. The group turned to look at her, and she hesitated. "I was nine. I remember because it was my birthday, and we were having a sleepover party. My first one. Do you remember, Darlene?"

Darlene's gaze skittered around the room, not landing anywhere at all, completely avoiding Reva. Her hands went to her hair, and she started pulling at it, as if she would get it tighter into the bun at the nape of her neck if there was any way to do it. Reva noted the new polish on her nails, a pretty shade of pink with tips a shade darker.

"Gran made me that princess cake, do you remember it, Crystal?"

Crystal nodded at Reva. "Yeah, I remember. Blue icing, white piping."

"And she brought us home because Daddy called and said he and Darlene were running late from the store. Gran had to get us back to the house because our friends were coming over, and someone had to be here for the party. When we got here, Gran hurried to decorate and prep a little because nothing had been done yet. Darlene was supposed to be home, getting it ready, but she hadn't come home. Then Jenn showed, and Keri, and their parents left them because Gran told them y'all would be here any minute. Stephanie had just moved to town, though…her parents weren't sure. They waited a while and let Stephanie stay and eat some pizza with us—Gran went ahead and cooked since y'all still didn't come home—and then we cut the cake, and you still weren't here. So, Stephanie had to leave."

"Gran was getting worried," Crystal broke in. "You could tell because she was pacing, kept looking out of the front windows. She tried calling the store, but there was no answer."

"And when you finally got here, you came through the back door. Daddy hustled you straight to your bedroom, Darlene. He came out and he was white as a sheet, said you'd gotten real sick."

"Jenn and Keri had to call the folks to come pick them up," Crystal added. "So that first sleepover party turned out to be not much of a party at all." Crystal looked at Reva, straight into her eyes, seeing the past together with her in a way only sisters can see each other. "We never did have a sleepover party. That was the first and last time we ever even tried."

"July 27th. That's when it all started, really. Maybe not the hoarding exactly, but that day was the day it started, right Darlene? It was my birthday, my ninth birthday."

Darlene's hand shook as she squeezed her hands into tight fists.

"I'm not going to talk about that day," Darlene said, but everyone in the room had to strain to hear her. She looked around the circle of faces, her eyes almost wild with anxiety. "That day didn't happen. We don't talk about that day."

"But we have to, Darlene, don't we?" The resolve in Reva's voice was forced—she had to dig deep to find it. "Because something happened that night that changed all of our lives, forever. It started all of this. Whatever happened, it brought us here. It brought Lindsay and this TV crew here. We have to deal with it."

"No!" Darlene snapped. "We can clean up the clutter. I'll clean up. If we straighten up the rest doesn't matter." Darlene stood up. "Let's go, then. We'll throw it all away. Isn't that what you're after? You want me to throw out all my things, fine. Just put everything I've been saving up in the trash."

Lindsay stepped in. "Darlene, I think what Reva's trying to say is that if we don't deal with what triggered your hoarding, we won't succeed with this cleanup. Or that, after we clean up the house, it'll just fill up again. Do you understand how that might be a concern for your family?"

"Come on, Darlene," Reva pressed. "It all goes back to that day. How else would you explain all the calendars in my old room?"

"Those are for the new store," Darlene said. "People like those picture calendars. We'll sell plenty of those."

"No, you won't sell any of those calendars," Reva said, frustration edging her voice.

"They're perfectly fine. I made sure all of them were perfectly fine," Darlene insisted.

Reva rubbed her temples. "Oh, Darlene, really? Is that what you did, pulling out July 27th from every single one of those calendars? Because if that's what you think, then we definitely need to talk about what happened that night. You're pretending that that one day—which also happens to be the day I was born—does not exist. Why?"

"I will not go back to that day!" Darlene sprang from the camp chair she'd been sitting in, knocking it over, and stormed outside.

Everyone followed as Darlene stomped through the yard and right on down the street.

Willie stopped them at the carport. "Let me go after her. She won't listen to nobody else, anyway."

"Then why weren't you saying anything to her in there, Willie?" Lindsay asked. "Never mind that now. Go see to her. I'll keep working through this with the girls."

Lindsay stood between Reva and Crystal with her hands on her hips, concern and confusion scrunching her face. "Do either of you have any idea what might have happened that night?"

"No, not a clue," Crystal said.

"Me, either."

"So, Darlene came home sick, your friends had to go home from the party. What happened after that?"

Reva and Crystal locked eyes, as if they had to somehow come to an unspoken agreement of how much to tell. Reva decided on as much of the truth as she could remember.

"Gran took us home with her that night. We stayed with her for a couple of weeks after. Daddy said that Darlene was too sick for us to come home."

Crystal nodded. "I don't remember how long it was before we came back home. It was a while. And then, when we did, Daddy said we had to be quiet while he was at work, that we couldn't disturb Mama because she was so sick."

"She cried a lot," Reva said, almost to herself.

"All the time," Crystal added. "It was awful, the sound of it."
"Like a keening animal."

Crystal stepped to the edge of the carport and lit a cigarette. "We stayed outside a lot for the rest of that summer."

"We didn't want to—I don't know, bother her isn't the right word. We didn't want to do anything that might push her further over the edge, I guess."

"We were afraid," Crystal said.

Reva's gaze snapped to her sister, recognizing the blunt force of simple truth in her words. "We were. I thought maybe she was dying."

"I was sure she was," Crystal said. "Daddy didn't have to worry much that we would bother her. I think we were both too scared. When she was crying, we were too scared of knowing what was making her cry, and when she was quiet..."

"We were scared that she had gone ahead and died." Reva dropped down onto the steps.

"It was like living with a ghost. A ghost of your mother," Crystal said.

"We were all living like ghosts," Reva said, near breathless from the realization of it. "That went on for a while, and then the stuff started piling up. And once it started, it was like a mushroom effect."

Crystal nodded. "Like she was trying to literally box herself in here."

Lindsay took Crystal's hand and pulled her so that she was close enough to take Reva's, too. "I'm sorry you girls had to suffer through that. It must have been so confusing. You were just kids."

No one spoke for a long while. It could have been minutes or hours before Willie and Darlene walked back to the house, Reva wasn't sure. They all watched in silence as Willie led Darlene past the driveway and up the little brick walkway to the front door, avoiding them entirely.

"Okay, ladies, I realize that today has already been fraught. Lots of emotional landmines here, for all of you, but we have to deal with the practical matters of cleaning the house out. Given where we are today, I think we should work on getting things set up for Dean and his crew out front. We're going to have to spread some tarps and put up tents, given this weather. That's where we can set up areas for Darlene to sort things to keep or donate. When we reconvene here in the morning, we'll start at the start, all together. We'll work from the porch and the front room first, and if we can get Darlene to cooperate, we'll split you off to work in other areas."

Reva laughed. "I suspect we won't be getting a whole lot of cooperation."

Dean gave her a resigned smile. "I suspect you're right, but we'll give it a try. I'll work with her on it, anyway. I can be surprisingly persuasive."

"One thing that might help is to have some insight into any positive motivators for your mother, things that might encourage her to really commit to getting the house clean and keeping it clean," Lindsay offered. "Is there anything you can think of that might help keep her motivated?"

Crystal coughed. "She doesn't much care about having people in and out of the house, not even family. You can already see her anxiety is through the roof. I don't know how we'll work around that."

"What about grandchildren? Reva, would it help motivate her to know that she'd be able to have your kids over more often if the house was safe for them to play in?" Dean asked.

Reva felt the color drain from her face. She wondered for a moment why he would assume she had children before the thought crossed her mind that, if she'd only given her mother some grandchildren, maybe it would have given her a reason to change.

"No kids for either one of us yet," Crystal answered. Reva couldn't look at her, but she was grateful for being let off the hook.

"The store," Reva said, sitting up straighter. "The idea of it, anyway. If we can give her hope that she could actually open a new store if she cleans this hoard out, that might help motivate her."

"Okay," Dean said, "what kind of a store?"

"Junk," Crystal said, laughing.

Reva couldn't help joining in with her, and Lindsay wasn't far behind. It was the sad truth. Darlene had spent years filling her house with junk for a store that everyone knew she'd never open. And now they were going to use the idea of opening a store to what? Convince her to throw out the very junk she thought she could sell in it?

"What we need," Reva finally said, catching her breath, "is one thing for her to latch on to. Crystal, if she were to open a store, what would be the one thing that would be her specialty item, one thing we could keep for her to actually put together in a shop to sell?"

"Oh Jesus, Reva, out of the mess in there?" Crystal waved a hand behind her.

"Yes, out of the mess in there. But please don't say the calendars. Hundreds of outdated page-a-days with July 27th missing does not a specialty store make."

"The books," Crystal said. "What if we focus her on the books and DVDs? She's got tons of them, and she actually halfway takes care of those."

"But does she take care of them thinking of reselling them, or of keeping them?" Reva asked.

"Hold on," Lindsay said. "We're on to something here, either way. A used bookstore...books and DVDs...if she's been keeping those items to resell, then giving her that area of focus could help us weed out the unrelated items. And those are items she could sell online and ship without a physical store."

"And if she's been keeping them simply to hoard them," Dean broke in, "then we can assume they're a layer of the cocoon she's spun around herself in there."

Reva nodded, catching up to the idea. "So, if that's the case, by focusing on starting her business by letting those go, she's freeing herself from that cocoon."

"It's an idea," Lindsay said.

"It's an idea," Reva agreed. "So how do we pitch this to her?"

"Wait," Crystal said. "Does it have to be a store? What if we could convince her to do something that doesn't require her keeping stock to sell?"

Reva cocked a brow. "Personally, I'd rather it not be, but—"

"Yeah, me too. I don't think she could manage another store. But maybe should could manage a new occupation, something she's already good at."

"What are you thinking?" Lindsay asked.

"Nails," Crystal said, grinning, holding up her own hands to show off her sparkling red nails. "She loves doing her nails, and

I've been letting her do mine, too. And I can already tell you that her polish is perfectly organized in her room. She's got a little station set up. She keeps that neat, organized. Maybe that's something we can have her hold on to, and she could maybe get into school or something."

Reva smiled. "That's a great idea, Crys."

Lindsay nodded. "I like it."

"Books and DVDs out, then," Dean said. "Even better."

The four of them continued to sort through the logistics of the first day of cleanup, until finally they agreed they had the best plan they could come up with without any direct input from Willie and Darlene.

Reva sat under the carport after the show's crew cleared out for the day, after Crystal retreated inside. She was so lost in her own thoughts that it took a while for her to notice that Caprice had come out to sit on her own front stoop. Reva raised a hand to wave, and Caprice grinned, waving back.

Reva thought that, if she ever had a kid, she hoped she'd be a lot like Caprice. Brave, smart, funny, unique. Entirely self-possessed.

And, in that moment, out of nowhere, she felt a pang of longing so intense, it took her breath.

When this was all over and her family was on the road to recovery, maybe she'd feel different about trying for another child. Maybe she'd feel different about law school, about working alongside Amelia at Owl's Roost.

If she had her family back, maybe she'd feel different about everything.

CHAPTER 20

The Help for Hoarders crew was busy spreading tarps and setting up tents when Reva pulled up to her parents' house for the first official day of the cleanup.

Alone. Because Tommy claimed he couldn't possibly leave a big job site running under two very capable crew supervisors over the weekend, especially since this big rain system was set to move in. Even though he'd been telling his crew he had to leave to help her here. There was talk of statewide flooding on the news, serious flooding. Reva had considered asking Help for Hoarders if they should hold off on the cleanup due to the threatening weather, but her need to somehow avoid the public humiliation that would come with the filming of the show was tempered by the ten days they had remaining to save the house. So, she trudged through the yard, picking her way between the bright blue squares spread everywhere, making her way to the front porch where Dean and Lindsay stood huddled in the corner.

"Hi guys," Reva said, taking the steps slowly.

"Hi Reva," Lindsay said. "Thanks for getting here early today."

"Where's everyone else?" Reva asked.

"Your parents are inside. Willie's doing his best to keep Darlene from panicking. Your sister is apparently staying elsewhere the last couple of days, but promised to be here by eight o'clock sharp," Lindsay answered.

Reva glanced at the time on her phone: 7:58. "Well, she's not late yet." The smile she gave them left little hope that Crystal wouldn't be late.

"We were just discussing strategy for the cleanup today," Dean said, leaning gingerly against the shaky porch railing, then thinking better of it. "Given the weather, I was telling Lindsay I think we should move this stuff from the porch on out to the yard, under a tent, and then move out what we can from the living room as well, so we have room to quickly move through the back of the house."

Lindsay nodded. "We'd like to start with your mom in the back rooms with a crew, see if we can have her sort through some of the things she's been collecting with the intention of selling," Lindsay explained.

Dean added, "If we can get everything sorted that's not damaged, we can get an appraiser out to look at anything that might have value."

Reva grimaced. "Guys, I don't know if there's going to be much of any value to be had here."

"But your mother's been collecting merchandise—"

Reva held up her hand to stop Lindsay. "My mother's being buying up piles of crap from a thrift store and barricading herself in the house with it. A solid ninety percent is damaged. Some of the new things that are still boxed could maybe be resold, but, if you're asking me, I say we help her keep focused on clearing it all out like we discussed yesterday, and donate what's usable."

"How hard do you think it's going to be for your mother to part with what she thinks of as collectibles, items for a shop, that she's believed will bring in some income?" Lindsay asked.

"Honest answer?" Reva asked, hands on her hips. "Impossible."

Lindsay gave her a confident smile. "Well, then, it's another day at the office for me, isn't it?"

"I'll have another crew start in the kitchen as well, sorting trash and items to move out front for your parents to go through. I think if we get a good start on allof that today, we'll have done well," Dean said.

Reva nodded her agreement as an older-model Dodge pickup truck pulled over in front of the house. Crystal spilled out of the passenger side, dressed moderately more appropriately than she had been on family meeting day, her skin-tight black tank top and jean shorts showing off every bit of curves she had. She would at least wobble less in the wedge sandals she wore—but Reva had an extra pair of Converse stashed in the car, if she could talk Crystal into them. She'd give her a few hours to tire of prancing for the cameras. Surely it must get old.

Dean gathered his crew into three teams in the front yard: one to work with Darlene in the back rooms, one to work with Willie and Dean in the kitchen, and another to work on the sorting out front. Reva had Crystal off to one side trying to convince her to wear a tee shirt on over the tank and was getting nowhere when she noticed him, dressed in athletic shorts and one of Dean's bright blue crew shirts. She wasn't sure at first, seeing his face in profile, the strong set of jaw beneath his beard, the prominent nose, hawk-like dark eyes...but the prosthetic right leg confirmed she was indeed seeing the man she couldn't believe would show his face at her parents' house again.

Billy Simpson.

"...and I don't know what your problem is with my tank top or my makeup, but I have a right to look my best when—Reva, don't walk away from me—"

But Reva was already halfway across the yard, stomping straight over the tarps this time as she made a beeline for Simpson. He was listening intently to Dean's instructions for the sorting crew, so he didn't see her coming before she grabbed his arm and tried at spinning him in her direction. He didn't budge.

"What are you doing here, Billy?" Reva asked, placing an unsavory emphasis on his first name as she said it, as if it tasted sour in her mouth.

"I'm working," he said quietly, stepping away from the group, pulling Reva along with him.

"I think we've had enough of your working over here," Reva said, jerking her arm away. "How could you show up here today knowing you're responsible for this whole situation my family's in?" Reva said, flailing her arms out to indicate the bustling TV crew, tarps, and cleanup team around them.

"First off, I'm not responsible for this whole situation. This problem existed here long before I came around," he said, his tone soothing, which only served to irritate Reva further.

"But if you hadn't meddled and called—"

"Reva, please," Simpson said, maintaining his cool tone, "rehashing how this came to pass won't do us any good. It may not be the way you'd hoped, but your parents are going to keep their house. And it's going to be a clean, comfortable, safe place for them to be. You have to want that for them, right? More than you want to be angry with me for starting this process? The end result is going to be worth it."

Reva clenched her fists, frustrated that all of his words rang true, that, in the end, regardless of her anger, he was right.

"I don't want you here," she said, since she couldn't argue with him. "How did you even get involved to begin with?"

Simpson shrugged. "Dean's a buddy of mine. When I heard his crew was contracted to handle the cleanup for this show on the news, I gave him a call and volunteered to help out."

"We don't want your help," Reva said, fighting the urge to stomp her foot in a childish attempt to add emphasis.

"Hey now," Dean said, having come to see what the trouble was between Reva and Simpson. "We need all the help we can get, Reva, and Simpson here is damn good help."

"Do you know he's the one who reported my parents to the authorities?" Reva asked.

"I don't know how many different ways I can tell you that there was absolutely no malicious intent attached to my concern for your folks."

"And yet look what's happened. My family drama is unfolding like a three-ring circus for the entire world to see. I'd say you've done enough."

"In all fairness, Simpson's not the reason Help for Hoarders is involved here," Dean broke in. "That was your sister's doing. Maybe instead of trying to manage my crew for me, you can take that up with her?"

Reva glared at Dean. "Oh, I aim to. But in the meantime, does he really need to be here?"

"Yes, he does," Dean answered firmly. "We have a tight timeline, and we're working against the weather on top of that. We need every set of hands we have here, including Simpson's. Maybe you two can steer clear of each other and we can get this done, okay?"

The two men both stood watching her for a response, and she suddenly felt foolish for insisting Simpson leave. After all, Dean was right. They needed all the help they could get. So, what if she couldn't stand the guy? He was there, which was more than she could say for her own husband.

"Somebody better let Darlene and Willie know before they catch sight of him," Reva said as she walked away, calling over her shoulder, "Willie'll likely try to shoot him."

"Long as he aims for my left kneecap and not my right," Simpson called back. "The fake leg is way more expensive to fix than the real one."

Reva almost stumbled over her own feet, horrified at the insensitivity of her own words and at the same time amused by Simpson's. She heard both men chuckling and jogged up the steps to the house, her face flushed with something more than embarrassment.

If she didn't already hate Simpson's guts, she might actually like him. And that made her mad as hell.

Reva followed Lindsay into the house and down the hallway, where Crystal was waiting with Darlene to get started on the back room that once served as a craft and sewing room. As Reva peered through the doorframe, now empty of a door, she tried to make sense of the stacks and stacks of boxes and bags crammed inside.

"Where do we even start?" she asked no one in particular, her brain, so accustomed to meticulous organization, struggling to make sense of the chaos set before her.

Lindsay signaled Terrance and placed a hand on Reva's shoulder. "We'll start right here at the beginning, the three of us, and we'll work with your mother to sort through these items and make some quick decisions about what will be kept, donated, sold, and thrown away."

She turned her attention to Darlene and continued. "Now, Darlene, the goal for us today is to throw away anything that is actual trash, that's been damaged, or is otherwise unusable."

Darlene nodded, and Lindsay continued. "And we're also going to donate as much of this as we possibly can, okay? Anything that you or Willie aren't currently using on a day to day basis needs to be designated to be donated."

"Well, most of it will be to keep, because we got it for my store." Darlene smiled at Lindsay, her expression hopeful.

"Let's talk about that, Mama," Crystal started.

"Darlene, we're not going to concern ourselves with stocking a store during the cleanup." Lindsay's voice was kind but firm as she pressed Darlene forward. "We discussed this yesterday. First things first, we have to deal with where you and Willie are right now, this minute. We can keep the things you need, so that you can live safely in your home and enjoy the space. That's it."

"But when we have all this sorted out it'll be the perfect time to open up a new shop, to start fresh," Darlene argued.

"Once we have all this sorted out you'll have a fresh start, I agree," Lindsay nodded. "But you need a fresh start beginning with the things you need, for the life you're leading now. And, right now, there is no store."

"But once this is taken care of..." Darlene trailed off as Lindsay shook her head.

"Darlene, do you have a place in mind to open a store now?" Lindsay asked.

"We'll lease a place in town, maybe one over in the strip by Right Way."

"And do you know how much a lease might run you these days, monthly?"

Reva's heart sunk at the look of confusion and panic on her mother's face. As much as she wanted Darlene to see reason, to take the steps necessary to clean up her home and live as normal a life as she could manage, she didn't relish seeing her hopes dashed, especially at the start of this process. What if she decided not to go forward with the cleanup at all, if they told her that her dream of some new shop to run was already out of reach?

"Darlene," Reva interjected, wrapping an arm around her mother's shoulders, "I think the point Lindsay is trying to make is that, for right now, we need to stay focused on getting the house right for you. Part of that is letting go of these things you've collected, so that you have space for the things you really need, like she said. We may be able to sell some of it, and we'll put that money away for you and Daddy to decide on something to invest in together, okay? But first, let's get your home where you can manage it. Then, we can see about the rest. Crystal had a great idea yesterday, something that you could do that wouldn't require you to keep stock for a store."

"Like what?" Darlene asked.

"I was thinking you could do something like a nail tech service, Mama. You're so good at it, and you obviously enjoy it."

"But that's just for me," Darlene argued. "I couldn't touch all those strangers, I couldn't—"

"We don't have to figure any of that out today," Lindsay soothed.

"I don't want to get rid of all my things," Darlene said, her voice shaky. "Maybe we can box them up and store them in Willie's shed, or get one of those storage units."

"That's going in entirely the wrong direction, Darlene," Reva said through gritted teeth.

Crystal let out a huff and pushed her way down the hall. "I need a smoke," Reva heard her mumbling as she headed through the kitchen.

"Okay, let's take a step back," Lindsay suggested. "Why don't we start by going through the items we have here in this room, and anything we agree can be sold, whether now or in the future, will go in that area outside to determine what we do with it next. Can we do that?"

Darlene's gaze flitted from Lindsay to Reva.

"Let's do that," Reva said, determined to be positive. "Come on, Darlene. I know you can do this."

"Just don't get rid of anything if I don't say," Darlene insisted.

"No one will get rid of any of this if you don't say," Lindsay assured her. "So, let's get started."

Three hours later, the women stepped back out of the room and surveyed the progress they'd made.

"Look, Ma," Crystal said, grinning, hands on her hips and Reva's Converse on her feet, "there's pink carpet under here."

Darlene giggled. "I forgot it was pink up under all that. I loved that carpet so when Willie had it laid. You girls would sit in there and play and play with your dolls while I was sewing or stitching."

"Well," Reva said, patting the top of the sewing machine, "soon you'll be able to start sewing again."

"Yep," Crystal said, pulling out the old wicker basket that held Darlene's knitting needles and yarns. "Knitting, too."

"That would be nice." Darlene stepped to the sewing machine and bent to brush off the seat of the old wooden spindle chair that sat beneath it.

"Okay, ladies," Reva said, "think we can push through these last few boxes to get into that closet?"

"No!" Darlene was on her feet and between Reva and those boxes in a flash. "Not in there."

"Darlene," Lindsay said, coming to stand beside her, near the boxes. "Why don't you want us to sort through what's in the closet?"

In response, Darlene held her arms out and shook her head furiously. "You can't open this closet."

Crystal and Reva exchanged a glance as Lindsay studied the three Tucker women.

"Does anyone want to tell me what's in that closet?"

"The inventory, what was left of it," Reva said quietly. "The remaining inventory from Darlene's dress shop. I remember one night, maybe a couple months after she got sick, Daddy brought it all in boxes in the back of his truck. He thought maybe we should get rid of it, but she told him to put it away in here. So, we stacked the boxes in that closet and shut the door. That was so many years ago. I don't think that door has been opened again since."

"Is that when you started using this room for your crafts and sewing, Darlene?" Lindsay asked.

Reva shook her head. "That's when she stopped, and when she started barricading that stuff in there."

"It has to stay in there," Darlene whispered. "We can't open that door."

Lindsay led Darlene to the chair at the sewing machine and knelt on the dirty pink carpet. "Why can't we take out the inventory that's in the closet? What is it you think will happen if we open the door to remove it?"

Darlene pressed her hands to her belly and began to rock, back and forth, as Reva had seen her do many times in the throes of a panic attack.

"Darlene," she said, stepping behind her to rest her hands on her shoulders, "whatever it was that happened, whatever made you close the store and lock all of this away, it can't hurt you now."

"I can't be in here with that door open," Darlene whispered, desperation in her eyes spilling over with tears as she clung to Reva's hand.

"Alright, then, let's walk outside and we'll let the crew bring it out and take it straight to the donation truck. You don't ever have to touch it or see it again." Reva shifted Darlene in front of her so they could make it down the hall together.

"Oh!"

Darlene drew up short when they rounded the corner into the kitchen.

"Wow," Reva said, smiling at Willie when he turned from unloading a cabinet to look at them.

"Where did it all go?" Darlene's voice hitched as she asked. She grabbed Dean's sleeve and tugged at him. "Where did you put all of my things?"

"Everything is outside, Miss Darlene." Dean took her by the elbow and led her down the steps under the carport, to the front yard. "See, it's all out here for you to sort, all of it that wasn't trash.

"Where is the trash?" Darlene walked toward the trucks lined up in front of the house. "Who decided what went in the trash?"

"Darlene," Lindsay called, jogging after her.

"Shit," Reva muttered, stopping short.

"Is she about to pull trash out the damn truck?" Crystal nudged Reva and they exchanged a look.

"Think we should get in there, or let Lindsay handle it?" Reva asked.

The cameramen both followed Darlene and Lindsay, which seemed to spur Crystal's interest in intervening.

"I'll take this one," she called to Reva as she pushed her way into the truck where Darlene was now yelling at Lindsay about her bags of plastic bags.

"How are you holding up?"

Reva cut her eyes at Simpson, who stood beside her watching the scene as Crystal alternated between attempts to help calm Darlene and adjusting her boobs in the tank top Reva had told her to cover up.

"I'm still trying to figure out why we can't just light a damn match and get this over with," she answered, her frustration bubbling up. She didn't want to talk to Simpson, but she appreciated somebody—anybody—asking how she was doing.

He laughed. "That would seem to be a simpler solution, but I'm sure that there are at least a few things here worth salvaging, right?"

"Eh," Reva said, tapping her chin with a finger, considering. "Nothing we couldn't live without. I already took most of the photo albums and such over to Gran's—well, my house, now. Far as I'm concerned, all of it can go in the dump. Unfortunately, Darlene is upset that her stash of plastic bags has been thrown in the trash, so we're obviously not all on the same page here."

Simpson glanced at her left hand, at the simple gold band she wore. "Which one's your husband?" he asked, looking around the yard.

"He's not here," Reva answered.

"Why the hell not?"

"Not that it's your business, but he's at work."

"On a Saturday?"

"He owns a tree clearing business, does some small logging jobs. He has two sites running right now and—"

"Hey, you don't have to make excuses for him. I'm just saying, if this was my family, I'd be here. Hell, it's not my family and I'm here."

"Well, this isn't his family, per se, it's mine. His family...God, they'll be humiliated by this whole mess if it gets connected to them. It's likely best he's not involved in this," Reva said.

"When I got back to Austin after rehab, my fiancee and I, we tried to pick back up where we left off, you know? In my mind, even though this deployment was a little more—explosive, let's say, than my others," he paused for effect and winked when Reva rewarded him with a laugh, "I figured I'd get rehabbed, go home, and things would be fine."

"But they weren't?" Reva asked, her curiosity piqued.

"They were for me, but Natasha...well, she had a little more trouble adjusting to my missing leg than I did. Which is somewhat screwed up, but whatever."

"She broke up with you because you lost your leg at war? That's more than screwed up."

"Nah," Simpson said, laughing, "I broke it off with her."

"Oh," Reva said, stepping back so she could better study his face. "Why did you decide to do that?"

Simpson's mouth twitched as he thought. "It wasn't so much that Natasha was bothered by my amputation, or embarrassed about it, it was that she seemed to think I was embarrassed by it."

Reva looked Simpson up and down, at his chiseled physique and features, dark hair, eyes full of fire, and wondered how anyone could miss the pure confidence oozing from his pores. Especially someone who'd been engaged to the man.

"You don't look the type to get embarrassed by much," Reva offered.

"Yeah, I'm not," he said, rolling his shoulders. She tried not to notice the way the muscles rippled beneath his tee shirt.

"It wasn't just her. It was everybody back home, handling me like I was broken, going on about my sacrifices, apologizing all the time for nothing, thanking me when all I did was my job. I hated it. But mostly, I hated the way Natasha was always worrying over whether I could do this or that, if I'd be comfortable, holding onto me like I might fall down any minute, like I hadn't had months of rehab and work with my bionics."

Reva couldn't help smiling at his self-deprecation. But damn, he was charming.

"So, you broke off your engagement because you couldn't tolerate her feeling bad for you?"

"Not exactly, Reva. I broke it off because I can't tolerate anyone treating me like I should be embarrassed for being a human with a past and challenges to overcome. It's not okay for somebody to treat you like you should be embarrassed of who you are. Who you are is just fucking fine. They have no right to be embarrassed by your folks getting help that they need—"

"Why can't you let this shit go?"

Reva and Simpson snapped to attention and hustled over to the garbage truck, where Crystal was on an epic tear, snatching things up and hurling them into the truck bed as Darlene watched on in horror and Lindsay scrambled between them, trying to diffuse the situation.

"Crystal, I need you to please stop what you're doing," Lindsay practically begged, while trying to keep an arm around Darlene, who was wailing now. Simpson took her off Lindsay's hands quickly and found a seat for her while Reva got hold of Crystal around the waist and dragged her away from the truck.

"What the hell are you thinking?" Reva gritted her teeth, determined to keep her cool with the cameras around, and determined to keep Crystal from making a complete spectacle of herself.

"Let go of me!" Crystal screamed.

Reva complied, and Crystal stumbled up against the house.

"Dammit, Reva, I was trying to get her see reason," Crystal huffed.

"That is not what you're trying to do here," Reva said, getting in her face so that only she could here. "Stop showboating and focus on helping get this done. Much more of that crap and Darlene is gonna completely decompensate."

"I've been here working all day just as hard as you have."

"Right now you're working at making an ass of yourself. Quit it or I swear to God I'll make them send you off the property," Reva said, calling up the icy stare she'd used to intimidate her sister into cooperation when they were children and she was acting out.

"Fine, you take her," Crystal spat. "I'll go help Daddy and the other crew and stay far out of your way, little miss perfect."

Reva rolled her eyes. "Please do, Crystal. And try to remember, this isn't a show about you. This is a means to an end for our family."

"One that I arranged, thank you very much."

"For all the wrong reasons, I'm sure. But come hell or high water, we're going to use this opportunity to get it right, so suck it up and get back to work."

"Okay, ladies," Lindsay broke in, pulling Crystal toward the house by the elbow, "let's all calm down and focus on what we're here to do."

"Please," Reva agreed, crossing her arms over her chest.

Crystal rolled her eyes at Reva and stomped to her car, muttering to herself the whole way. Reva and Dean watched her drive away in silence, until finally Reva said, "Well, this has gotten off to a fantastic start."

"Seems Simpson's coming in handy, at least," Dean said, grinning as he nudged her shoulder.

She shrugged. "You know what would really come in handy?"

"What's that?"

"A bulldozer," she answered, forcing herself to head back toward the house, when what she really wanted to do was run.

CHAPTER 21

"Tommy, I've tried to call you three damn times. Pick up the phone! I need to talk to you about what happened at my parents' today. And I need you to come tomorrow. Please. I'm coming to find you. I really need you right now."

Reva tossed her phone to the passenger's seat in frustration, having left a message after her third failed attempt to reach Tommy.

The sky darkened quickly as Reva drove over to Blossom Hill. Tommy wasn't at the Ramirez site. "Gah, he's gonna be all the way over in Bluffton."

The drive wasn't that long, but it felt like an eternity that evening. The first spatters of the torrential rain expected for the entire state began to splash against the windshield. Reva flipped the wipers on the slowest setting and turned up the radio. She hummed along to Chris Stapleton, making the series of turns to reach the logging site. Reva had expected to drive into a nest of activity, knowing that Tommy would likely have the whole crew loading equipment onto trucks to get everything out of the wood before the rain started in earnest. She was surprised to find the site already empty of equipment. Tommy must have gotten a head start on shifting everything to the sheds out on his parents' property.

But, after making the drive back over to check for him there, Reva was disappointed again. The equipment was indeed parked in the stalls as she'd expected, but Tommy's truck was nowhere in sight. She pulled into the driveway and sat for a minute, debating whether or not she should go inside and check in with Amelia. She tried Tommy's cell phone again.

"Still no answer," she muttered. "Where could he be?"

Reva jumped when a horn blew behind her. She checked the rearview mirror and saw Jeremy's truck pulled in perpendicular to her car. A second later, he tapped her window with a knuckle, grinning.

"Hey Jeremy," she said, rolling the window down and returning his smile.

"Hey now," he said. "You meeting up with Tommy over at the Sugar Shack?"

"Oh, is that where he is?"

"Yeah, a few of the guys were headed over once we got everything out the woods. Gonna be an epic storm, they're saying."

"Sure is, from what I'm hearing. You know it's getting rough when all the weather reporters make an appearance, and they're swarming us," Reva said.

Jeremy shrugged. "I reckon we'll get through like we always do. Tell Tommy I gotta go see a man about a truck," he said with a wink. "I might catch y'all later."

"Sounds good, Jeremy. Have a good night. Make sure you check under the hood."

She could hear him laughing until he slammed his door. It was dark now, past eight o'clock already. Reva realized she was hungry, and more tired than she'd been in her entire life. She would stop in at the Shack, have a cheeseburger and a beer, and get Tommy home to tell him about the day, and to talk about their future.

Pulling into the lot at the Sugar Shack, Reva scanned the rows looking for Tommy's truck, guessing it was around back, where there were wider spaces. She drove around to the back side of the building and spotted the big red Dodge down at the end of the row of work trucks lined up along the chain link fence that bordered the property.

Reva smiled as she parked in the row across from him and turned off her headlights. Tommy had backed into the space, and he was still sitting in the driver's seat, hat on, head back, eyes closed...he'd fallen asleep.

During the first few years they were married, there had been nights Reva would hear Tommy's truck pull up outside and know that it would be a good half hour before he'd make his way inside. At the time, he'd been nursing a regular pot habit, and he'd have a smoke before he came in for dinner. She always gave him that time to himself in the evenings to unwind a little. But some nights, the time would stretch on, and she'd wander out to find him asleep in the truck, the radio playing, hat in his lap, a slight smile playing on his lips, as if he was having the most pleasant dream. And there was one time she'd found him with the door of the truck open and one foot out, as if he'd fallen asleep as he took the step out of it.

Of course, he'd quit the pot smoking as their fertility issues dragged on, hoping it might help them achieve a healthy pregnancy. But he'd still always taken that time coming in.

He'd been such a handsome boy, all those years ago. A handful of a boy, wild, but still he'd been hers. How different could things have been if had Tee Jae survived? How different the bond might have been between Reva and his family.

She would try and rectify all of that now, start over. They would figure something out about her going to law school later. But she made up her mind to try to make a real family with Tommy, like she always planned. This cleanup at her parents' place could be a fresh start for them all around.

Tommy's head lolled to the side, then his chin dipped forward. Reva stepped out of the car and moved to the passenger side door of the truck, thinking she would quietly open the door and snuggle up to him on the bench seat, wake him up with a kiss. It had been too long...

But when her hand met the handle of the truck she saw inside, through the window...a woman, a woman's ass in the air, her husband's right hand inside the woman's shorts. And his left hand, the one where his wedding band glinted back the light from the parking lot as it gripped the back of the woman's head, which was planted firmly at his crotch.

It took her too long watching to put the picture together in her mind, to process blonde hair and her own Converse kicked off in the motherfucking floorboard of her motherfucking husband's truck.

She was standing in the back lot of a bar watching her sister give her husband head.

"Oh, oh God no."

She heard the words, and she thought maybe they'd come from her, but it sounded like something other than her voice, something primal, inhuman, breaking loose from the stranglehold that was cutting off the supply of air to her lungs.

Whatever it was, Tommy heard it, too. And he saw her. He saw her seeing him and Crystal in the truck doing things that he should never have thought of doing with her sister. Reva stumbled back when his eyes met hers, as if he'd slapped her in the face. Punched her really. He could have punched her straight in the face and it would have hurt her less than seeing what she had just seen that she would never ever be able to forget.

Reva sat in the gravel of the parking lot, unsure how she'd ended up on the ground, but feeling the sting of scrapes in her palms, filling with blood. She studied the angry red lines, flexing her fingers, refusing to look up to see her husband—

"Reva, let me explain."

Tommy was on his knees in front of her, buckling his belt. She laughed at the absurdity of the entire scene.

His belt had not been buckled in the truck. She didn't care if he buckled his belt now. She didn't want him to explain.

All she could do was laugh.

"Reva, please," he said, taking her by the shoulders. "Are you okay?"

She laughed harder at the question. How could she possibly be okay? Her sister had been in her husband's truck and his penis had been in her mouth. Was that just a moment, two minutes, before?

"Reva, hey, everything okay?" Another voice behind her, one that had quickly become familiar.

"We're fine," Tommy said, holding up a hand. "This is personal business."

"She doesn't look fine." Simpson stood beside her, his hands on his hips as he looked from Tommy to Reva.

"Listen, I told you man, we're fine. This is personal business between me and my wife."

"I was talking to her," Simpson said, reaching a hand to Reva's shoulder, drawing her attention from Tommy to him. "You okay?" He asked again.

"No," Reva answered, her voice as shaky as her knees. Simpson took her hand, pulling her to her feet.

"You fell," he said, a crease forming between his brows. "I didn't see you inside. Tipsy much?"

"No, I—"

"Man, you need to back off," Tommy said to Simpson,

stepping in front of Reva.

Simpson stood his ground, watching Reva over Tommy's shoulder, until the passenger door of Tommy's truck opened and Crystal stumbled out. Reva thought her sister must have been delighted. All eyes were finally on her. A few other people had gathered around in the lot, curious about what was happening between Tommy and Reva, but no one stepping in to intervene like Simpson had. People around New Hope knew Tommy's short fuse, especially when it came to Reva. Simpson didn't know—and Reva sensed that, even if he did, he wouldn't much care.

"What's happening?" Crystal asked, her words slurring. "Tommy, where'd you—"

She stopped dead in her unsteady tracks when she caught sight of Reva. Reva took a step toward her, her hands balled in tight fists.

"I want you to know," Reva said, her voice so quiet that everyone had to strain to hear her, "if you had been any other woman in that truck with my husband, I would be ripping your hair from your head by the root right now."

Crystal shook her head and made a sound something like an uncomfortable laugh. "We were just talkin', sis."

"You were talking? With your face in his crotch and his hand in yours, you were talking? Tell me, *sis*, what exactly was it you were discussing with my husband's—"

"Shit, Reva, not here," Tommy said, reaching for her arm.

"Don't touch me!" she shouted, pushing against his chest, forcing him away from her, toward Crystal. "Don't you ever touch me again!" She shoved him again, hard, and he held his hands up to steady himself.

"Let's go home and we'll talk this through, you and me. I'll get one of the guys to take Crystal. We'll go home, and we'll sort this out."

"You don't have a home to go to, you piece of shit cheating asshole," Reva spat through gritted teeth. "Do not ever step foot on my property again. Take her wherever you damn well please, as long as it's nowhere near me. I don't want to see either one of you ever again, you hear me? Ever."

Tommy made a move toward Reva that Simpson shut down immediately. Reva heard Tommy tell Simpson to get out of his way, and then a loud thump as Simpson invited Tommy to have a seat. She saw as she got in her car that he had Tommy by the collar, on the ground, keeping him from following after her. When she was safely inside the car with the doors locked, Simpson backed away from Tommy and over to her passenger door.

"Let me in," Simpson said, "please."

Reva fumbled with the door lock and let him climb in the passenger seat.

"You get us out of the parking lot and pull over. I'll drive you home."

Reva stared at the man beside her for a long minute. "What are you doing?"

He gave her a half smile, a sad one, and squeezed her hand that was resting on the gear shift. "I'm seeing you home safely, and making sure that shithead you're married to doesn't give you any trouble tonight."

"Thank you, but he won't," Reva said, though she wasn't entirely convinced of that herself.

"Yeah, well, humor me. I'm not entirely sure what happened back there, but I got the gist, and the way you're shaking right now you really shouldn't be driving. Let me help."

"You are hell bent on helping me, aren't you?" Reva said, shaking her head and throwing the car in drive. She watched Tommy, Crystal, and the little crowd gathered outside the Sugar Shack, watching her pull away with Simpson.

He smiled, a real one this time, his dark eyes crinkling at the corners. "I've already set my mind to it, yeah."

CHAPTER 22

Reva didn't drive far before pulling over so she and Simpson could change seats. They were quiet the rest of the way home, with Reva only speaking to tell Simpson when to turn where. When they pulled up the drive and parked behind the house, they sat together in the car in silence for a long moment.

"Thank you," Reva said. "I could have gotten home on my own, but…"

"Yeah, I know you could have. I didn't feel right about leaving you to your own devices after the hell of a day you've had."

Reva laughed. "You must think—Lord, I don't know what you must think. I don't even know what I think. I mean, my life right now, this moment, is something I don't even recognize. It's not like everything was fine and dandy before, but…it feels like somebody lit everything on fire all at once."

Simpson grimaced, dropping his chin to his chest. "I'm sorry for playing a part in all of this, Reva. I hope you know that what I did, calling in for help for your parents…it was my intention to help them. If I'd known…"

Reva shrugged. "I know that. And, at the end of the day, something had to be done about their place." She blew out a slow breath. "But I'm still trying to sort out how we work through all of that as a family, and after the physical cleanup, how everything else gets fixed, and now, this."

Simpson nodded slowly. "Looks like you're in the midst of a shit storm."

"An epic shit storm with an epic flood on its heels. Who will survive?" She said dramatically. "Doesn't look like my marriage will."

"I hope you don't mind my saying this, but your husband is a complete douchebag."

"You don't say?" Reva said, rolling her eyes.

"So, when you drove in at the Sugar Shack, he was in the truck…"

"With my sister. Who was performing oral sex on my husband. Who had his hand—you know what? Can we talk about something a little less embarrassing if we're gonna talk? I think I've been humiliated enough in front of you for one day." Reva's voice quaked as she spoke, and she knew she was dangerously close to breaking down.

"You hungry?" Simpson asked, opening the door of the car. "Because I could eat."

Reva sighed and heaved her tired body out of the car. "You know, I was earlier, but maybe I lost my appetite."

"Did you have dinner?"

She shook her head as she unlocked the back door. Simpson stood behind her on the bottom step. She thought she should tell him to go home, that she needed to be alone.

But, as humiliated and exhausted as Reva was, she didn't want to be alone. She knew if she went inside her house—Gran's house—all the ways she was now truly alone would start to settle into her chest and smother the life out of her.

Because this house, as much as she loved it, felt truly empty without Gran in it.

And Tommy wouldn't be coming home tonight. Deep down in her heart, in her bones, in her soul, she knew that Tommy wouldn't be coming home to her ever again. She couldn't imagine ever looking at him and feeling anything other than disgust.

Her marriage was over. If she didn't know how to sort out anything else, that was clear.

"Umm, Reva, we going in?"

"Oh," she said, startled out of her thoughts by the sound of Simpson's voice. "Sorry, yeah."

Reva flipped on the lights and pointed at the bar stools. "Have a seat," she said, sliding her shoes into their place and padding into the kitchen. "What can I get you? Something to drink? I'll figure out something for us to—"

Simpson took her by the shoulders and pushed her out of the kitchen to the sofa in the adjoining living room.

"Sit," he said. "You've had a hell of a day."

"But you're hungry—"

"And I know you'd never guess it, but I can cook."

Simpson had the refrigerator open and was scanning the shelves as Reva looked on.

"How do you feel about omelets?" he asked as he sat the egg carton on the counter, followed by sliced mushrooms, spinach, bacon, and shredded cheese.

"I feel fine about them," Reva answered. She curled her legs beneath her on the sofa and pulled the old quilt from the back, wrapping it around her.

"Good, because I happen to make amazing omelets."

Reva watched Simpson as he moved around the kitchen, finding the bowls and the pan he needed, opening and closing cabinets and drawers, making himself at home. She noticed how gracefully he moved, how at ease he felt in his own body, prosthetic or not, and she realized that it had been a very long time since she'd felt that kind of comfort within herself.

Had she ever felt comfortable in her own skin, really?

The thought that she had not suddenly overwhelmed her. It was clear, though, when she thought back over her life…the discomfort of her childhood after her mother's hoarding began, all the hiding she did, of her family life and her home and what she worried would manifest in her as well. Her marriage to Tommy right out of school, the attempt it was to redefine herself, to become someone she wasn't, someone she could never really be. Her failed attempts to carry a child, the way her body refused to cooperate with the greatest wish of her heart, or what should have been.

She'd never felt that comfortable in her own skin.

"How do you do it?"

Simpson glanced up at her as he whisked the eggs for the omelets. "You whisk the eggs like so, and heat the pan to—"

"I know how to make an omelet, Billy," she said, a sarcastic bite to her words but a smile on her face.

"How do I do what?"

"How do you—how are you so much entirely who you are?"

Simpson's face scrunched as he considered her question. "I don't know, Reva. I mean, who else would I be?"

"Yeah, but you're so, like, confident and sure of yourself. With everything you've been through, you still carry yourself like you've never hit a bump in the road in your life. How does one achieve such swagger? I would like to know where I can get some."

"Wow," he said, laughing. "You think I'm all confident and sure of myself, eh?"

She nodded, resting her chin on one hand. "Yes, I do. For example, look at how you took control of this little situation tonight. You didn't even hesitate before getting involved, you stepped in. And you made sure I was okay, rather than stepping back and leaving me to deal with Tommy on my own, like everyone else did, if you didn't notice."

"I guess stepping back isn't in my DNA, Reva. Obviously, I've faced some challenges, but I don't care if I'm on one leg, no legs, or eight legs. I'm a soldier. I will always stand up for those who need defending. Especially when it's someone I care about."

Reva paused at his words. "But you barely know me."

"Sure, we just met, but I feel like, because of the situation, I understand you on a different level than most folks I know. And I kinda owe you a solid, so…"

He flipped the omelet he'd been frying in the air and it landed in the pan perfectly.

"I could never do that," Reva said, unable to keep the wonder from her voice.

"It's all in the wrist," Simpson said, plating the omelet and finding the forks.

"Tell that to Tommy."

Simpson's eyes went wide for a second before a deep rumble of laughter escaped from him. "Wow, you're something else, you know that?"

Reva shook her head. "It's the hurt talking. I'm a smartass when I'm hurt. Usually, I'm polite to a fault. Full control."

"Well, then," he said, setting the plate and a glass of water down in front of her, "may I never receive a smartass remark directed at me. Again. Because I'm pretty sure I fielded plenty the day we met."

Reva laughed, shifting to lean over the coffee table and the delicious-smelling omelet. Her hunger returned instantly, leaving her mouth watering as she cut into it, melted cheese and bacon and mushrooms spilling out onto the plate. She took the first bite and closed her eyes, savoring the flavors as they filled her mouth. "Wow, that's so good."

"Mmhmm." Simpson was back at the stove, working on his own dinner. "You're welcome."

"Thank you."

Reva watched his back as she ate, the muscles of his broad shoulders flexing under his soft cotton tee shirt as he moved at the stove, tapering into a narrow waist and a tight...

She nearly choked, had to fight off a coughing fit, as she recognized the drift of her thoughts.

She would not be that woman who took revenge on her cheating husband by hooking up with the first man who cooked her an omelet. And, even if she was, it would not be Billy Simpson. She reminded herself that she didn't even like this man.

Reva took several long gulps of her water to try and cool the heat of her cheeks, watching Billy closely as he plated his food and poured himself a glass of water, then joined her in the living room, choosing to sit beside her on the couch rather than across from her in the armchair.

"You all good?" he asked her, grinning as she polished off her last bite. "Need me to make you more?"

"Oh no, you eat." Reva shook her head and pushed her plate away, suddenly self-conscious about...everything. She scooted to the end of the sofa and tucked her feet beneath her again, covering up with the quilt she'd abandoned while she ate.

"You wanna talk about it?"

"Nope." Reva wrapped the quilt closer to her as Simpson focused on his plate.

"Good. I don't want to talk about it either," he said.

Reva leaned her head against her hand, her elbow propped on the back of the sofa. "What else is there to talk about, right? Before we met, my life wasn't going that great, but I was managing it."

"And now?"

"And now, it's a damn disaster," she said. "My parents are going to lose their house if we don't get it cleaned up, like, tomorrow. My sister is an addict. And she's apparently been giving my husband...well, you already know. Which means my husband is cheating on me with my sister. I have failed to carry three babies to term, but everybody wants me to try one more damn time. And I got in to law school but I can't afford to go without a grant and I'm pretty sure my boss is sabotaging whatever chance I had of getting one."

Simpson was staring at again, his jaw slack. "Well," he started, taking his time, "I'm a trained master of chaos. I'm sure there's something we can do to negotiate a way through this situation. And if that fails, I'm also pretty handy with explosives."

Reva burst into laughter, caught off guard by his response to her litany of complaints. "Any help you can offer up is most appreciated," she said, settling back into the cushions. "Actually, I haven't thanked you for coming to help with the cleanup at my parents' house. I know you're feeling some responsibility for turning them in, but you could have let it be, especially after I tracked you down and lit into you the way I did. Most people wouldn't have bothered, but you did."

Simpson gave her a quick smile. "You're welcome. Honestly, it's my pleasure to help them. I would have done it whether you lit into me, as you say, or not. But yes, I knew when I reported them that there would be consequences, so I'm glad I was able to follow up and pitch in. It was always my intention to help. Getting to know you is a bonus, too. I know you feel like things are crazy right now, but there's some crazy amazing in there, too. Getting accepted to law school is a huge deal, Reva. Congratulations. Seriously."

She felt herself blushing again and rushed to move the topic of conversation away from her. "Tell me something about you," Reva said. "I'm bored as hell with my own whining."

Simpson's gaze met hers. "What would you like to know?"

"I don't know…where you're from, how you ended up here, what your family's like, why you're still single…"

"Where I left my other leg?" he threw in.

"Billy!"

They laughed together, and he finally said, "It's generally the thing people ask me about first now."

"Fine, then," Reva said, "even though I already know the short answer, where did you leave your other leg?"

Their laughter faded, and Simpson's face took on a more serious shadow before he spoked again. "As you know, it was blown to bits somewhere in the desert in Afghanistan."

Reva held his gaze with hers, determined not to look away, to let his story, his reality, make her uncomfortable. She sensed how much he would hate that, and she desperately wanted him to not regret this moment of openness with her.

"That had to fucking suck," she said, remembering not to say thank you, or I'm sorry.

"It definitely fucking sucked, Reva."

"Do you want to tell me the story? I mean, I guess I know Scott's story. But I haven't heard yours."

So, he did. He told her about the mission he was on with Scott and Kedrick, about how he and Kedrick were hit on the ATV, how they couldn't find Scott in the chaos…about the drive back to the outpost holding his dead teammate up on the ATV, all the while unable to check his own wound, but knowing his leg was all but lost. He told her about tumbling off into the dirt when they made it, of immediately falling unconscious. Of dreaming the most horrible dreams until he woke up in a hospital room in Germany, missing his right leg from above the knee.

That the loss of his leg hurt significantly less than the loss of Kedrick, and what he'd thought was the loss of Scott.

"When I got back to the United States, I went straight to a facility in Pensacola that specializes in rehab for amputees. I had to work hard to adjust to my body in its new form. And yes, you'll notice there are words I don't use. Disabled is one of them."

"I don't look at you and think disabled. Although I don't think of disabilities as anything to be ashamed of," Reva offered.

"Neither do I," Simpson said, "but the label didn't feel right on me, so I never accepted it. My body is strong, healthy, and whole. I'm still a whole person. I had to learn a different style of balance, different ways to build and use my strength. And I've done it so well that, frankly, I'm stronger than I've ever been in my life, in every way."

Reva reached for his hand out of some instinct, and he let her take it. It felt like the most natural thing in the world. "I can see that," she said. "The fact that you've gone through so much—not just the physical, but the mental and emotional stuff that came with it—the fact that you came through all of that and you came out on the other side stronger, it gives me hope. It makes me believe that there's another side to what I'm facing, if I can shift my perspective. You make me want to be a stronger version of myself when all this chaos is behind me."

Simpson squeezed her hand and grinned at her. "I think that might be the nicest thing anyone's ever said to me."

"Thank you," Reva whispered. "Thank you for finding me and seeing me."

"You'll be fine, Reva. Better than fine. This chaos, as you call it, it's alchemy. Let it forge you. Don't let it break you down."

"I won't."

"I won't let you forget," he whispered.

Suddenly she was so tired, she could barely keep her eyes open. She thought she would just rest them for a moment, let her head drop to the soft cushions she'd piled behind her, relax a bit...

"Reva, time to wake up."

She must be dreaming, though there was no way she'd been asleep long enough to be dreaming. But she couldn't immediately pinpoint the owner of the decidedly female voice telling her to wake up, so she must be dreaming.

"Reva, wake up."

Her eyes popped open and she nearly fell off the sofa when she saw Bay Ramirez and Leigh Anne LaFleur leaning over her.

"Wh—what are y'all doing?"

"Don't freak out," Leigh said, plopping down in the side chair. "Simpson called Scott to come pick him up last night, and we came to check and see how you were, but you were out like a light."

"I slept so hard," Reva said through a yawn. "Oh my God, y'all came to check on me. What have you heard?"

"Everything," Bay said, handing Reva a cup of coffee.

"Gah, did Billy have to spill all my dirt?"

"He wasn't fast enough," Leigh said. "Paige Docherty called me before you'd even slung up gravel out of the Shack's drive, and I got three texts from the bar while I was on the phone with her. Funny how half my Sunday school class was at the bar on Saturday night."

"Well, shit." Reva took a sip of coffee and nodded her thanks to Bay. "When did y'all get here?"

"A little after eleven," Leigh said. "Simpson said he slept in the recliner for a while too before he called Scott."

"And I called Leigh to come with me because I thought it might be nice for you to have family here," Bay added.

"I still can't believe what's happening. This—this is not my life."

"I can't believe my stupid cousin is so damn stupid," Bay said. "What I mean is, this should definitely not be your life. You're a good girl, Reva. Tommy's a fuckup, if you'll excuse my language."

Leigh laughed. "When did you start asking people to excuse that mouth of yours?"

Bay rolled her eyes.

"What time is it?" Reva asked, jumping to her feet and sloshing coffee.

"A little after seven," Leigh said.

"Shit. Shit shit shit."

"It's Sunday. Where do you have to be?"

"At my parents' house. That's a whole other nightmare I'd love to wake up from."

Leigh and Bay exchanged a look.

"What?" Reva asked, picking up on the weird vibe.

"I was wondering if your sister will be there," Bay said.

"God, I hope not," Reva called down the hall. She came out of the bedroom buttoning her jeans. "I really don't think I can deal with her today. But I'm gonna have to deal with her sometime. Shit."

"You try not to worry about that today," Leigh said.

"Listen, thank y'all for coming and staying, even if I was sleeping away. I appreciate you being here for me. I gotta get myself ready to go, though."

Bay and Leigh both hugged Reva, and they left while she ran to brush her teeth and pull her hair up. She studied herself in the mirror, and wondered for a split second if she could really do this today. But she was determined to see this cleanup through for her parents, Crystal or not. She would not let her sister derail the progress their family had been making.

She thought about Simpson, about his determination to see himself as whole, even after the injuries he'd endured, regardless of the physical, emotional, and psychological pain he'd had to overcome.

If he could go through everything he'd gone through and come out stronger on the other side, then so could she.

"Starting today, starting right now," she said to herself, "I'm taking my life back. And nobody better try and stop me."

CHAPTER 23

"Oh, thank God," Lindsay said when she saw Reva walking up Willie and Darlene's driveway, waving her over from where she stood with some of the crew beneath a tent. "I thought both of you girls had bailed on us today."

"Sorry I'm late," Reva answered. "Crystal's not here, then?"

"She called your parents earlier and said she suddenly has the flu," Lindsay said, holding her hands up as she shrugged.

Reva gave her a quick nod and exhaled her relief, trying to keep her expression neutral. "Good, then. We'll likely move faster without her causing drama. Let's get going."

Lindsay's brow furrowed, but she didn't argue.

"Do you think we should check on her, Reva? She didn't come here last night, and we don't know where she is," Willie asked. Concern knotted his features.

Reva almost had to bite her tongue to keep from launching into how little she cared where her sister was, or what she might do to her if she showed up. "No, I'm sure she's right where she wants to be. Let's not waste the time we have with this excellent crew here, okay? We can get this tackled while we have the help. Time's ticking."

"But, what if something's happened to her?" Darlene asked, folding her arms across her chest. "I think we should check on her, Reva. You should call and see where she is, see if she needs—"

"Mama," Reva broke in, "she already called you, right?"

Darlene nodded.

"So, you know she's alive, and conscious?"

Darlene nodded again.

"Let's not use this as an excuse to stall out, okay? You're doing great. We're going to do this together, you and me and Willie. Crystal has to learn to take care of herself."

"Wait," Darlene grumbled. "Just wait a minute. I want to see what's under the tents and in that shipping container before we start on another room today." She turned her back on Reva and started wandering the yard, picking up and putting down items they'd already sorted from the living room and kitchen.

"Oh, no you don't," Reva said, taking Darlene by the shoulders and turning her around. "We don't have time to redo what's already done. Forward motion, okay?"

"But—"

Reva leaned in and whispered, "I believe in you, Darlene. You've got this, okay? You're doing so well. Now, let's go."

With that, Reva strode up the steps and into the house, trusting that Darlene and Willie would fall in line. Terrance greeted her in the hallway with a warm smile.

"Hey, Terrance. Do you know where we're getting started today?"

"Your mother's room," Lindsay answered from behind her, and Terrance nodded.

"I was waiting for everyone to come on inside before I find somewhere to set up in there," Terrance said.

"Well, then, let's find you a spot."

Reva pushed through the door to Darlene's room and took in the space.

"Terrance, I think there's plenty of room right over here between the door and the dresser. Looks like the pileup here is in the far corner and on the bed."

Clothes, books, and myriad boxes of whatnots were stacked high in the room, but Darlene had left space for her chair, and a path to the bathroom, so there was at least room to move. Anxious to get started, to keep her mind and body moving forward, Reva dove straight in, directing Willie and Darlene behind her.

A few hours into the day, Reva stood from where she'd been crouched to hand things back to Willie.

"Lord, Darlene, I didn't even remember that you had a desk in here," Reva said, as the surface of the old roll-top appeared from beneath the enormous pile of books in the corner of the room.

Darlene's hands fluttered up to her mouth, where she pressed them tight against her lips.

"Did you remember?" Reva asked her, unable to read her

mother's reaction.

"I remember," Willie chimed in from the far corner, where he sat picking through the contents of more grocery bags than Reva cared to count. "We mainly used it for bookkeeping and whatnot with the store."

"Don't—" Darlene hesitated on the word, having removed her hands from her mouth and clenched them into tight fists at her sides.

"Let's finish clearing the books and then we can deal with the desk." Reva passed an armload of paperbacks off to Darlene and shooed her. "Take those on outside. We don't have too much more to go."

With Darlene out of the room, Reva made quick work of clearing the rest of the books away from the desk, making neat piles behind her that Darlene could easily carry out. The roll-top had been open beneath the pile of books for years, and when she tried to pull it forward, it stuck. With a sigh, she pulled out the narrow drawers one by one, left to right, finding an assortment of pens and pencils, decomposing rubber bands, ancient stamps, and dust bunnies. She dumped the contents into an empty bag as she removed each drawer, thinking she could toss it all in the trash without Darlene needing to even touch it.

Reva pulled out the last drawer expecting to find more of the same, but when she glanced down to check the contents, saw that this drawer had a lone black jewelry box inside, one with an emblem atop that she knew she'd seen before. She set the bag of trash aside and lifted the box from the drawer, running a finger over the design.

"I had forgotten."

Reva startled at her mother's voice, so light, so close behind her.

She turned and held the box out. "What had you forgotten?"

Darlene studied the box, an odd, wistful look overtaking her features.

"Your pearl."

Reva felt something squeeze in her chest, as if by uttering those two simple words her mother had reached into her rib cage and stopped her heartbeat, knocked the breath from her lungs. She wrapped her fingers around the box, willing herself to breathe.

"My pearl?" The question was barely a whisper of breath, and hardly a question at all.

"It's been so long, I'm surprised I recognize the box. But I'm sure that's it." Darlene stared at Reva's hands, nodding, a slight smile on her face as her mind wound its way back through the clutter to a clear memory. The cameramen and cleaning crew seemed to sense the mounting tension between mother and daughter, drawing closer in, catching the scent of unfolding drama.

"If it's mine, why was it here?"

"Well, that's a good story." Darlene perched on the edge of the bed, settling in to spin a tale in a way Reva remembered suddenly from her childhood, when she'd fed Reva and Crystal a steady dose of fairytales, ones that would lead a young girl to dream of princes, glass slippers, diamond rings and tiaras…

Pearls.

"I'd like to hear it," Reva said, lifting the lid from the cardboard box and carefully removing the royal blue velvet clamshell it held. She knew what was inside without opening it—she could feel it down to her bones—but she wanted to hear her mama tell it.

"She brought it here, did you know? Right up to the front door. Knocked and knocked, waited and waited out in the heat. Why on earth you had to get married in June…"

"Who waited, Mama?"

"That Amelia Patterson, of course." Darlene nodded toward the front of the house as if Amelia was out there knocking at that moment.

"Did you ever answer?"

Darlene shrugged. "Your daddy came home and she was still standing out there on the porch. Didn't even sit in one of them chairs we had out there. Looked for the longest time like she couldn't decide whether she was comin' or goin'."

Reva flinched at the thought of Amelia standing on her parents' dusty little front porch, trying to decide whether she should wait it out or leave and resign herself to a second trip. Had she peeked in the windows and seen what was inside? Reva's stomach flipped at the thought of her then future mother-in-law realizing what her son's wife-to-be had come from, realizing who Reva really was.

She'd always assumed what Amelia must have thought of her, since she didn't gift her with a pearl at the wedding. She couldn't yet process the fact that Amelia had not withheld the pearl. What she'd assumed of Amelia for all these years had been wrong. Amelia had known exactly who she was, who she came from, but she intended to welcome Reva anyway.

"And when Daddy got home, did he talk to her?"

Darlene nodded. "He came in with that box there," she said, pointing at Reva. "Told me all we had to do was take it over to the jeweler on Edisto who does them Pearl Girl necklaces, and I could pick out whatever I thought you'd like best, no charge to us at all."

Reva pressed her thumbnail in the seam of the velvet box and lifted the lid. Inside lay a fat, luminous pearl. Her pearl. It had never been set—her mother would never have taken it into the little shop on Edisto where all the pieces for the Pearl Girls were created.

But her daddy could have done it. Or her aunt. Even Crystal could have managed back then. They could have asked Amelia to have it set herself. Instead, her pearl sat buried in her mother's hoard for ten years, and like the pea beneath the princess' mattresses, it had been the unknown source of many sleepless night for Reva. She choked back a sob and tried to compose herself, remembering there were cameras filming every word of this, every shattering heartbeat, every tear that tumbled down her cheeks.

Reva crossed the space between them and knelt in front of Darlene. "Why didn't you do it?" she whispered. "I mean, I know you would have never taken it to get it done yourself, but why didn't you ask Daddy? Or Crystal? Anybody? I could have done it myself, even."

"I thought maybe I'd be able to do it for you, honey. Really, I did."

"No, Darlene, you knew you'd never be able to do it," Reva said, shaking her head furiously. She pushed to her feet and held the pearl under Darlene's nose. "How could you, Darlene?" Reva asked, trying and failing to keep her voice from rising. "How could you take this from me?"

Darlene smiled, a patronizing, slight smile that cut Reva to the core. "I didn't take nothing, baby. I kept it right here, see?"

"I don't mean the pearl!" Reva shouted, turning away from Darlene, unable to look at her anymore. "All I've wanted, all these years, was to be a part of a family—to be a part of my husband's family. And you let me believe, from the day I married him, that they didn't want me. That they'd never accept me. I spent my wedding day wondering why—why would Amelia have shut me out of a family tradition that, so far as I know, *no one* had ever been excluded from? Why would I be the first? She was so cold to me the entire day, so distant, and all I could figure was that she didn't think I was good enough for her son. Do you have any idea what that's done to me, to us, all these years?"

"You're blowin' this all outta portions, Reva," Darlene said, her jowls shaking. "I explained it to Amelia at the wedding. Or—well—I told her what I could tell. It was fine."

"What do you mean, what you could tell?"

"When she came to see the necklace when you were getting dressed, I told her you wouldn't be wearing it, that you'd rather have something from your own mama for your wedding day. And she didn't say a thing about having any problem with it."

Reva closed her eyes and squeezed the clamshell together in one hand, her fingernails digging in the other. "You told her I preferred to wear secondhand costume jewelry from the thrift shop than wear a precious pearl that had been in her family for generations, one that would have signified my official induction into the Pearl Girls? You told her that, and thought it wasn't a problem?"

"She didn't say a word."

"You really don't get it, do you? This pearl, this gift from Amelia to me, is how generations of women have been bonded together in that family. It's not just a necklace, Darlene. It's an honor and a privilege to be part of that group of women. Lord, what Amelia must have thought when you told her I didn't want to wear this on my wedding day! What a complete snub that must have felt like to her, a rejection of something so precious to that whole family. And here I am, coming from nothing, turning my nose up at the whole thing. Do you get that's what it must have seemed like to her?"

Darlene's cheeks flamed red. She huffed out a breath. "What was wrong with what I gave you for your wedding day? And don't you dare tell me you come from nothing. Just because we ain't rich and fancy don't make us nothing. All this ain't nothing!"

Reva nearly doubled over laughing. When she recovered herself, she spread her arms and twirled around, scattering some of the trash on the floor. "You're right about that, aren't you? All of this sure ain't nothing. It's a damn dumpster in here."

"You watch your mouth!" Darlene shouted, curling her fists in her lap. Her eyes darted around the room as if she was looking for an escape, for Willie to step in and shield her from any challenge. But it wouldn't happen this time. The Help for Hoarders crew had crowded the little available space in the bedroom, blocking the door, letting the scene play out between mother and daughter. It was obviously the kind of high drama they hoped for in the hopelessly dysfunctional families they helped.

If a show was what they wanted, Reva thought, a show was what they'd get.

"My mouth is no filthier than this shithole we call home," Reva yelled. "It's no filthier than you lying to me all these years. Do you realize what this did to my life, to my marriage, for ten years?"

"If Amelia cared about whether you wore that pearl or not, she didn't let on—"

"Darlene, I cared," Reva said, stifling a sob. "I cared so much about this pearl. It's not just a piece of jewelry to wear on your wedding day. You know who the Pearl Girls are—what the Pearl Girls are. I mean, for God's sake, it was all Leigh could talk about when she and Ethan were getting married. This pearl," Reva said, lifting the box in front of her as her voice cracked, "it's a symbol of belonging, a symbol that you're a part of something greater than yourself. This pearl means something. It means family."

"You have a family, Reva, whether you care about us or not," Darlene said, lifting her chin. "Maybe we ain't enough for you, but it ain't like you don't have anybody. Just because you don't even call us Mama and Daddy anymore don't mean we're not still your family."

Reva shook her head as the pools of tears in her eyes spilled over and down her cheeks. "All I ever wanted—" She paused, the emotion rising in her throat almost too thick to speak through. "All I ever needed was for us to be a real family, like I remember us being when I was little. Do you remember, before you got sick, how happy we were? This house—this mess—it was a happy home. And then everything changed, overnight. I didn't understand it, not then, and not later. So, when Tommy and I got married, yes, I was excited about being a part of his family, too. I wanted so much to feel like part of that kind of family again. I still don't understand what happened to you, but it's always seemed like you took our family away from us. And now, it's like you took my second chance at a family from me, too. How could you, Darlene?"

Darlene turned her eyes to the popcorn ceiling above her and swayed a few times before letting out a gutteral moan that slowly inched its way up into a roar. Reva held her ground as the crew continued to block a protesting Willie from the room. Focusing her attention, Reva took her mother's hands in hers.

"It's just you and me, Mama. Tell me."

Bringing her gaze back to Reva, Darlene whimpered and fell back to the bed, jerking her hands away to cover her face. Reva dropped to a knee in front of her. "Tell me," she whispered.

"I was at the shop, closing up for the day. It wasn't too late yet, but it was winter. It was dark already outside, so I knew there wouldn't likely be anybody else to come in. So, I went up front and turned the sign, locked the door. They were walking by right then, those two boys, lookin' in on me." Her voice started to shake, and she clinched her fists tight in her lap again, as if she would fight off the memories returning to her if she could. "Something about the way they was lookin' wasn't right, but then the phone rang."

Darlene paused, her eyes focusing past Reva, the look on her face one of near horror, as if she were watching something terrible play out on a screen in the distant past. Reva waited for Darlene to continue.

"It was your daddy on the phone. He was late coming from work, so I was gonna have to wait on him at the shop. It was the third night in a row, and I was mad, fussin'. I wasn't thinking about the back door, that it was still unlocked. And I was fussin' so hard I didn't hear it open."

Reva closed her eyes and rested a hand on top of her mother's still-clinched fist.

"One of 'em grabbed me by my hair while I was still layin'

into Willie. I didn't even let go of the phone at first—it yanked right off the counter onto the floor with me. And it was them two black boys who'd been lookin' in at me out front, had to be. The big one, the one who was so tall, he held me down on the floor while the other one went through all the drawers in the desk. I'd already emptied the register, so the cash bag was right there in my purse. All they had to do was to take it and leave. I thought they would take my purse and leave."

"But that's not what happened?"

Darlene shook her head, her eyes still fixed on something beyond Reva. "The big one, he took the phone out of my hand and hit me right across the face with it, then threw it against the wall. I could hear your daddy calling for me, asking me what was going on. The whole time he was hearing…"

Reva slipped the pearl that she was still holding into her pocket and took Darlene's other hand. "All this time, all these years…you and Willie didn't tell anybody, did you? Did you even report it?"

"No!" Darlene's gaze snapped back to Reva, a look of alarm in her eyes. "By the time Willie got to me those boys was long gone. He wanted to call the police, but there wasn't any way I was lettin' him. All they'd took was thirty-eight dollars and seventeen cents in that bag. Didn't even take my purse."

"But, Darlene, they attacked you. They—"

"No!" Darlene grabbed Reva by the arms and shook her hard. "You hear me? Nobody needs to know about anything about this!" Her eyes wild, she shook Reva once more. Her voice dropped to a whisper. "We're gonna pretend like it never happened. I'll take some days off sick and we'll go back to normal."

Reva reached a tentative hand to her mother's cheek, willing her back to the present moment. "That's not what happened, Mama. You tried to pretend it didn't happen, but you weren't able to. Now I understand why. Now I understand why everything changed, why you shut yourself away from the world like this. Listen to me, though, Mama. You don't have to be a prisoner to that one night for the rest of your life."

Darlene wiped at her face with the backs of her hands. "Nobody can know about what them boys did," she whispered.

"Nobody else has to know." Reva turned to give a pointed look to Terrance, who had already dropped the camera to his side. "I promise you, it won't leave this room, if you promise me that starting now, you'll get the help you need to deal with this."

"I don't know if I can," Darlene said through her tears.

"You can. I'll help you," Reva said, pulling Darlene into a hug, rocking her back and forth. "Lord, Mama, all this time, why didn't you let me help you?"

"There isn't no way to help me, so long as those boys are still out there. I can't be on my own outside of this house. I can't."

Reva pulled back and gave Darlene what she hoped was an encouraging smile. "One thing at a time. Let's get this place straight so you can really live in it. Then we'll tackle whatever's next."

For the first time in more years than she could remember, Reva's mama reached for her and hugged her. "I'm sorry about your pearl. I really did mean to see to it when Amelia brought it. I just..."

"I know. I understand now. It's not important."

Darlene's eyes went wide. "You can't tell Amelia. She can't know why—"

"Don't worry, I won't tell anything you don't want known. Okay?"

"Okay," Darlene nodded.

Reva turned to Terrance and Lindsay, still hovering at the door. "I think we maybe need to break for the day. And none of that stays, understood?"

"Understood," Terrance said, placing a hand on Reva's shoulder. "We'll take care of it. Don't worry."

"Can you come tomorrow?" Lindsay asked Reva. "We can work out staying, and I'll talk to Dean. We can't hold this over for next weekend with the weather."

Reva nodded. "I'll make it work." She pushed past them into the hall, where Willie stood, his eyes and face as red as her own. "She'll need you, Daddy," Reva said, giving him a quick hug. "I've got to take care of something."

"I'm sorry, baby," Willie said, squeezing her hard.

"It's alright. It'll be alright," she whispered.

Finding Caprice waiting outside under the carport, Reva tried to find the words to explain what she must have heard. Reva had seen her lurking around outside, listening at the windows. She pulled the girl into a tight hug and whispered her apologies. When she finally let her go, Caprice chewed the side of her thumb, never meeting Reva's eyes.

"I got the gist of your mama's story, Miss Reva, but don't worry, I won't say nothin' about it to nobody."

"Thank you, Caprice," Reva said. "I guess we have a little better understanding about Mama's attitude over some things now."

"I reckon. So, is that why your mama doesn't like black people? Because some black boys hurt her?"

"Listen," Reva said softly, "my mama had something traumatic happen to her, and she's going to have to work through what damage that's done to her way of thinking. I'm going to make sure she works on it."

Caprice nodded. "Bad and good comes in every color. Even yours."

Reva hugged Caprice close again. "You speak the truth, young one. You should run on back home. I gotta go take care of some things."

"Yes, ma'am," Caprice answered, seeming hesitant to leave as she looked out across the road to her double-wide.

"Caprice, you okay?"

The girl nodded. "Yes ma'am," she said again, then pointed to the truck. "Ray's over there. I might wait out here a little bit, 'til my mom comes home, if that's alright with you."

"Okay, that's fine," Reva said, her stomach doing a weird somersault. Reva noticed that Caprice stayed outside whenever her mother's boyfriend was around. She worried over why. "You sure everything's alright?"

"I'm sure," Caprice said. "You go on and don't worry about us over here. I'll keep an eye out."

"Okay," Reva said. "If you need me, Caprice..."

Caprice smiled. "I know, Miss Reva. I'll call."

But, as Reva backed out of her parents' drive and watched Caprice sitting tucked away in a corner of the carport, she did worry. For Darlene, and for Willie, and, now, as she watched the sweet child chewing on the edge of her thumb, afraid to go home, she worried for her, too.

GINA HERON

CHAPTER 24

The Owl's Roost was busy on Sunday afternoons, with patrons picking up late lunches or early dinners after church, or just coming in for dessert. The bells on the door sounded when Reva walked in, but she knew that no one would register them over the chatter.

She paused just inside the door, uncertain of what she would even say to Amelia. Lucky for her, her mother-in-law was nowhere in sight. Reva knew she was probably in the back, hustling up orders for the floor staff. They'd worked alongside each other in the kitchen enough for Reva to know the rhythms of the restaurant.

Reva hugged the interior wall of the room as she made her way to the kitchen. She studied the old high school photographs Amelia had hanging as she went, pausing at the now legendary ones of Marco, Scott, and Bay Ramirez. It had been Marco's high school football photo that triggered Bay's questions about a potential link between the man and her husband, and as it turned out, Marco was, in fact, the father that Scott had never known.

Further down the wall, there was a picture she'd forgotten of her and Tommy their senior year. It took her breath how handsome he was in his football uniform, and how happy she looked snug against him, her pom-poms gathered at her waist. Without thinking, she yanked the photo from the wall. A sob caught in her throat, and all at once one of the girls at the counter noticed her. Reva heard her call back for Amelia.

"Reva," Amelia said as she hurried to her side, concern and relief mingling in her voice. "Honey, come to the back."

Reva let Amelia lead her as she clutched the photo to her chest and fought off her tears.

Once in the office, Reva sat down in the chair where she was guided and watched Amelia carefully as she circled behind her desk, wondering what she might be thinking, under these circumstances. Was she relieved that Tommy and Reva's marriage might be over? That Tommy might get out of this unequally paired, childless marriage?

But that was the kind of thinking that Reva would have done before the pearl was found, that required her to forget that the snub she'd assumed Amelia guilty of years before had not, in fact, happened.

Amelia wasn't happy about this. And that made Reva even sadder. She choked down a sob.

"Tommy's been at the house since last night," Amelia said, sitting down heavily, turning toward Reva, looking everywhere but her face. Her eyes were red-rimmed, her face blotchy. It was obvious that, in the moment, she could barely hold it together. She propped her elbows on the desk, fumbling with a ragged tissue in her right hand.

Reva nodded. "I figured that's where he would go. Home."

"Reva, you must know, he is absolutely heartbroken."

"Is he?" Reva said. Her words strangling in her throat. She realized that she hadn't cried—hadn't shed a single tear—since seeing her sister and her husband together in the parking lot. It was seeing Amelia, the person she'd be trying for years to please, that finally broke her.

Amelia was crying again herself. Crying for her. For Tommy. "He's made the biggest mistake of his life, doing this to you," she said.

"It's unforgivable."

"Oh, Reva, I should hope not. As horrible as it is, I hope that maybe in time you can forgive him."

Reva shook her head fiercely at the thought of forgiveness. Maybe the possibility would come with time, but she couldn't imagine that moment yet. Forgiveness would be somewhere far into the future for her husband, and for her sister.

She had lost them both last night. The realization broke her open, and she covered her face as the sobs came fast and furious.

How much more could she lose?

"Oh, honey," Amelia said, coming over to wrap her arms around Reva's shoulders, her own tears spilling down her cheeks.

"I don't understand how he could do this to me, and with her," Reva choked out. "It's sick, both of them make me sick!"

"If it helps at all, he's sick over it," Amelia told her. "Threw up all night. And I told him it serves him right. Even if she was throwing herself at him, like he said—"

"You tell him that doesn't even matter, who did the chasing. I don't even care. The bottom line is my husband and my sister have been carrying on behind my back for Lord knows how long, when he barely ever even touches me."

Amelia gave her a pitying look. "Oh, honey, do you think maybe that's the problem?"

"Ugh, of course it's part of the problem," Reva said. "We've been through so much with the babies, and I'm not sure—it's complicated. But my sister? How could he do those things with my own blood and lay his head down by mine at night, like it's nothing at all to him? Honestly, I can't even claim I'm surprised that Crystal would do this. It's not like she's ever had the clearest judgment in these things. Why not my husband? What does it matter to her?

"But Tommy? Tommy knew if I found out—when I found out, because nothing you do in the dark around here stays in the dark for long—he knew how bad it would hurt me. Especially now."

Amelia rubbed her back and snatched her a handful of tissues from the box on a little table behind her. "He told me what's going on at your parents'."

Reva laughed. "Of course, he did."

"I reckon I always knew about the problems over there, but I didn't know it had gotten to this point."

"It's been so bad for so long," Reva said, twisting a tissue in her fists. "So, on the one hand, I'm grateful something's finally getting done about it, and that my mama might get some help for what's caused it. What she's been through…we didn't know. Only Daddy knew, and he thought the best thing to do was hide things, pretend they didn't happen. Let her bury them under her hoard."

"And now it's going to be on TV for the whole world to see."

Reva gave a slow nod. "I'm sorry about that. I know it's a bit humiliating. Maybe it's not such bad timing for a split with our families?"

"Don't you ever think that, Reva," Amelia said. "I know we

haven't been as close over the years as we should have been, but I've always known what a precious thing Tommy had in you. Whether he's forgotten it or not, I haven't."

"Hey, speaking of us not being as close as we should have been…there's something I need to tell you. Or, first, show you."

Reva reached into her purse. Amelia watched with interest as she riffled through it, finally retrieving the blue velvet box that held the pearl Amelia had intended for Reva years ago.

"You should know," Reva said, setting the box in front of her on the desk, "that I had never seen this until today."

"But—what—" Amelia reached for the box, held it in both her hands, studying the emblem embroidered in silver thread on its top. She carefully opened it.

"We found it today, buried under Darlene's hoard of books."

Amelia's jaw dropped. "She lost it?"

Reva shrugged. "Not at first, no. At first, she didn't know what to do with it. When you brought it over to her, she had the right intentions. It was something she thought she'd be able to handle.

"But then she did what she always did with something she was supposed to handle. She put it off, and put if off some more. Finally, when it was pretty much too late to do anything about it, she decided it wasn't that important a thing, after all."

"She decided that your becoming part of the Pearl Girls wasn't that important for you? Without asking you how you felt about that?"

"You have to understand," Reva started, "that with Mama…well, it becomes about the story she tells herself in her head, to get out of doing things that scare her. Like letting people inside the house, going to unfamiliar places, interacting with anyone she sees as threatening, which unfortunately eliminates a lot of folks." Reva rested her head in her hands. "So, in an effort to avoid any of those things, she'll twist the story up in her head so that she doesn't have to deal with it. By the wedding, she'd convinced herself that I'd rather wear something she picked for me, since you'd helped pick my wedding dress. And, rather than ever giving me the pearl, she'd stashed it in a little cubby in her desk—it's one of those rolltop secretaries with the tiny drawers—and proceeded to bury it under a mountain of books. I swear, by the time we cleaned through it, we'd all forgotten a desk had ever been there. It was completely covered."

"So, you never even knew I'd given her the pearl to have your pendant made?"

"Nope," Reva answered. "And I never knew that she told you I didn't want to wear it."

"All these years…"

"You'd think with her illness, with this disease that's so skewed her thinking, that her mind would function at a more basic level, right? But it takes cunning to deceive the both of us, and in such a way that neither of us felt like we could ever mention this pearl to the other. I don't know if it was blind luck that she executed the whole thing that well, or if she's that smart. But she knows me well enough to know that I could have never brought myself to ask you why I wasn't welcomed into the Pearl Girls when Tommy and I got married. She knew how badly it hurt me—and on my wedding day, even—but it was easier for her to hurt me like that than it was for her to find a way to get that pearl to me the way you intended."

Amelia dabbed at her eyes. "I don't understand why she wouldn't have asked me to take care of it myself, Reva. I handed it off to her because I thought she'd like to be a part of that process, and that she'd be able to pick something that you'd love. The pearl from me, and the design from your mother. But I'd have been happy to have it set myself. Thrilled, really." She gave Reva a sly smile. "I secretly prefer to get to choose myself, you know."

Reva smiled, too. "She didn't mean any harm, but, God, did she ever cause a great deal of it. I spent all these years thinking…"

"Thinking what, sweet girl?"

"That y'all didn't want me. That I was an embarrassment to you," Reva wiped at her eyes with the backs of her hands. "God, Amelia," she said, fighting a sob, "I can't tell you how many tears I've shed over not being welcome in your family. But I couldn't bring myself to ask you why. So, I licked my wounds, and I tried to prove myself worthy. I kept the house spotless, so if you ever stopped by you'd know for sure I wasn't like Darlene. And I finished school, worked straight through so that we didn't have to borrow any money for me to go.

"Of course, I tried to give you grandchildren. Over time, when that didn't seem to be in the cards…I figured you didn't want to waste a family pearl on someone you didn't think was good enough *and* turned out to be infertile. You know, in case Tommy came to his senses, divorced me, and married someone who—oh God." Reva covered her mouth with her hands, the color draining from her face.

"What's wrong, Reva?"

"What if—Amelia, what if they—"

Amelia shook her head, realizing what was running through Reva's mind. "Absolutely not. There is no way that my son and your sister will have anything else between them, Reva."

"But what if there's already a baby?" Reva whispered. "What if she gives him what I wasn't able to?"

Amelia knelt in front of Reva and grabbed both her hands. "Don't you even think such a thing, you hear me? Don't even let the thought cross your mind again. That was a terrible, awful mistake and he will never make it again."

"Tommy would like to try again. I've been the one holding out, not because I can't, physically. I don't know if I could survive losing another baby, Amelia."

"Oh, honey…maybe the two of you can still somehow work this out? You could still have the family you always wanted."

"I can't imagine how. No one has ever done anything so hurtful to me in all my life. For all of Darlene's craziness, the whispers and jokes in school, Crystal's out of control behavior, Willie's denial…this is even worse than not getting that damn pearl."

"I can't believe you never even knew I'd delivered it for you."

"Why didn't you ask me why I wouldn't wear it? You must have been shocked at the idea I didn't want to be part of the Pearl Girls."

"I was mad as hell, to tell you the truth," Amelia said, crossing her arms over her chest. "When Darlene told me that you weren't wearing the pearl for the wedding, hadn't even had the pendant set, I stormed right across that church to the choir room where the boys were getting dressed and told Tommy he was calling the wedding off immediately."

"You did not!" Reva said, eyes wide.

Amelia nodded. "Oh yes I did. But my mother dragged me out before I had a chance to explain why and forbade me to say another unpleasant word that day."

Reva shook her head. "If I recall, you didn't say many more words that day at all."

"I was livid. You can thank Violet for calming me down enough to keep me from throwing all that food in the trash before the ceremony was over. Told me over her dead body would I throw all that hard work away."

"Y'all must have all thought I was out of my mind, and so ungrateful. But why didn't you ask me about it, Amelia? All these years, and you never once thought maybe you should ask me why I didn't want to be a Pearl Girl?"

Amelia huffed out a breath. "I reckon I was too proud to give you the satisfaction of thinking I'd come begging you to accept a place with us if you didn't want one. My feelings were hurt, too. As much as you must have felt rejected by us, I felt rejected by you, too."

"I'm really sorry for that," Reva said. "If I had known, I promise you, I'd have worn that pearl proudly on our wedding day. And I'd have never taken it off after, ever. I had such high hopes marrying Tommy, of what it would be like to be part of a real family, you know? A good, solid, normal family without so much baggage to carry."

"Well, don't be so sure about that," Amelia said. "We've all got our things. Maybe not as externally obvious as your family's, but things nonetheless."

"I've exerted so much effort over the last ten years trying to show you that I was worthy of your acceptance, and because you felt like I was the one who rejected you, I never even had a chance." Reva laughed. "It's all so clear now, really. And so very, very sad."

Amelia ran a hand over Reva's messy hair. "Maybe now that we know, we can right at least some of these wrongs. I know I intend to."

"I don't think I can figure that out today. First, I gotta see that my parents make it through this cleanup so they don't lose everything they have."

"I am truly sorry that you've had all of this to deal with, Reva. I knew, but...I guess I didn't really know. I thought your mother needed to pull herself together and clean up the house. I had no idea this kind of illness could run so deep and cause so much damage, and to a whole family. As irritated as I am at what she did, I'm sad for her that she's suffered so much. If I'd known I would have tried to help y'all get her the help she needed."

"You could have tried, but, unless you did what Billy Simpson did, getting the authorities involved, you wouldn't have gotten anywhere with my family."

"But it would have been nice, my darling, to have gotten somewhere with you at least. I'm truly sorry that you felt shut out for all these years. It wasn't intended."

Reva gave Amelia a sad smile and shrugged, handing the pearl to her. "I guess there's nothing to do now but figure out how we carry on from here. But I won't be needing this."

"Reva, no," Amelia said, her plea shining through fresh tears in her eyes.

"I have to go," Reva said, getting to her feet quickly and moving to the door. "I'm sorry, Amelia."

She grabbed her purse, bolted from the office, and ran to her car before Amelia could follow, tears streaming down her face. She didn't want to change her mind. She couldn't. But she wasn't ready to face the way she was breaking Amelia's heart.

She still didn't know how she was ever going to patch up her own.

CHAPTER 25

When Reva dragged her tired body up the steps at Gran's house—now, hers, alone—she closed the door, locked it behind her, and leaned against it, soaking in the blissful quiet of the space. She let her eyes drift over the clean surfaces in her kitchen and den.

Wandering through the spaces, she stashed the mail in its tray, which was stacked too high for her comfort. She ran her hands across countertops and tabletops, opened cabinets to take in her neatly organized dishes, pots and pans, and pantry items. In the living room, she straightened a few books on the bookshelves, checked for dust, and refolded the throws on the back of the sofa and Tommy's recliner. She checked the artwork to make sure each piece was level. The room was cozy and tasteful, much like Gran had left it. Reva's additions had been mostly books and a few family pictures. She had an aversion to stuff almost as strong as Darlene's desire for it.

Reva stopped to study a photograph of her and Tommy for the second time that day, another one from years they were well past. She pulled it from the shelf and eased herself onto the couch, careful not to move to quickly, feel too much in a rush, so that maybe she could avoid another complete unraveling.

The young couple smiling out from the picture were just two kids she didn't know anymore. She turned the frame over and placed it face down on the coffee table. That happy couple was so incongruous with their present-day failing marriage, she couldn't stomach the thought of it.

What if, on that day when they married, things had been different? What if Darlene had given her the pearl, rather than burying it beneath all those lies?

Reva took a deep breath and let it loose in a sigh. There was no use in speculating what could have been. She'd finally held that pearl in her hands today, for a brief moment. What good could it have done her? It wasn't like it was some talisman of protection that could have stopped her world from crashing down around her.

"I need all the energy I've got to deal with what is," she said out loud, surprised by the rough edges that remained to her voice after her earlier breakdown.

She pushed herself off the couch and marched her tired body to her kitchen whiteboard, which she erased completely without looking at the list she'd made before. What could she do today, right now?

Start the laundry. She knew there was a hamper full by now.

Just her laundry, though. Tommy's could go in fire barrel out back later.

And the dishes. She eyeballed the sink, where a lone coffee cup from the morning remained. Billy must have cleaned up while she'd been asleep the night before.

She sorted the laundry and started the machine, willing herself not to think about the pile she left on the back porch for burning.

A shower, then, to wash off the day's work. Reva allowed herself to linger beneath the warm stream of water, took her time with her nighttime routine, focusing on feeling normal.

Focusing on everything she could except being alone.

Alone.

She let the word sink in and the fresh tears flow at the thought of how utterly alone she was in the world. Gran, who had been her one constant source of strength and comfort, was gone. She couldn't turn to her for advice or solace. Her marriage was over—she couldn't see any way around that after what Tommy had done. The family she'd hoped to be accepted into all of these years, that hope was gone. And her sister…gone.

After everything, she couldn't help but worry for Crystal, and she was frustrated with herself for it. She shut off the water and dried quickly, throwing on her pajamas before trudging down the hall to the den, where she jerked down the photo Gran had hung of the two sisters when they'd been in middle school. Gran had taken the photo herself, down at the beach on Hilton Head, the backs of their heads bent close over something they were studying in the sand. They'd drifted so far apart over the years, and for what

Reva had always thought were good reasons.

But could that have been different, too? Should she have tried harder to help Crystal clean up? Reva couldn't help but wonder, if she'd done more... if she could have gotten Crystal the help she needed at some point over the years, would it have saved their relationship and her marriage?

She had tried. Gran had tried. Her parents, God love them, had tried in their own way.

Her sister was lost to her now, completely.

And then there was her career. She wanted to be excited about law school, but it seemed like she'd chosen the worst timing ever to reach for that particular star. Gran had left her in a position with the house and inheritance that she knew she'd be okay on her own, but affording law school and another place in Columbia would be an entirely different matter.

A tap on the glass of the back door startled Reva out of her swirling thoughts. She glanced from the door to her purse on the counter, where her phone was firmly in the OFF position, because she didn't want to talk to anyone. Not Tommy, or Crys, or anyone from work, or Amelia.

"Go away!" she shouted, not getting up to check who it was.

There was a pause, then, "Okay, but I have wine and brownies. And I'm taking them with me."

At the sound of Billy Simpson's voice, Reva couldn't suppress a smile. She shook her head as she walked to the door and swung it open.

"How much time for one brownie and all the wine?" she asked him, cocking a brow.

Simpson smiled and shrugged. "I can hand them over, or I can stay as long as you'd like me to. Either way is fine by me. Just thought you could maybe use a little comfort food, if not company."

"Brownies are comfort food?"

"They're what I know how to make, so yeah. You're welcome."

"Thank you, Billy. You weren't wrong, but you should have called first." Reva stood aside to let him in.

"I actually don't have your phone number," he said, walking to the kitchen and grabbing wine glasses from the rack.

Reva followed and pulled down plates for the brownies. "I guess my phone's been off all afternoon anyway, so…"

Simpson laughed. "Well, then, I'm glad I came on over. Seriously, though, if you don't want company, I can respect that. I didn't mean to intrude, but at the same time, I keep thinking things can't get crazier for you and then I watch them actually get crazier."

Reva sighed. "Let's go sit outside while there's still a little light?"

He nodded and followed her out. Reva realized as she led him down the little path to Gran's swing by the marsh that she was in her pajamas, face scrubbed, hair piled on her head, and she didn't feel at all self-conscious. Nor did she feel put out by his coming over unannounced, even though she knew she would have if it had been pretty much anyone else that day.

The two of them sat down in the swing, and Reva traded Billy a brownie for a wine glass and took a long sip. The light was still lingering late into the evening, and she spied Lucy standing still, looking out over the water. Reva raised a hand slowly and pointed her out to Billy.

"That's Lucy," she whispered. "She's out here all the time, since my Gran died."

Billy didn't say anything, but nodded his recognition of the blue heron. Reva saw the lines of his face soften, his deep brown eyes melt a little, as he studied the scene.

Lucy's head swiveled in their direction. She looked from Billy to Reva, as if to say hello… or goodnight… and then took to wing over the marsh. Billy's eyes lit, and he reached over to squeeze Reva's hand, then let it go.

They sat in silence another few minutes, finishing their wine and watching the sun set.

"Thank you, Simpson," Reva whispered.

He paused a beat, then grinned and bumped her shoulder. "You're welcome. Also, you just called me Simpson."

Reva laughed and drained her glass. "Yeah, maybe I did."

"Does that mean we're friends now?"

"We might be," she said, nodding.

And she realized she meant it.

CHAPTER 26

The activity around the Tuckers' place was at a fever pitch when Reva arrived Monday morning. Reva had gone by the office early and caught some things up, then left Macon a note. She would be by later. He'd have to handle it for the day.

The sky was a heavy sheet of gray hanging low overhead, and the rain poured without any sign of ceasing.

"What's happening?" Reva said, sloshing through the yard and into the group gathered beneath a tent. They formed a tight circle around Lindsay, trying to stay at least a little dry.

Willie joined the huddle at the same time Reva did. "It's all this rain, and the extra water from the way they diverted it from the creek with the bridge construction last year. We're flooding faster than I've ever seen."

"We've got an extra moving truck on the way so we can load up everything y'all plan to keep," Dean said. "A couple of my guys are out back already, packing up the workshop. That should go pretty quick."

Reva nodded, looking around the tent. "The rest won't be quite so simple, I guess. Where's my mom?"

"I'm here," Darlene said, coming down the steps faster than Reva had imagined she could move.

Willie rushed to Darlene's side with his umbrella and walked her to the tent with his arm around her. His tenderness with Darlene, his steady faithfulness, after everything they'd been through, left a lump in Reva's throat. Somehow, she'd never noticed the example her daddy had set for her, the kind of man he was, and the kind she should have been looking for.

Lindsay turned her attention to Reva. "We've been talking, and I don't think it will be safe for you parents to stay here at the house tonight. We're going to try and empty the things they'd like to keep, including the furniture, given the threat of flood. The kitchen and living room are already clear. We need to finish the bedrooms today, and the bathroom."

Reva nodded. "I agree, they can't continue to stay here with the house emptied out and the weather like this. There's plenty of room for them to stay with me at Gran's."

Darlene glanced back over her shoulder at the little house that had been her fortress for so long, her turmoil over leaving it showing on her face.

"Mama, I know it's scary, but I'll make sure you're comfortable, okay? We'll put the things you think you'll need in the truck Dean has coming, and we can park it right by the house so you can get to it."

"That's a fine plan, honey," Willie answered with an encouraging nod to Darlene. "I can bring in anything you need."

"What about Crystal? Is she—" Lindsay began.

Reva shook her head. "No. Crystal won't be here today. She's—she, umm—she's still got that flu."

She tried not to notice the flare of red creeping up Dean's neck. He knew—likely most of the people milling around knew—about Tommy and Crystal, what happened at the Shack.

But her parents didn't know, and they couldn't afford another big disruption on this last day of cleanup. Reva scanned the muddy edges of the property, the water churning ever closer to the home where she'd grown up, that had become so much more a prison to her mother than she'd ever realized.

"She okay? Maybe we should check on her, make sure she doesn't need anything," Darlene asked, her gaze skittering from spot to spot. Reva sensed an underlying current of hope from Darlene that maybe she could still escape all of this. Even though so much progress had been made, it would be so easy for her to slip right back into her pattern, her cycle. Reva realized they were on a razor's edge with her, and likely would be for a long time.

"I already checked up, and she's fine," Reva lied. "Mama," she said, reaching for Darlene's hand, squeezing it, "I know this is hard for you, but we have to hurry."

Darlene squeezed back. "We're going to lose the house, aren't we?"

"Let's focus on one thing at a time," Lindsay said, coming over to place her hand over Reva and Darlene's joined hands.

Just then, a huge moving truck rambled onto the road in front of the house, followed by two SUVs full of...

The Pearl Girls.

Reva's heart hammered in her chest as first Scott Ramirez, then Simpson, stepped down from the truck cab and headed toward the tent. Amelia, Violet, Leigh Anne, Elizabeth, and her sister Caroline spilled out of the SUVs and followed on their heels.

"What the—"

"Reinforcements," Scott said before Reva could finish her thought. "Dean said we need extra hands over here today, so I found some. Bay sends her love, but she is literally about to pop. We left her at Blossom Hill with Mel."

Simpson gave Reva a wink.

"But, we—I—" Reva tried again, but words failed her. She stood slack-jawed as the Pearl Girls surrounded her and her mother, huge smiles on their faces.

"We're here to help, and we won't take no for an answer," Violet said, tucking her hair behind her ears and pulling herself to her full—yet still slight—height. "Where do we start?"

Reva glanced over her shoulder at her mother, who seemed to be folding in on herself in the presence of the other women. "I don't know if this is the best idea, if she can manage with all of you here," she said, locking eyes with Amelia. "It's been an emotional week for her. She's not ready to confront...well, anything else, I guess."

Amelia nodded her understanding, then went to Darlene and took the other woman's hands in hers.

"Darlene," she began, "it's so good to see you, honey."

Darlene nodded, her lip quivering. "Amelia, I want to tell you I'm sorry. I didn't mean no harm about that pearl."

"Oh, I know, I know," Amelia said. She gave Darlene a quick hug. "That's all behind us now, isn't it? Let's focus on today, and getting things squared away for you and Willie."

"She's right," Lindsay said, waving her arms in an attempt to get everyone's attention. "Now's the time for us all to pull together for a fresh start. Are we ready to load this truck?"

"We're ready," Willie answered, resting his arm over Darlene's shoulders. "Let's let Darlene choose what she wants on the truck from inside the house first, and whatever room's left we can load in what's packed from the shop."

"No, start with the shop," Darlene said, a soft smile indicating her surprising level of calm. "They're already packing it and we can keep everything from in there. We'll take what we need from the house, clothes and family heirlooms, not that we have much, but anything the girls might like to have."

Reva looked from Darlene to Lindsay, whose face showed the same mix of shock, concern, and delighted surprise Reva felt. "Mama, you sure? Because what we leave inside today may not make it through the rest of this storm."

Darlene scanned the yard, the waters rising, rising toward the house, then watched Scott and Simpson loading the first boxes from the shop into the back of the truck.

"I'm sure. For the first time in a long time, I feel like I have something to look forward to, like maybe with some more help I can figure out a way to have a real future outside of those walls. It won't make sense dragging all this junk along, will it?"

"No, it won't," Reva agreed. "I think it will be wonderful to leave as much of this behind us as possible."

"Then let's do it. We'll bring just what we need, our clothes and such. Pictures, and my laptop. And my chair."

"If you're willing to let go of everything else, I'll even spring for you a new chair," Willie said, squeezing her close.

"No, I need my chair," Darlene said firmly. "Everything else can go."

"Okay, then," Lindsay said, clapping her hands together," let's organize into groups and get going."

Lindsay paired up a group with Darlene, one with Reva, and one with Willie, and they all moved quickly through the house, filling trash bags with things to throw away, stacking boxes for the donation truck, and choosing what would matter most to load into the moving truck for Darlene and Willie to carry forward with them, wherever that might be. Reva kept a worried eye on the rising water as they moved to and from the house. It seemed that Mother Nature herself had determined to wash away the wreckage of her family's past and take the little home they'd share together with her.

And, even though she was relieved her mother was able to find a way to let go of the hoard of memories she'd been drowning in, and the things she'd barricaded herself away behind, Reva felt a surprising sense of sadness creeping in around her heart. There had been a time, before Darlene had been so deeply wounded, when their family had been happy here. Before she'd been broken—before they'd all been broken—there had been so much love here.

Reva didn't know where, or how, but she was determined, as she watched her parents let go of everything they had, to help them find that love and happiness again.

GINA HERON

CHAPTER 27

Reva was late getting in to work on Tuesday, still exhausted from the of hard labor at her parents' and the evening getting them settled into the guest bedroom at her house. She figured she'd beg forgiveness when she saw Macon and stay late to smooth it over, blame it on the rain that was somehow still falling, but the note from him on her monitor was her first clue that her plan may not go as well as she'd anticipated.

See me when you get here.

She gave herself a few minutes to breathe and log in to her computer before she made her way to his office, tapping on the door before sticking her head in.

"Please come in, sit down," he said.

Reva paused for a moment, then complied with Macon's request.

"Are you alright?" she asked, eyeing him carefully. Macon was nearly always impeccably groomed and dressed, so his appearance that morning was startling. He sat with his socked feet up on the corner of his desk, eyes closed, his blond hair a disheveled mess, glasses tossed aside, loose tie, rolled up sleeves.

He rubbed his hands over his face and cracked his eyes open to slits. "I think I should be asking you that, shouldn't I?"

Reva started to sweat as she considered the events of the last several days. Which humiliating bit had he heard? Probably all of it, especially since Elizabeth had been at her parents' helping the day before. "Oh, I—"

"Listen, Reva, word's gotten around about what happened with Tommy and Crystal. Obviously," Macon said, clearing it up for her.

She shifted her gaze to the packed bookcases that lined the wall beyond his desk, the slow burn of humiliation creeping up her neck to her face. "I'm okay. Hurt and angry, but I'm dealing with it."

"On top of dealing with the situation at your parents' house."

Okay. That, too, then. "The cleanup is over. But the house—"

"Did they lose it?"

"Not yet, but it seems likely they'll lose it to the storm, rather than the county. I don't know that it's worth salvaging at this point at all."

"Is that the worst thing that could happen?" he asked.

Reva hesitated. "Given all the bad things that have happened here recently, I'm afraid to question what the worst thing that could happen might be."

Macon gave a sad laugh. "I feel that deeply today, Reva." He stretched his arms over his head and leaned back further in his chair, closed his eyes again.

"Is something wrong, Macon? You seem a little out of sorts yourself."

"What about you and Tommy?" he asked, keeping the focus of their conversation firmly on her and her issues.

"We're done," Reva said, clipping the words. "I assure you, it won't be a problem here at work."

"Are you sure about that?"

"Of course. I've never had any problem performing my duties, regardless—"

"Not what I meant," Macon broke in. "Are you and Tommy over, for good?"

Reva took a deep breath and let it out. "Things haven't been good between us for a while. Aside from what happened at the Shack, our marriage hasn't been a real marriage since we lost Tee Jae."

Macon held up a hand when it seemed she couldn't continue. "Listen, I get it. You're hurt, and you're angry. But don't you think maybe you could have prevented that little transgression on his part if you had been a bit more present in your marriage here lately?"

"Wh—what?" Reva whispered, her chin trembling. She felt like she'd been slapped in the face.

Macon rolled his eyes at her as if he'd lost all patience. Reva took in the room again, noticing an overnight bag beside the sofa that sat under the broad window, the open bottle of Scotch sitting on the end table beside it. "Did you stay here last night?"

"Things haven't been exactly right in my marriage for a time, either," Macon confessed. "Liza, you know she struggles with depression, anxiety. All of it."

Reva's face clouded with concern. "No, I didn't."

Macon picked up a pen and twisted it in his hands, then tossed it back on the desk. "It's been ongoing since she was a teenager. Maybe earlier. If I had to guess, it started when her mother ran off."

"They never found out what happened with her mother, did they?"

Macon shook his head. "I think it's always going to haunt her. And I've done everything I can think of, Reva. But I can't keep this up with her. I can't."

Reva studied the backs of her hands folded in her lap, unsure of how to respond to such personal revelations from Macon. "What are you going to do?" she asked quietly.

"I'm going to insist that she do what she should, Reva. Same as Tommy should be doing with you."

"Macon, with all due respect, I have no idea what in hell you're going on about." Reva sprung to her feet and crossed her arms over her chest.

"What I'm going on about, Mrs. Patterson, is the fact that all of you women don't think anything is ever good enough for you. You can't be satisfied working here as a paralegal. Oh, no. You need to upend your family's life so you can go to law school. Never mind that your husband would like to start a family sometime before you're middle aged, or that he has a business to run himself. And then you're surprised when he slips up one night out of—"

"Slips up?" Reva hissed. "Slips up? You call having sexual relations in the parking lot of a bar with my sister a slip-up?"

"I'm just saying to keep it in perspective," Mason argued back. "Here he is providing for you, building something for you, and it's never enough, is it? You go and get some big idea about law school, like you're going to be the next Juliette or something. But you don't come from that kind of background, Reva. That kind of money. Juliette's father bought her a seat at the table. How blind do you have to be not to see that?"

Macon crossed the room to his bottle of Scotch and poured himself a fresh drink.

"It's a little early, don't you think?" Reva said, turning to face him.

"I'm calling in sick today," Macon said. He swirled the amber liquid in the crystal highball glass and leaned his head back. "Do you realize that now Liza has it in her head that she should go back to school, too? Pursue her passion for art, she says."

"Is there a good reason why she shouldn't?" Reva asked, her blood simmering closer to a boil.

"Yes, Mrs. Patterson, there are plenty of good reasons why she shouldn't, the first of those being that I absolutely forbid her to."

"Macon, you do realize that she's your wife and not your child?"

Macon gave her a sneer. "Yes, I do, but if she wants to behave like a child—"

"All I see right now are the grown men in this town behaving like children. What is wrong with—"

Reva was making her way toward Macon, determined to get in his face, when something caught on her shoe. She bent down to grab it and realized almost too late what it was.

"Oh, for fuck's sake. You have got to be kidding me."

Macon's face suddenly flared red, almost purple, when she kicked the lace thongs toward him. "I'm guessing these aren't Elizabeth's?"

"Reva, please don't—"

"Macon, you don't. Don't even try to explain this away or blame your wife for your indiscretions. Here you sit, going on about how we women ought to know our roles, right? That's what you've been trying to get at with me. I should know my place and stay in it? Well, when are you men gonna stop acting like two-legged dogs and lead your families with some integrity? Whatever happened to men who took vows and meant them, Macon? Men who know how to love and cherish what they have so they don't lose it, so their wives don't have to pick up so much of their moral and ethical slack—"

"Macon?"

Reva hadn't heard the door open behind her. She turned at the sound of Elizabeth's voice, mouthed *I'm sorry* to her friend, and turned back to Macon.

"I quit."

Reva squeezed Elizabeth's hand as she walked by. Her hands shook as she grabbed her purse. She left her computer on and the work stacked where it had been when she came in late. She could feel Macon's eyes on her as she hurried down the hall to the kitchen, where she exited the back door without even making sure she closed it.

As she drove herself home, her body shook uncontrollably. She replayed those few moments in the office with Macon over and over in her mind. What had Elizabeth heard? And did it matter? What had she already known about her husband's infidelities, of which Reva was certain this wasn't the first.

And why did Elizabeth stay? It was the thing Reva was trying to reason out as she pulled back into her own driveway to find her very own cheating husband standing at the bottom of her porch steps with a gun aimed at his chest.

GINA HERON

CHAPTER 28

"Mama, put that thing down."

"I will when he leaves," Darlene said, fury shaking her voice.

"It's okay, Mama. Please. I think we got enough going on without somebody getting shot today," Reva coaxed, getting between Darlene and Tommy. She fought down her own anger and frustration and kept her voice and expression steady, calm.

"I heard what you told your daddy last night," Darlene said, aiming the gun higher, over Reva's shoulder. "You told him this sorry excuse of a husband you got cheated on you, and that's why he's not staying here."

Reva nodded and took the first step up to the porch. It was easy to forget how observant, how sharp, her mother was, in spite of her illness. If Reva had told Willie that Tommy had cheated with Crystal, her husband would likely already be full of bullets. Thank God she'd kept that little detail to herself.

"You're right, he is sorry," Reva agreed. "Where'd you get the gun, Mama?"

"From my purse, where it always is."

Reva wasn't sure why she was surprised, after all she'd learned in the last few days about her mother's traumatic past, that she kept a gun nearby at all times.

"Well, that's handy. How about if you go put it up, though?"

Darlene's gaze drifted to Reva, then back to Tommy. She lowered the pistol and slipped on the safety. "Are you sure? When I looked out the window and saw it was him I heard pullin' up, I figured he'd leave if I didn't answer the door. But then he went back to his truck, and was coming with the keys. I didn't figure you wanted him walking on in here like it's still his right."

Reva turned to face Tommy, keeping herself between him and Darlene. "You're right, I don't want him here," she said, fighting hard to keep her voice and her expression flat. "But I can handle him, okay? Go on back inside."

"Are you sure you want to be left alone with him?" Darlene asked.

"It's fine, Mama. Thank you for looking out, though. I can take it from here."

Reva heard the door open and click shut behind her. She took a steadying breath, then another.

"What do you want, Tommy?" She heard her own voice, sure and steady, and marveled at the fact she didn't choke on the words. In her mind, all she could see was what she'd seen the last time she laid eyes on her husband.

Tommy and Crystal.

"Thank you for not lettin' her shoot me," Tommy said, his face pale and sheened with sweat.

"Don't thank me. The only reason I stopped her is because if somebody gets to shoot you, it ought to be me."

Tommy wiped at his face with the back of his hand and groaned. "What's she doing here, anyway? I thought y'all were supposed to be cleaning out their place." His gaze drifted to the moving truck parked near his shop. "Don't tell me you brought all that trash over here—"

"It's none of your business what I bring over here, or why. You gave up that right the moment you decided to have sex with my— my sister."

Reva couldn't control the tremor in her voice any further. She turned and took the last three steps up to the porch and sat on the edge of one of the pristine white rockers, staring past Tommy to the edge of the marsh behind the property. The last few days, in the quiet moments, she'd imagined over and over how this conversation would go. It had to happen sometime. She'd lined up the perfect insults, the most damaging, cutting things she could come up with to say to her cheating husband.

But none of the words would come now. All the sadness, all the anger, it expanded, filling her lungs and pushing out the air, pushing until her throat and eyes felt the sting. Here was the man she had loved since she was a teenager, her entire adult life, and she couldn't even look at him.

"Reva," Tommy said his voice barely above a whisper, thick

with emotion. "What happened to us?"

He was kneeling in front of her, his eyes wet with tears and searching her face as she continued to stare past him.

"Do you really need me to tell you what you did—"

"No, that's not what I mean," he broke in, shaking his head. "I know what I did with Crystal. I know that it's unforgivable, and I don't know how I can ever make it up to you. What I mean is, what happened to us?"

Reva closed her eyes, searching for words, for an answer to the question she'd asked herself so many times, and still coming up empty.

"Do you remember the trip we took for our first anniversary?" Tommy asked her.

She nodded. "St. Augustine. We stayed in that little bed and breakfast with the view of the bridge."

"We laughed when they said it was haunted."

"And then the shower kept turning itself on in the middle of the night." Reva felt her lips involuntarily curving toward a smile.

"You thought it was funny." Tommy gently touched her knee.

She opened her eyes. "You were completely freaked out and insisted that we find somewhere else to stay."

"And you dragged me into the shower. You said the ghosts were just making a suggestion."

"That was a good night," Reva whispered.

"One of many."

"We had some good times, Tommy. But in between the good times, we've had some rough spots, too."

"We've always worked through them. C'mon, babe. We can work through this, too," he pleaded, his voice quaking with emotion.

Reva got up and walked past Tommy, leaving him on his knees.

"Do you care to know why I'm back home this morning, Tommy?" she asked, leaning against the railing as she turned to face him.

"I didn't think—"

"Yeah, I know you didn't. You rarely think about anything but yourself, do you?"

Tommy pushed to his feet. "That's not—"

"I quit my job this morning."

"You what?" Tommy's brow furrowed, his lip curling into the smirk that Reva had grown accustomed to the past few years.

"I quit—"

"I heard you. Why would you do that?" Tommy rested his hands on his hips, his tone incredulous.

"Because my boss is a chauvinistic asshole who is also cheating on his amazing wife, and I'm not spending another minute of my time working for him."

"Nice one, Reva. Love the sarcasm, but what are we gonna do without you working?" Tommy threw his hands up. "Your job is what we count on for steady income, insurance—"

"Are you kidding me right now? You're worried about my paycheck and health insurance? Our marriage is on fire because you had sex with my sister, my parents' house is not only cleaned out but flooded out, and they didn't have insurance so I have no idea what's next for them, I've been afraid to even think about kids again since Tee Jae, and my gran died and I'm drowning in all of this grief and you—you're worried about health insurance?"

Tommy's shoulders dropped. "We can figure it all out—"

"You can figure it all out for yourself. And I'll figure it out for me, on my own. You asked what happened to us. We grew up, Tommy. We grew up, and we grew apart, and instead of the fairytale we got the cliché, the disillusioned, unhappily married couple who'd stay together if they had kids. But we didn't, and we don't have to. We don't have to make each other miserable, and I don't know how I'll ever look at you again and not re-live the most miserable experiences of my life. There were good times, sure. But they're over. This is over, Tommy."

"If we could—"

"No. I'll send your things to your mama's. Don't come back here again. Goodbye, Tommy."

Reva held her shaking hand out toward his truck. It took him less than a minute to decide whether to fight for her or give up.

As she watched her husband drive away for the last time, a fresh wave of grief shook her shoulders. Reva knew there wasn't any other way forward, and that she would move forward, but it didn't ease the pain she felt, letting go of her past.

CHAPTER 29

The next Saturday morning, Reva drove her parents back over to their house to meet with Lindsay one last time. Willie and Darlene sat in the back seat together, holding hands. Reva was touched by the simple gestures of love between her parents, but she was also worried about how they'd both react to what she already knew was a total loss of their home.

"So, I talked with the crew yesterday," Reva started, choosing her words carefully.

"Louder, honey, we can't hear you," Willie said.

"I talked with the crew yesterday," Reva repeated. "They got everything else out of the house, but I want y'all to be prepared. They weren't able to salvage anything else, and the waste collection company picked up the containers yesterday."

"So, everything else is gone, then?" Darlene asked.

"I'm sorry, Mama. It is."

No one spoke again before they arrived at the little house they'd left to the flood a week before. When they pulled up, it looked much the same as it had, minus the hoard.

But when you looked closer, you could see signs of the damage. A hole in the roof. A fresh sag in the porch so deep that the boards had pulled away from the thin porch columns. The windows left open by the crew in hopes of drying out all the water on the inside.

"Hi Lindsay, Dean." Reva greeted them with hugs and anxious smiles.

Willie and Darlene were slow to get out of the car. Willie finally stepped out, then walked around to help Darlene. Reva followed.

"Mama, remember all the work you've done," Reva said, holding Darlene's gaze as she tried to look past her to the house.

GINA HERON

"The goal was to clear everything away, right? We're letting go of all that junk from the past that's been holding us back, like we talked about. We're doing it together."

Darlene looked from Reva to Willie and nodded.

"Mr. Willie, Mrs. Darlene," Dean said, coming over to greet them. "I know these aren't the best of circumstances, with the flood and all, but I hope you'll be happy with the work the team did this week. Everything is cleared away, so you can at least have that peace while you make the decisions you need to make now."

"And we don't have to necessarily rush with that," Lindsay chimed in. "Let me show you where we are with the house, and then we can talk.

The fire marshal joined them under the carport, along with Terrance, and they began the tour of the now-empty home Reva had grown up in.

"Mr. and Mrs. Tucker, I'd like for you to know, you both did such a great job clearing the house," the fire marshal began. I've been here with Dean and the crew this week, and the work you did before the storm was commendable. Had it not been for the flooding, the house would have been in fine shape."

Darlene scanned the kitchen, taking in the empty space where the little dining table had been, the clear, scrubbed counters. The sink even sparkled.

But, Reva noticed, when you looked lower, you could see that the wooden cabinets had swollen and were bowing at odd angles. The linoleum, which hadn't been in the best shape, was now curling up and away from the subfloor, a distinct buckle evident right at the center of the room.

Willie sighed and wrapped an arm around Darlene. "Be careful walking here," he cautioned quietly.

Reva laughed quietly. "Wouldn't you know, we clear all the stuff out, and the house takes on so much water during the storm that you still can't safely walk through it."

Lindsay kept her eyes on Darlene. "How are you holding up? I know this is a lot to take in, both with everything emptied out and the damage. Are you okay to move on?"

Darlene shook her head.

"Mama, it's okay," Reva began.

Darlene reached for her and squeezed her hand. "Thank you,

baby. Thank you for helping us, and for taking us in, and for being here. I'm okay to move on, to let go like we talked about. But I don't want to see any more here, okay? You and your daddy go on through. I don't need to see more."

"I'll keep her company outside," Dean said, reassuring Reva and Willie. "Y'all finish up here."

So, Reva and her father held hands and listened as the fire marshal assessed the damage to their home. Their uninsured, flooded out, total loss of a home.

"Now, the shop out back will be fine once it's dried out. It's on cement, and is mostly metal, so we'll check the wiring for any damage, and drywall and insulation can be easily replaced or repaired."

"I'm gonna go back there and take a look," Willie said, heading back through the kitchen.

Reva stood with Lindsay and the fire marshal in the den, looking up at the sky through the hole in the roof.

"How in the world did that happen?"

"Seems like it just fell in."

"If they'd have still been staying here…" Reva started, but couldn't finish the thought.

Lindsay squeezed her shoulder. "But they weren't."

Reva turned to the fire marshal. "So, now that the house is cleaned up, and they're not staying here, how much time do we have to decide what to do with it?"

"As long as you keep the power off, and no one is staying here, take your time."

"Thank you," Reva said, her voice thick with gratitude. "I know when Simpson first called you over here, we didn't exactly welcome the intrusion, but my family needed this. If he'd never come, and never called you, we'd still be stuck exactly where we were, or worse. So, thank you."

"You're most welcome," he said, smiling.

Reva turned to Terrance. "Let's go check on my folks."

Lindsay went to the shop with Reva to gather Willie. When they got back to the street, Reva was surprised to find Simpson had pulled in behind her car. The sight of him standing with her mother and Dean brought a smile to her face.

"Hey," she called as they approached. "What brings you over

this way?"

"Well," he said, taking her hand and pulling her aside, "I was looking for you, and when I didn't find you at home, I figured this would be the next best place."

"Simpson, you do have my number now. You could have called."

He scratched at his stubble and shifted his weight. "Yeah, except I really needed to see you in person. Actually, I need to take you somewhere."

Reva looked around. Lindsay was chatting with her parents, and Terrance was packing up. "I—guess I could take off from here. But where are we going?"

"Thing is, I'm not supposed to say."

Reva crossed her arms over her chest and gave him a look.

"Do you trust me?"

"Ahh, maybe? C'mon, Billy. What's this all about?"

He sighed and studied her, considering. "You promise you'll come? I think it's important."

"What?" she asked again.

He reached for her hand again. "It's your sister."

CHAPTER 30

Reva was lost in her own thoughts on the drive to wherever they were going. She must have trusted Simpson, because by half an hour into the trip, she was completely lost geographically, too. After so abruptly quitting her job on Tuesday, and coming home to find Tommy there waiting on her, she'd spent a couple of days in overdrive, cleaning everything to a shine, changing the locks at the house, clearing Tommy's things and boxing them up so someone could get them from his shed. Then, she'd spent a couple of days in bed, letting her parents take care of things while she slept off the wave of despair that seemed to take her out at the knees without warning.

She'd thought about Crystal. Of course, she had. Even if she was trying not to care, not to worry, she wondered where her sister was sleeping, if she was eating, and if she was getting high.

Her parents worried, too, but they seemed accustomed to Crystal disappearing. Willie said she'd be gone for days at a time. Each time Darlene asked if Reva had heard from her, she deflected.

And every day that passed without a word from Crystal, Reva remained somewhere between relieved and panicked. One way or another, that was about to be over.

Reva realized with a start where they were headed.

"Why are we going to Edisto? There's no way…"

Simpson glanced at her, seeming to consider what to tell her and what to keep to himself. "Ramirez asked me to bring you here. He said it had something to do with your sister. That's all I got."

When Simpson pulled into the drive at Pearl's Place, he wished Reva luck and told her to call him when she was ready to go home.

"So, you're leaving me to fend for myself here?" she asked, incredulous.

"I'm meeting Ramirez at the bar. We'll be close enough to hear you ladies if it comes to blows."

Reva took a steadying breath. "Is Bay here?"

Simpson nodded. "All of them are."

"What if I don't want to do this?" Reva whispered.

Simpson laughed. "I don't think you've wanted to do anything that you've had to since we met, but here you are, doing it all anyway. Take a deep breath, Reva. Go in. Get this behind you so you can move forward."

Reva turned to study the handsome face she was growing to like more and more. "What's in it for me?"

Simpson shrugged. "Closure, if you need it. A chance to heal what's broken with your sister. And, when you have in fact survived it, I will reward you with an adventure of some sort."

"Promise?"

"I promise. Go."

Bolstered by Simpson's encouragement, Reva got out of the car and made her way to the house, walking in without knocking. The Pearl Girls were gathered there, scattered through the kitchen and living area, obviously waiting for her. She looked around at the faces of the women who were her friends, her family, and almost ran from the room. But she forced back the flush of emotion and pushed forward.

"Why are we here?" Reva asked Amelia, who sat at the table with Violet.

"Your sister's outside," Amelia answered bluntly.

"Oh, no," Reva turned back to the door, but Bay blocked her way. "Simpson said this had something to do with her, but he didn't say she was here. I don't want to see her. Not today, not ever."

"Reva, hear her out," Bay said. "I can't even imagine how upset you are, how angry, but just hear her out. She's your sister. Trust me when I tell you, you need to fix this if you can."

"You know you're about to go into labor any minute, Bay, right?" Reva asked.

"Don't change the subject." Bay rested her hands on her enormous belly. "This is important."

Amelia rested a hand on Reva's shoulder. "I cannot believe what my son has done—what my son and your sister have done—

but I blame him more than I can blame her. I love that boy, God knows, but he can be a complete ass sometimes. I don't want to think about how that might be my fault."

"They're both grown," Reva said. "They got nobody to blame but themselves."

"There's some truth in that, Reva, yes. But your sister, everybody knows she's not well, that she doesn't make the best of decisions. Yes, she could do better, and she has to own that. And how a woman does this to her own sister—well, I'll never understand it. Family doesn't betray family that way. But Tommy of all people should have known better."

"What Amelia's trying to say, I think," Violet said, taking over, "is that they both should have known better. But the fact of the matter is, your sister has a problem with addiction that clouds her judgment. Tommy has no such excuse for what he's done, aside from being a giant ass."

"Mama," Bay said, her eyes wide.

"Well, it's the truth," Violet continued. "But we'll have to deal with Tommy another time. Tommy is not what we're here for today." She stood up and took Reva in her arms, into the warmest hug Reva had experienced in a very long time. "Today we're here for you, sweet girl. For one of our own."

"Thank you for that," Reva said, her voice barely more than a whisper. "But, Tommy is family, and obviously I can't—I don't think I can—"

"You're our family, too, Reva," Amelia said, reaching into her purse and pulling the now familiar blue velvet box out. "You're a Pearl Girl. Regardless of what you decide you need to do about Tommy, this right here is a lifetime membership." She opened the box and pulled out the pearl, now suspended on a chain, the pendant in the shape of eternity, with the pearl secured in the center. "I'd be honored if you'd allow me to put this on for you, like I should have on your wedding day."

Reva nodded her head, tears closing her throat. Amelia stepped behind her and clasped the pearl necklace around her neck. Reva's fingers found the pendant, and she looked around the room at her fellow Pearl Girls—Violet, Bay, Leigh Anne, Elizabeth, Caroline—all here to support her through one of the worst times of her life. It was support she'd stopped dreaming she'd ever had, and it was overwhelming.

"Thank you all for being here for me. For Crystal. I'm sorry, but I don't think I'm ready to face her. Not yet."

"We understand why you feel that way, but it's going to be an important first step for the two of you to heal," Bay said, taking Reva's hand. "Believe it or not, Crystal feels pretty awful about what she's done. And, deep down, I think she just feels pretty awful about who she is. That she's a person who'd do something like this to her sister."

"You girls didn't deserve to suffer through what you did growing up," Amelia said. "Neither one of you deserved it. You're a strong one, Reva. You held things together—yourself, your family, your world—you took control of everything you could to counterbalance the things you couldn't. Crystal, she's not so strong. She got lost in the chaos. I'm not saying she's not responsible for her bad choices—she absolutely is. But all she's ever known is self-destructing. This is just another way to ruin whatever's good in her life."

"Crystal needs help," Bay said. "I know she's been to rehab before, but she needs serious intervention, and sustained help to get her life together. We're going help you see to it that she gets whatever she needs."

Reva wiped the tears from her cheeks and folded her arms over her chest. "I want that for her. I do. I can't—I don't—I don't know if I can ever forget seeing them—"

"So, go out there and tell her how you're feeling," Bay said. "Tell her how her actions have hurt you. Be honest with her about that, about the fact that you don't know if you can ever look at her the same. Tell her she has to get better. That it's the only chance she has."

Reva squeezed Bay's hand and nodded. Leigh handed Reva a sweater and pushed her toward the back door.

"She's out there. Take as long as you need," Leigh said.

Reva found Crystal sitting on the steps of Pearl's Place that led onto the beach. There was a slight chill in the wind that was whipping the waves into a frenzy, sending the sand dancing up in stinging swirls. Dark clouds hung low, clinging to the coastline. Reva wondered if they'd ever see the sun again.

She sat down beside her sister, quietly, wrapping her arms

around her knees.

"Chilly out here for August," Crystal said, after they'd sat in silence for several long minutes.

"Mmhmm." Reva squinted, looking out over the water, the wind and the salt air stinging her eyes. "Crazy weather. Crazy times."

"I know I need to say I'm sorry, Reva." Crystal's voice cracked, and she took a minute to compose herself. "But how can that ever be enough for what I did?"

"It's not," Reva said, holding back her own tears.

"I could tell you I was drunk, and high. I was both. I could tell you Tommy made me do it, but that would be a lie."

"And you've lied to me enough."

"I don't deserve your forgiveness. I'm not gonna ask for it."

"You're right about that, and honestly, I don't know if I'll ever forgive you for this." Reva started to cry then. "But I'm always going to love you. I need you to get better. You're all I had when we were little, you know? You and Gran."

Crystal leaned into Reva, sobbing. "You're all I've ever had," she said through her tears. "You're the only person who ever really loved me."

"We can't keep going like this, Crystal." Reva took her sister by the shoulders. "You have to get clean. Not for me or for Mama and Daddy, not for anybody but yourself. You deserve better than being sick, like Mama. You have to get well."

"I don't know how to be better," Crystal whispered. "It feels like something's bad inside of me, Reva, like something's broke and I don't know how to fix it."

"You didn't deserve what you had to go through growing up," Reva said, echoing Amelia's words from earlier. "I'm sorry that I left you."

Crystal laughed, wiped at her nose. "By the time you graduated and got married, I was never there anyway, Sis."

"That may be true, but maybe if I'd been able to give you a safe place to go...I should have given you a safe place to go when I left. You're the baby sister. I should have taken care of you."

"Mama should have taken care of us, Reva. Isn't that really the problem here?"

Reva sat stunned at the simple, astounding truth Crystal spoke.

"But she couldn't."

Crystal shook her head hard and fumbled with her cigarettes, struggling to light one against the wind. "No, she could have."

"Crystal, you weren't there the last part of the cleanup. You didn't hear what—why Mama is the way she is. Some things happened to her. Bad things—"

"Lots of people have bad shit happen to them, and they don't disappear on their families. Our mistake—all of us—was letting her get away with it. She should have gotten some help if she needed help. Daddy should have gotten her some help to deal with whatever it was." Crystal stopped and took a deep, shaky breath. "I'm sorry for whatever happened to her. But it happened to us, too. It happened to us, too, and we couldn't even name what happened so we could deal with it. I don't want to be like her, Reva. I don't want to hide from my problems. I don't want to kill myself trying to escape anymore. I need help."

Reva wrapped her arms around Crystal, gathered her up into her lap as if she were a child. "Then you'll get it. You'll get it, I promise."

"I'm so sorry, Reva," Crystal whispered. "I'm so sorry for what I did to you. You didn't deserve that, either."

"No, I didn't," Reva said. "But I will try to forgive you. If you will promise me," Reva pulled back to look into Crystal's eyes, "If you will promise me that you will stop with the pills and the booze, Crystal, promise me that you'll get clean, and that you'll stay clean, that you'll keep up with your therapy and you'll let me help you, I will do my best to forgive you for what you've done. Because I know this isn't you. This—this has never been you."

"Do you remember that time we were playing by the tree line at Gran's, and we found those baby bunnies?"

Reva nodded, laughing. "I remember. We put them all in our hats and brought them back up to Gran's house. We were so excited thinking we were going to raise those baby bunnies and take them home to be pets."

"Until Gran told us they'd likely die before sun-up the next day if we didn't get them back to their Mama."

"But I was sure that we could keep them alive, that we could just read up about what they needed to eat and drink, and love them, and they'd be just fine."

"I knew what Gran was saying was true, though. They needed their Mama. We had to take them back."

"I finally gave up the argument."

Crystal grinned. "Finally. You've always been stubborn as hell, you know."

"I'm never quick to concede, I know. But it was like you knew, right down to your bones, that Gran was right. And rather than being sad about not getting to keep those bunnies, you were excited that they would get to be back with their mama, where they belonged."

"It was more important that they got to be free than it was that I got to keep them with me."

Reva squeezed Crystal's hand. "Just like it was more important for me to have the freedom to get out, to get away from our family's mess, than it was to keep me trapped in it, too."

"I was sad to be without you. Scared, really. But, at the same time, I knew if you could make it, then maybe I could, too." Crystal shrunk into the blanket she was wrapped in. "I sorta lost my way somewhere."

"I want you to remember that that's who you really are, Crystal. The drugs, the drinking, the partying, that's all what you got lost in. It's not who you are. You're the girl who'd give up her own comfort, her own security, so that the people she loves could live the life they want. But you gave up so much that you got trapped in this disaster. It's your turn now, okay? It's your turn to get free. And we're going to see you all the way through it."

"Reva! Crys!"

Reva turned to see Leigh running toward them, waving her arms.

"The baby!"

Reva and Crystal scrambled up from the steps, brushing away the sand from their clothes. "The baby's coming?"

Leigh nodded frantically. "Bay's water broke. We have to get her back now!"

Reva ran with her sister, hand in hand, like they had when they were kids.

And she realized, just like all those years ago, together they'd make their way back home.

GINA HERON

CHAPTER 31

A year later

"This is my reward? I don't think I want my reward."

Simpson laughed as he and Reva stood at the edge of the field, watching as the small plane was prepped for takeoff.

"I promised you an adventure. We're doing it."

It was true, he'd promised her all those months ago that if she survived the life storm he'd met her in the midst of, he'd take her on an adventure. She hadn't known him quite as well then. She hadn't known how important it was to make him be more specific.

"Do you trust me?" he asked with the sly grin she'd grown to adore.

Yes. She did trust him. He asked her all the time, every time he'd challenged her to stretch outside of her comfort zone since they'd met. Simpson had been there, supporting her during her divorce that was finally official. As she helped her parents through the demolition of their former home, and the building of their modest, brand new open floor plan house that Darlene and Willie kept as tidy as Reva's own place. He'd driven her back and forth to visit Crystal during her four months of rehab, and had helped her find work for Crystal when she came home. He'd helped find a fellowship she qualified for to assist with paying for law school, and made the trips with her to Columbia to find a studio apartment, where she'd stay during the week when classes were in session. He'd helped her come up with a plan, and she knew he'd be there to help her along the way with everything she needed.

"Yes, Billy," she said, laughing, near hysterical with nerves. "I trust you. But this—"

"I've done it a hundred times, at least. You'll be fine. I promise," he reassured her.

Reva tried her best to pay close attention during the instruction before takeoff. Simpson was unnervingly calm and disinterested. He knew the drill. Once again, he was along for the ride with her. Then, they were suiting up, and running through what would happen on the plane with the instructor one more time.

All the while, Reva was thinking of how her family would react to this story that night. She and Simpson would be joining her parents and Crystal—and Caprice, who had become Darlene's right hand around the house somehow—to watch their Help for Hoarders episode together. Today was a day to celebrate how a life that had fallen apart could be beautifully stitched back together with love.

Loading into the plane was a blur, and then they were taking off. Simpson held her hand as they climbed to thirteen thousand feet.

"You ready?"

Reva couldn't hear the words above the noise of the plane's engine, the wind outside the open door, but she could read Simpson's lips just fine.

"No," she mouthed back, shaking her head furiously.

"It's about that time," the instructor yelled right by her ear. As he hooked in with her, Simpson took her hands and squeezed them. "You can do this."

God, how he believed in her.

She shook her head again. "No, not yet," she shouted.

"Reva, you're ready," he insisted.

"Almost."

Reva leaned closer, grabbed Simpson's face in her hands, and kissed him for the first time.

"Now I'm ready," she said, smiling as the other jumpers cheered around them.

And she jumped.

THE END

ABOUT THE AUTHOR

Gina Heron is a native of South Carolina, where she currently lives in her hometown with two children. She has a degree in English Literature from Francis Marion University. She's had a long career in the software development industry and continues to work in research & development for a global marketing firm. She also provides productivity coaching for individuals and small businesses.

Gina loves hearing from friends and readers at www.ginaheron.com.

Made in the USA
Columbia, SC
07 July 2020

13318249R00138